Satin Doll

by

Joe Cosentino

A Jana Lane Mystery

Satin Doll

Cover Art by *Debbie Taylor*

The Wild Rose Press, Inc.
PO Box 708
Adams Basin, NY 14410-0708
Visit us at www.thewildrosepress.com

Publishing History
First Vintage Rose Edition, 2016
Print ISBN 978-1-5092-0727-5
Digital ISBN 978-1-5092-0728-2

A Jana Lane Mystery
Published in the United States of America

Jana Lane, America's most famous ex-child star, *ran down a dark hallway in the north wing of the Capitol, causing the row of senators' office doors to become a blur of brown. Sweat soaked through her beige business suit as her heart pounded in her ears. She turned a corner, and Jana's heels skidded to a halt on the marble floor as she screamed at the sight of—*

Jana gasped and looked up at her husband's handsome face. *Thank God it was just a dream.*

Brian leaned back against the gold circular headboard under the ruby-red satin canopy bedcover. "It must have been one heck of a nightmare."

Jana noticed her beige satin nightgown was soaking wet. She pushed off the silver satin sheets. After walking past the island fireplace without looking into the floor-length oval mirror, she headed into her walk-in closet and changed into a pink silk replacement.

"Care to tell your husband about it?"

She sat at her pink crushed velvet-trimmed vanity, looked in the mirror, and brushed her long strawberry-blonde hair. "I don't want to tell you."

"Why not?"

"I know what you'll say."

"Whatever happened to innocent until proven guilty?"

Jana placed the gold brush back on the vanity. "I was being chased by someone at the Capitol."

"The Capitol Theatre?"

"No, the Capitol…in Washington, DC."

Brian ran a strong hand through his thick chestnut hair, and said like a television announcer, "Courtesy of Jana Lane's next film, *Madam Senator.*"

Dedication

To Fred, for everything over all these years
~*~
To Melanie and the staff at The Wild Rose Press, Inc.
~*~
And to everyone who loved
Paper Doll and *Porcelain Doll,*
and begged for another Jana Lane mystery.

Chapter 1

1983

Jana Lane, America's most famous ex-child star, ran down a dark hallway in the north wing of the Capitol, causing the row of senators' office doors to become a blur of brown. Sweat soaked through her beige business suit as her heart pounded in her ears. She turned a corner, and Jana's heels skidded to a halt on the marble floor as she screamed at the sight of—

Jana gasped and looked up at her husband's handsome face. *Thank God it was just a dream.*

Brian leaned back against the gold circular headboard under the ruby-red satin canopy bedcover. "It must have been one heck of a nightmare."

Jana noticed her beige satin nightgown was soaking wet. She pushed off the silver satin sheets. After walking past the circular fireplace without looking into the floor-length oval mirror, she headed into her walk-in closet and changed into a pink silk replacement.

"Care to tell your husband about it?"

She sat at her pink crushed velvet-trimmed vanity, looked in the mirror, and brushed her long strawberry-blonde hair. "I don't want to tell you."

"Why not?"

"I know what you'll say."

"Whatever happened to innocent until proven guilty?"

Jana placed the gold brush back on the vanity. "I was being chased by someone at the Capitol."

"The Capitol Theatre?"

"No, the Capitol...in Washington, DC."

Brian ran a strong hand through his thick chestnut hair, and said like a television announcer, "Courtesy of Jana Lane's next film, *Madam Senator*."

Guilty as charged. Jana got back into bed. "I hope this isn't a premonition...like the last time." She nestled her cheek into Brian's mountainous chest. It smelled woodsy, and it felt like home.

Brian placed a muscular arm around her shoulders. "Remember what happened during shooting on *His Obsession* last year?"

"I was nominated for an Oscar," Jana replied into Brian's pectoral muscles. She crinkled her nose. "But I didn't win."

"You also nearly got killed. Not to mention what happened during *Sugar and Spice* when you were eighteen."

She looked up at him. "I want to do this movie, Brian."

His hazel eyes turned into slits. "Simon and Jackson want you to do this movie."

Jana sat up, meaning business. "*I* want to do this movie."

Brian took her hand. "Tell me why?"

She wrapped her legs around his. It felt like two thin twigs twining around a tree trunk. "I'm forty-one years old."

"Older than me."

She slapped his bottom playfully. "Not by much."

He tossed back his mane. "I'm still younger."

Jana shared a laugh with her husband then gazed out the window at their five acres of land leading to the Hudson River and Catskill Mountains in the distance, like charcoal cutouts reaching up to the gray sky. "It's terrific that the architecture firm is doing so well."

"Thanks to my blood, sweat, and ulcers."

"And I love being your wife and the kids' mom, but—"

"I get it. You need more than that. But, babe, we have all the money we'll ever need. Why can't you do your AIDS fundraising, go to your church with the lesbian minister, have lunch with Jackson, and be happy?"

Jana sat in the yoga position and faced Brian. "I know this is hard for you to understand." *It's hard for anyone to understand, including me.* "For most of my childhood, I was an actor."

Brian scratched his washboard abdominals. "You weren't just an actor, babe. As Simon never lets us forget, you were the *biggest child star in the galaxy*."

"During my adult years…when I tried to run away from it, a part of me was…dead. I was lost…empty inside. Making *His Obsession* made me remember how much I love it." She squeezed his hand. "And how much I *need* it."

He looked like a lost little boy. "But you need me, too, right?"

"Right."

"Good."

They shared a long, passionate kiss. His lips felt warm and wet. She ran her fingers down his V-shaped back. "I'd be lost without you, Brian."

"I love you so much, babe." After a tight hug and another kiss, Brian said, "Do you feel better?"

"Much."

"Good."

They shared a longer, even more passionate kiss.

Jana came up for air first. "I can think of one good thing about my nightmares."

"What's that?"

"Come here, I'll explain it to you."

They giggled and slid underneath the sheet.

****

Jana saw Brian off to work the next morning, pulled on indigo spandex pants with a matching sweatshirt, sneakers, and headband then hurried across the hall to her home gym, where she worked out to Michael Sembello's "Maniac" and Irene Cara's "Flashdance…What a Feeling." As Jana gazed into the floor to ceiling mirrors and watched the forty-one-year-old woman stretch, run, lift, grunt, and groan, she wondered what happened to the young girl who tamed wild tigers, scaled treacherous mountains, and body-surfed on a ten-foot wave in her old movies.

Out of breath and soaking wet, Jana ran back to her bedroom and into the master bathroom. She turned on the gold falcon faucets, took a quick shower in the huge glass stall then dried off with a fluffy powder-blue O monogrammed towel. Thankful for her five-foot two-inch height and petite frame, Jana put on tight jeans, a pink off-the-shoulder sweater, and crimson jellie shoes. Then she teased her hair, applied turquoise eyeshadow over her eyes, highlighted her cheekbones with pink blush, and rubbed a bit of pink gloss onto her lips before hurrying down the spiral staircase.

Jana entered her two-island kitchen and found Devon, eleven, and Ed, seven, spinning on swivel chairs in the breakfast nook as buckwheat waffle pieces flew through the air like space grenades.

"Launching space torpedo one!" Devon placed a piece of waffle on his fork, wound up, and fired at his brother.

Ed lobbed a butter patty at his brother's nose. "Space station under attack!" With syrup dripping from his forehead onto his new shirt, Ed screeched, "Mommy, can we see *Return of the Jedi* again on Saturday?"

Jana replied, "Ask your father." *After I wring his neck for taking you to see it last weekend.*

Grace Effington, the children's new nanny, raced by the glass table, the glass wall, and the stone fireplace, following Brian Jr., two, into the butler's pantry.

"Climb! Pull down!" Brian Jr. shouted joyously.

"No, B.J., wait!" Grace looked a great deal older than her twenty-five years.

Jana took in a deep breath. As she counted to ten, she thought about how cute her children were as babies, and how much cuter they would be at twenty-one.

Feeling like a captain entering a disheveled barracks, Jana ordered Devon and Ed to finish their breakfasts. Then shape shifting into a private assigned to mess hall duty, Jana cleaned up the kitchen as well as her two sons, handed them their lunch boxes, kissed them goodbye, and stood at the large front door waving to the school bus at the white-columned front gates of her estate.

Jana closed the door and sat in the window seat of her front hallway, under the cathedral ceiling. As the morning glow penetrated the skylights and illuminated the stained-glass window and prism chandelier, Jana noticed her arms were bathed in a rainbow befitting America's one-time sweetheart.

Jana's maid opened the front door and stepped into the hallway. Rubbing her lower back, she said, "That heavy door will be the death of me. Why are you sitting on the window seat?"

"Hello, Theresa. I'm waiting for Simon."

The elderly woman looked down at the saffron marble floor. "The kids' shoes scuffed this floor. I need to mop it now." Theresa checked her gold watch—a Christmas gift from Jana. "I only have a couple of hours before my first soap opera."

Jana sighed.

As Theresa entered the kitchen, the doorbell rang.

Jana shouted, "I'll get it."

Jana opened the door to Simon Huckby. Her agent, somewhere between sixty-five years old and rigor mortis, wore a chartreuse and lime jumpsuit with a peach ascot and lemon waist pouch. After kissing the air around her cheek, Simon announced, "Baby doll! You look fabulous."

Who said an agent isn't worth ten percent? Jana walked Simon through the hallway, past the toy-laden play room, and into the all-glass sun porch, where they rested on bougainvillea print seat cushions atop white wicker rockers.

After Jana served him herbal iced tea from a silver carafe, Simon raised his Jana Lane glass and said, "To the biggest and brightest child star in the galaxy."

Who is dimming at forty-one. Jana took a sip of the mint tea then returned it to the white wicker and glass end table. "How's Cornelius?"

Simon helped himself to a pecan cookie on a silver tray. "He dropped me off on his motorcycle. It took us only five minutes to get from Rhinebeck to Hyde Park." He giggled. "Cornelius is such a *devil*." Simon's brown eyes grew like soaked raisins.

Jana smiled at the vision of Simon at barely over five feet tall riding behind a nearly seven foot tall Cornelius.

Simon wiped a tear from his sunken cheek. "When Jonas passed away, I thought I'd never love anyone ever again." He patted her knee. "Except for my star client." His face softened. "But then Cornelius came along. And I was miraculously given a second chance at happiness!"

Brian Jr. raced into the sun porch. "Mama!"

Jana scooped up her child, and bounced him on her lap while kissing his cheek. "How's my big boy?"

"This adorable little fellow will one day have his name up in lights—under his mother's," Simon said taking B.J.'s hand.

B.J. replied between giggles, "Simon…Mama's yagent."

"I'm sorry, Jana." Grace Effington stood in the doorway of the sunroom trying to catch her breath. Grape juice and maple syrup stains lined her cream-colored blouse, and chocolate stains laced her indigo skirt. "I thought I could catch him."

"It's fine, Grace." Jana took in Grace's short sienna hair, small features, and thin figure. "Would you like a cookie?"

"No, thank you," Grace replied with a tense smile.

"You didn't eat any breakfast," Jana said, always a mom.

"I'll eat something later."

"Simon, this is Grace, B.J.'s new nanny."

Simon looked at Grace suspiciously. "How long have you been working for my baby doll?"

"Only a week." Grace smiled, revealing a row of straight white teeth. "I was desperate for a job...and a place to live, and Jana took me in."

Simon looked at Grace like a guard checking in a refugee at Ellis Island. "Where did you come from, Grace?"

Is this the Spanish Inquisition? "Grace's husband was killed in the US Embassy bombing in Beirut."

Simon raised a dramatic hand to his mouth. "That was only two months ago."

Grace nodded sadly. "We were married for only two months. I was a mess. My only living relative...my cousin in Westchester took me in...temporarily. After I was well enough to look for work, a local agency sent me here. I got lucky."

"We're the lucky ones." Jana kissed B.J.'s nose. "Aren't we, B.J.?"

"We lucky," B.J. announced merrily.

"I'm sorry for your loss," Simon said, giving Grace the once-over.

"Thank you," Grace replied.

Simon added, "It must be quite an honor for you to work for the one and only Jana Lane."

Grace replied, "Yes, it is. Like everyone else, I really enjoyed *His Obsession*."

"And I'm sure, *like everyone else*, you adore my

girl's childhood movies," Simon said.

Grace looked down at her beige sandals. "I'm afraid I've never seen any of them."

Uh-oh.

Simon clutched his hands to his heart as if going into cardiac arrest. "You never saw *Daddy's Girl* or *The Adorable Orphan*?"

The young woman shook her head bleakly from side to side.

"Or *The Girl Detective*?"

Grace shook her head no again.

"*The Cowgirl and the Bandit*? *The Littlest Farmer*? *Jungle Girl*?" Simon flailed his arms like a patient in an insane asylum as his voice grew louder and higher pitched with each film title. "*Young Mermaid*? *Pink Ballerina*? *The Pirate Princess*? *The Cutest Scientist*? *Surfs Up*?"

Before Simon burst a blood vessel, Jana said, "Simon, Grace is only twenty-five years old. You can't expect her to have seen movies made before she was born."

"I most certainly can! Jana Lane was every child's best friend and protector. You are part of American history." Simon reached into his waist pouch and gently removed an antique doll with strawberry-blonde hair, crystal-blue eyes, and rosy cheeks, wearing a pink satin gown. "Every girl in America had this Jana Lane doll."

"Ja Lane doll!" B.J. reached for the doll.

Simon held it close to his caved-in chest.

Jana gave B.J. back to Grace. "Simon, that's all ancient history. Nobody cares about any of it anymore."

"I care!" Simon rose and glared at Grace like a schoolteacher confronting a tardy student. "Jana Lane's

The Small Sailor film paved the way for women to join the navy. *Girl Astronaut* led to Sally Ride becoming the first American woman in space on the Space Shuttle Challenger—just this month. You should watch every Jana Lane movie on videotape and honor your heritage as a woman!"

"I'm sorry. I will." With tears in her dark eyes, Grace took B.J. by the hand and hurried out of the sun porch.

Jana rested back on her rocker. "Simon, you frightened that girl. And where did you get that old doll?"

He returned the doll to his pouch with the precision of a plastic surgeon operating on a celebrity. "I found her when I moved out of my house in LA."

"Was that difficult for you?" Jana patted his tiny hand.

Simon looked off into the distance. "Yes, it's my final goodbye to Jonah." He grinned. "But now I'm closer to *you*."

Lucky me.

Simon scratched his bald pate. "Speaking of LA, I spoke with the brass at Masaka Productions." He sat down on the rocker. "Filming on *Madam Senator* begins the first of August. One week of shooting in Washington, DC when Congress is on vacation, then six weeks in a studio in New York City. So you'll only need to be away from your family for one week."

Jana looked out past her heart-shaped swimming pool and cabana. The rays of the sun illuminated the azure river, teal mountains, and periwinkle sky in the distance like a painting under a spotlight. "I see."

"What's wrong, baby doll?"

I could never hide anything from you, Simon. "I've been having nightmares…about Washington, DC."

"Jitters before starting a new film is to be expected, doll face."

"This is more than jitters, Simon. It's the same kind of dreams I had about *Sugar and Spice* and *His Obsession.*"

A worry line joined the wrinkles on Simon's forehead. "Tell Mama all about it."

Jana closed her eyes. "In each dream, I'm running down a hallway in the Capitol…past the offices of US senators."

"Who are you running to?"

"That's just it. I'm running *away*…from something or someone."

"Who?"

She looked at him. "I wake up before finding out."

Simon took her hand. "I'll come with you to DC."

"Thank you, but that won't be necessary. I have over a month to get myself together."

"Not exactly. The producers of the film have arranged for you to shadow Cassandra Castle for a week—as research for the film."

Jana slapped her knee. "I *knew* the film script was based on Senator Castle."

"*Loosely* based." Simon adjusted his ascot. "She hasn't sanctioned the film or agreed to put her name on it, but she *did* say yes to interviews."

Jana felt her eyes double in size. "That's wonderful! She's a hero of mine."

"Heroine, baby girl."

"She's one of the only two women in the US Senate, and she's a tireless champion for women's rights, children's rights, gay rights, healthcare, education, the environment, racial equality." Jana paced the sun porch, nearly knocking over the tiffany chandelier and banging into the hanging white wicker swing. "She's also a graduate of Vassar College like me. How amazing it will be to talk about politics with the junior senator from Ohio!"

She reached for a pillow from the glider and pressed it against her chest. "I can also ask about her father. He was a terrific senator. And I can inquire about government funding for AIDS research. I wonder if she's heard about my two fundraisers for AIDS? Do you think she knows who I am? I wonder if she's seen any of my movies. She's about my age, I think, so maybe she has. I can't wait to talk to her about her rise from assemblywoman to congresswoman to senator!"

Simon stood and wrapped his thin arm around her shoulders. "Slow down, baby doll. You can ask Cassandra Castle as many questions as you like when you interview her for the film."

"When is that?"

"In three days."

Jana fell back onto the glider. "Three days! I can't possibly fly to Washington, DC for a week in three days."

"Why not?" Simon sat next to her. "Devon and Ed have only one week left of school. You can take them with you and make it an educational vacation. I'm sure they'll learn more about history and government in Washington, DC than from their over-the-hill matron teachers."

"Their teachers are in their twenties."

"What do young people nowadays know about

history and government? They haven't been around that long. Devon and Ed will get firsthand experience at the Jefferson Memorial, Washington Monument, Lincoln Memorial, and Smithsonian Museum. And you'll have them back before they need to leave for summer camp."

Jana leaned back on the glider. "And what about B.J.?"

Simon waved his little hands as if swatting an invisible fly. "Your new nanny what's-her-name can take B.J. to the National Zoo and wave at the monkeys. Kids love monkeys. Why, I'll never know." He elbowed Jana in the ribs. "And Brian will love the Naval Heritage Center and US Navy Memorial." Simon wet his finger and ran it across his eyebrow. "And make Brian take you to see a show at the Kennedy Arts Center or at the Ford Theatre."

"You've got this all figured out, haven't you, Simon?"

"I've been watching over you since you were six years old, baby doll, and I have no intentions of ever stopping."

She kissed his cheek and smelled makeup base. "All right. I'll ask Brian tonight."

Simon left and Jana fed B.J. his lunch in the kitchen—careful not to disturb Theresa's soap opera viewing. Then she played an intergalactic video game in the play room with the returning Devon and Ed, fed them their dinners in the kitchen, gave B.J. a bath in the upstairs bathroom, and tucked them all into their beds with a bedtime story. Next, Jana checked each of the three bedrooms to make sure all overhead lights, desk lamps, flashlights, and space game lights were off then she came down the spiral staircase and greeted her husband.

Brian yanked off his tie and jacket and threw them over the banister. Then he wrapped his arms around her and pulled her into his strong chest and torso. After a long kiss, he asked, "How's my girl?"

"Bursting to ask you about something."

The bags under Brian's eyes dropped to his cheekbones. "I had a long day. I have something to tell you, babe. Let me change, kiss the kids, and meet you in the dining room in a half hour."

She kissed his strong chin. "Sounds like a plan."

A half hour later Jana and Brian sat on either end of the long maple table in their dining room, taking in the luscious scents of Theresa's Moroccan chicken smothered with sweet potatoes, asparagus, olives, prunes, and cinnamon. Jana smiled at how adorable Brian looked in his sweatshirt and jeans with his chestnut hair falling over his ears and forehead.

She took a sip of white wine from a crystal glass then released the white silk napkin from her silver napkin holder and placed it onto her lap. Moving the napkin holder around the white lace tablecloth, she asked, "How are things at the company?"

Brian dug into his dinner like a rescued castaway. "You don't want to hear my complaints."

You're right, but what are wives for? "Sure I do."

He didn't need further coaxing. "Remember how miserable I was as a landscaper?"

"I think a wall in the study still has a fist hole in it."

"And remember when I opened the architecture business, how long and hard I went after wealthy clients?"

She released her famous dimples. "I vaguely recall the five-course dinners I hosted here."

"Now I have more clients than I know what to do with, and I'm up to my bloodshot eyeballs with work."

"Isn't that a good thing?"

Brian wiped gravy off his chin with his napkin. "Good for business. Bad for my sanity...and stamina."

She looked at her reflection in the maple and glass China cabinet. *You can do this, girl.* "Then what I have to tell you should be good news."

"What's that?"

Here goes. "I've arranged for a little...vacation...for all of us."

Brian's neck stiffened. "A vacation? Where? When?"

"In three days. To Washington, DC." *Why do I sound like a frog with a human caught in its throat?*

"Babe—"

"Please don't say anything, Brian. Let me explain everything, and then you can tell me all the reasons why you don't want to do it."

Brian put down his fork, mimed zipping his lips, and waved his hand for her to continue.

Jana pushed away her untouched plate. "Simon arranged for me to follow Senator Cassandra Castle in Washington, DC for a week...as research for *Madam Senator*...starting in three days. I've cleared it with the school to take Devon and Ed. Grace is happy to come along for B.J. I know you are incredibly busy at work, but you just said you need some time to wind down or you'll collapse. We have plenty of money, so if you lose a client, we'll manage." *Thank goodness I'm an actress.* "I think this trip will be a fun vacation, but also a great opportunity to teach our children about our government and the importance of being active citizens." *Okay, I'm rambling.* "Please don't say no before giving it a chance."

Brian asked, "Are you finished?"

Totally—after you bite my head off. Jana nodded.

Brian walked to Jana's end of the table, bent down, and kissed her cheek.

"Is that the kiss of death?" Jana asked.

Brian sat in the chair next to his wife. "It sounds great."

Jana's jaw dropped to the silver candle holders. "You *want* to go?"

"I'm looking forward to it."

"In three days from now?"

"I'll be packed and ready."

"And you understand this is a one-week—seven-day vacation in Washington, DC?"

"I do."

"And you are Brian Otley of Hyde Park, New York?"

"That's me. What did Theresa leave us for dessert?"

Jana began eating her cold dinner like a revived shock victim. "Before we move on to dessert, what is it you wanted to tell me?"

A devilish grin filled Brian's handsome face. "I got a government contract to design a new wing in the Capitol for more senate offices. I have to go to Washington, DC next week for meetings."

Jana chased Brian around the table and caught him against the purple peacock wallpaper. "You think you're very clever, don't you?"

"No, I think *you're* very clever. That's why I married you."

Jana rested her hands on Brian's strong neck and they shared a kiss. "I called Jackson and he said we can stay with them."

Brian's shoulders slumped.

"He's our best friend, Brian."

"Who we never see."

"Because of his crazy schedule as a congressman going back and forth to DC."

"He comes home every third week."

"And meets with local business leaders, union leaders, religious groups, veterans, lobbyists, and community leaders."

Brian pouted. "Everybody but us."

"So this will give us an opportunity to visit him in DC. Jackson and Adam have a beautiful second home on a lake with two guest rooms. The kids miss seeing one another, and Jackson said they can all stay in Tyler and Topher's bedroom. You know Devon and Ed will love that."

Brian leaned against the wall. "I'm *touched* that the congressman has the time for us. I thought Adam took up most of Jackson's time nowadays."

Jana felt like a UN arbitrator. "I don't understand why you don't like Adam. He's an ex-Navy man like you. When his wife went off the deep end, he did the right thing and raised his two children. Are you jealous because Jackson is so devoted to him?"

"Of course not." Brian scratched at his hair.

"Is it because Adam didn't ask you for help when he and Jackson built their house in Washington, DC?"

"Come on, babe, I'm not childish like that."

Since when? "Then what is it?"

"There's…something about the guy I don't like."

"Well, can you get past that *something* for a week?" She hooked her fingers into his belt loops. "For me and the kids?"

His strong hands cupped her bottom. "What do I get if I say yes?"

"We'll think of something."

****

Over the next three days, Jana packed enough clothing, food, toys, games, diapers, cosmetics, hair products, and over-the-counter medicines to open a department store. With the hired limousine filled like a circus clown car, Jana and her family waved goodbye to Simon and Theresa as the driver headed across their brick driveway past the two stone columns. Upon reaching the street, Ed shouted, "Are we there yet?"

Sitting next to his brother, Devon cried out, "Washington, DC is far away. It'll take us at least an hour to get there."

Not to be left out, B.J. screamed from his car seat next to Grace, "We go Waton!"

Jana sat through countless sing-a-longs, car games, snack attacks, and bathroom breaks. She was thrilled when the frazzled driver pulled up to Pennsylvania Station. Brian paid the porter a small fortune to help, and the Otleys, their nanny, and their luggage were finally on the train to Washington, DC.

Jana arbitrated Devon and Ed's arguments over who would sit next to the window, and the train left the tracks amidst screams of delight from the Otley boys. Grace served lunch while Jana read stories about trains that could to the children bouncing in their seats like trampolines. To Jana's shock and elation, all three boys (and Brian) drifted off to sleep halfway through the three-and-a-half hour train ride.

When they reached Union Station in Washington, DC, Jana breathed a sigh of relief at the sight of Adam Stokes, in jeans and a sweatshirt, waving at them from his minivan. Adam was as tall as Brian but even more muscular in stature. He loaded their luggage into his car quickly then drove them through the inner city to the Washington Channel.

Sitting between Adam and Brian in the front seat, Jana glanced back at Grace and the children, making sure they were all right, then she turned to Adam. "Thank you for picking us up."

"My pleasure." Adam ran a rugged hand through his chestnut hair. "Check out the Potomac River out the window. It's the fourth largest river in the United States."

B.J. agreed. "Four!"

"That's right, B.J." Adam winked at B.J. in his rearview mirror. "The Southwest Waterfront area has been under development since the 1950s. Jackson wanted to do his part by building our house as part of the lakefront renovation."

"Lakefront?" Brian whistled. "Jack must be doing pretty well as a congressman."

Adam's thick neck muscles tightened. "My pension from the Navy helped."

"And Adam is a contractor," Jana said as she squeezed Brian's knee. "I'm sure the house was built economically and beautifully."

Brian sneered. "How long have you and Jack been living there now?"

Adam replied, "We started building during Jackson's first term in office."

"Who was your architect?" Brian asked.

"Somebody we found locally."

Jana felt Brian's bicep tighten under hers.

"We've been living there over a year now…when we aren't in our Hyde Park house."

"Which you got in the divorce proceedings, right?" Brian added.

Jana squeezed Brian's knee harder, stopping before she cut off the circulation. *The next squeeze will be higher up.* "Adam, I was so sorry to hear that your ex-wife is in a psychiatric hospital."

Adam nodded with sadness in his hazel eyes. "She's been suffering from manic depression for many years. It was rough on the kids…and on me. I had my own problems…with coming out. I'm sure Jackson told you."

"Yes." A line separated Brian's forehead. "But Jackson hasn't told us much lately. Come to think of it, we haven't seen Jackson since you and he…took up house together. Or I guess I should say, *houses.*"

Jana took Brian's hand—and squeezed. "Won't it be great to see Jackson and Adam's new home?"

"Sure." Brian added with a tight jaw, "After all this time."

Jana said quickly, "Adam, your children are fortunate to have such a loving father." She smiled. "And now they have *two* loving fathers."

Hearing about Adam's children, Devon whined, "When do we get there?"

"We want to see Tyler and Topher!" Ed chimed in.

Grace settled them down. "We'll be there soon,

guys."

Adam drove up the driveway to their house, and Jana marveled at the large A-frame. It was surrounded by emerald-green grass and Kelly-green trees leading to a peaceful cerulean lake matted by a hazy sky. The moment the car stopped, the children leapt out of the minivan like unboxed springs.

Topher and Tyler, ten-year-old blond-haired and blue-eyed twins, raced out of their carved oak front door and greeted Devon and Ed. "Yeah, Devon and Ed!" cheered Topher.

"Come see our boat!" cried Tyler.

Grace ran after them as all four boys hurried to the dock behind the house and onto Adam's rowboat.

Adam excused himself. "I better go make sure the kids are safe."

Brian and Jana stretched their legs, and Jackson came out of the house and scooped Jana up into his arms. At six feet six inches tall, he made Jana feel like a child meeting Santa Claus.

Thank goodness I wore a sweater and slacks.

Jackson returned Jana to the ground, and she took in his tight curly black hair, wide nose, and twinkling dark eyes. The self-described *Afro-homo* smiled, and the two best friends burst into tears.

"I missed you so much, hon," Jackson said while wiping his eyes on the sleeve of his sweatshirt. "How crazy is it that you have to come all the way to DC to see me?"

Jana searched in her bag for a tissue. "I know how busy you've been in Hyde Park."

Jackson groaned. "It seems like I'm fundraising, meeting with community groups, hearing people's problems, dodging lobbyists, or dealing with issues at home every minute. Believe it or not, hon buns, I look forward to coming to DC for my meetings in Congress."

"But you love it." Jana grinned at her best friend and wiped her eyes.

"I know it's crazy, but I do," Jackson replied.

Brian leaned against the minivan, wearing a tight blue polo shirt with the collar turned up and even tighter jeans.

Jackson said to Jana, "Hey girl, who's this gorgeous hunk of man-meat, your chauffeur or your bodyguard?"

Brian grinned from ear to ear and gave his friend a bear hug. "So you still remember me?"

Jackson laughed. "*Remember* you? Ask Adam how many times I still call him Brian. He insists I only went with him because he resembles you." He nudged Jana's side. "Any chance of us switching men in the middle of the night?"

Tears of laughter ran down Jana's cheeks. "I missed you so much, Jackson."

"Ditto." Brian put his arms around Jana and Jackson. "Here's to old home week."

"It was nice of Adam to pick us up at the train station." Jana grabbed a piece of luggage.

Jackson screamed, and Jana dropped the luggage like a ball of fire. "Don't either of you touch those! Adam and I will take care of that. Let's get you both to the guest room, so you can, as they say in gay Paree, *freshen each other up.*"

They walked toward the house of natural wood, glass, and stone. Jana said, "Your new home is beautiful, Jack."

Jackson beamed. "Adam worked with a local architect. My man is an amazing contractor. Didn't he do a great job, Brian?"

Brian winced. "Great."

Jana enjoyed watching Jackson play tour guide. He led them through the rustic stone hallway to the cathedral-ceilinged great room with a limestone floor-to-ceiling fireplace then out onto the huge wraparound porch, where they waved to Adam and the children on the boat. Continuing the tour, Jackson walked them through the enormous eat-in kitchen with a wood burning stove, spacious dining room surrounded by wooden columns, and a den laden with overstuffed chairs and sofas, carved wood benches, and end tables. Finally, they went up the knotted wooden steps to five bedrooms, including a guest room for Jana and Brian, and one for Grace and B.J.

After Jana and Brian unpacked, napped, and freshened up, they welcomed the boys returning from playing at the lake. Next, the adults bathed and fed the four children, and tucked them into their bunk beds— set up with blankets as space stations. Topher and Devon shared one bunk bed, and Ed and Tyler took the other. Since Jana's boys were on the lower bunks, she was able to kiss Devon and Ed goodnight. She winced as Brian followed after her, bumping his head on an upper bunk.

Jana and Brian looked on as Jackson and Adam kissed Topher and Tyler.

Adam said, "Do you two know how much we love you?"

The boys nodded. Topher said, "We love you, too,

Daddy and Papa."

Jackson hugged the two boys. "You're our boys."

Tyler added, "Papa Jack, promise you won't ever leave us?"

Jackson choked back a tear. "I promise, honey."

Then Jana checked in on B.J. and Grace in the next room. As Jana entered, Grace hung up the phone.

"Everything all right?"

Grace's face flushed. "I called...my cousin in Westchester...to tell her we arrived safely in Washington." She pulled at the sleeves of her hoodie. "Is that okay?"

Jana smiled. "Of course."

"I like Waton!" B.J. cooed.

"I like it, too," Jana kissed then covered her two year old in his carved sleigh bed next to Grace's carved canopy bed. Then Jana said to the young woman, "After B.J. falls asleep, come down and join us for dinner."

Grace sat on an oak rocking chair next to the window, avoiding Jana's gaze. "I'll come down for something later."

Jana took Grace's hand. "I can only imagine how difficult it must have been to lose your husband, but you have to eat."

"I will."

"Promise?"

Grace raised three fingers. "Scout's honor."

A half hour later, Jana, Brian, and Jackson sat around the huge carved oak table in the dining room looking out the glass wall at the swirls of pink, violet, and tangerine painting the cobalt sky. Adam served lemon chicken, scalloped sweet potatoes, broccoli almandine, and spinach salad with beets and goat cheese in a creamy avocado dressing presented beautifully on large ceramic plates.

Jana said, "Adam, this is absolutely delicious."

Jackson blew a kiss to Adam who caught it and placed it over his heart.

Brian said through a clenched jaw, "You build houses, cook gourmet meals, take care of the kids. Is there anything you don't do, Adam?"

"Clean the bathroom," Jackson said.

"Guilty," Adam replied pouring everyone white wine. "I don't believe in hiring a housekeeper, cook, landscaper, or even a nanny. It keeps me humble and in good shape taking care of the house. Besides, *I* want to raise my kids, not have some stranger do it."

Brian looked like a pit bull scratched by a kitten. "Those things are a necessity for people who *work*."

"What *work* are you doing in Washington, DC, Brian?" Adam asked.

"I'm meeting with Senator Josiah Maxmillion, the majority leader of the Senate, about a government contract I won to design a new extension for senate offices in the north wing of the Capitol."

"I wish they'd do that in the south wing for the House." Jackson moaned. "My office is so old and small it must have been used by Lincoln for clandestine meetings with his male lover—standing upright." He winked at Jana who giggled into her wine glass. Then Jackson turned to Adam. "This is quite a coincidence. Huh, Adam?"

"What do you mean?" Brian asked like a child wanting to be let in on an adult joke.

Adam cleared this throat. "Senator Maxmillion is

meeting with *me* about a government contract I won as the contractor—on the same job."

"That's wonderful!" Jana toasted Brian and Adam. "You'll both be working together. Brian designing and Adam building. You'll make a great team. And you can carpool to the Capitol!"

Adam and Brian looked as happy as a mismatched couple on a blind date.

"With this new contract, how will you have the time to do all your chores around the house?" Brian asked, looking like a dog unwilling to give up a bone. "Think you might have to hire a nanny?"

Adam cut into a piece of chicken. "Not likely. I believe people can do whatever they set their minds to doing. It's all about priorities."

Jana pressed her foot over Brian's. "I'd lose my mind without Grace. In only a short time, she's become one of the family."

Jackson asked, "Why didn't she come downstairs for dinner?"

"Good question." Jana speared a broccoli. "She's had some personal issues."

"Grace lost her husband in the US Embassy bombing in Beirut," Brian explained.

"How horrible," Jackson said between bites of his salad.

"It's a wacky world," Adam added.

"How do you mean?" Brian asked like a kid drawing a chalk line on the street and raising his fists.

Adam replied, "Tell him, Jackson."

Jackson nodded at his partner. After a deep breath, Jackson said, "We didn't want to discuss it in front of the kids."

"Discuss *what*?" Jana asked, feeling the acid rise in her stomach.

Jackson put down his fork. "Maxmillion is the senior senator from Ohio, a conservative, and a pretty sure bet to run for president."

"We know that," Jana said.

Jackson replied, "But what you *don't* know is Maxmillion also started a new campaign." It looked like Jackson had swallowed a worm. "*Protect the Children.*"

"What's he protecting the children from?" Jana and Brian asked in unison.

"Evidently…*us*," Adam replied.

Jana slid to the edge of her seat. "Care to explain that one?"

Jackson said, "Senator Maxmillion has presented a bill that just passed the Health, Education, Labor, and Pensions Committee. Since his party controls the Senate, he's the chair of that committee."

"What's the bill?" Brian asked.

Jackson answered, "It prohibits homosexuals from raising children."

Jana gasped. "That's insane!"

"Wait a minute." Brian looked deep in thought. "Tyler and Topher are Adam's *biological* children."

Jackson explained, "The bill goes broader than banning gay people from being able to adopt children. The law states that a gay person or a gay couple *cannot raise children outside of the institution of marriage*, regardless of the circumstances."

"But it's illegal for gays to marry," Brian shouted.

"Hence the catch twenty-two," Jackson said.

"What about heterosexual people who are widowed

or divorced, or straight couples who aren't married but are raising children?" Jana asked mystified.

"Evidently, that's okay according to Maxmillion's bill," Adam said.

Jana felt her face flush. "Jack, you're a lawyer. This can't be legal!"

"Everything is legal until a court says it is illegal," Jackson explained. "Reagan has appointed so many conservative federal judges to the bench, the law may slip through the court system."

"But surely this so-called *law* won't pass the full Senate," Jana said.

"I'm not so sure," Jackson said. "Conservative senators need to play the role of hero to their right wing constituents. In order to be a hero protecting others, you need a villain. It seems we've been cast in the role."

Brian threw down his napkin. "But the House is controlled by the Democrats. It'll never pass there."

Jackson swallowed hard. "I'll do my best to stifle it, but I'm only one of three openly gay congressmen. The closet gays in the House will be afraid to stand up to Maxmillion for fear of being outed by association. Maxmillion and his ilk have a great deal of lobbyist money. They are also working with the wealthy, more conservative religious leaders to appeal to the fear, ignorance, and hate in people under the guise of protecting their children. With that kind of fervor, the Democrats in the House may be afraid to vote it down."

"Whatever happened to true conservatism—letting people lead their own lives?" Brian asked with his head in his hands.

Jana added, "And true liberalism—fighting for justice and equality for *all*?"

Brian asked, "And what does Maxmillion propose to do with the children currently being raised by gay people? Take them from their homes and put them in orphanages?"

"That's about the size of it." Jackson tented his long, shaking fingers.

Jana collapsed back into her chair. "This is completely insane!"

"That's probably why it's getting play in the Senate," Jackson said.

"And *I* have a meeting tomorrow afternoon with Maxmillion," Adam explained.

"So do *I*," Brian replied like a kid not wanting to share his candy.

Jana said, "Won't it be difficult meeting with someone who opposes…or at least pretends to oppose your rights as a parent, Adam?"

"Not exactly. Maxmillion probably doesn't know about my home life."

"And when he *does*?" Jana asked.

Adam grinned like the Cheshire Cat. "All the better. I'm looking forward to *sharing my thoughts* with the senator."

Jackson replied, "Don't be surprised if Maxmillion dodges the bullet. He's a skilled politician with an amazing track record of getting what he wants."

Jana stood slowly like a volcano heading for eruption. "We have to stop this before Maxmillion and his ilk brand gay people with pink triangles as they did in the Holocaust." *Pink! That's it!* "Jackson, as you know I'm in DC to shadow Senator Cassandra Castle for researching my role in *Madam Senator*."

Jackson nodded.

"Isn't she the senator who wears pink satin dresses?" Brian asked.

Jana paced across the wide-planked hardwood floor. "*And* she's the junior senator from Ohio, a liberal who has fought hard for the rights of children...and for gay people. When I interview her tomorrow, I'll ask her to speak to Maxmillion and advocate for us."

Jackson and Adam shared a weak smile.

"What?" Jana asked.

"I don't think that will do any good," Jackson said.

"Why not?" Jana asked.

Brian asked, "Because Cassandra Castle has been mentioned as a possible Democratic vice presidential candidate?"

"That's not the problem," Jack said.

"Then what *is* the problem, Jack?" Jana asked.

Jackson waved his glass of wine. "The problem, honey, is according to *Wake Up Washington*, Cassandra Castle and Josiah Maxmillion are lovers."

Chapter 2

The next morning Jana rose early, got breakfast for the kids, and changed into a marigold business suit with shoulder pads, matching heels, and an ivory and gold pendant. After kissing the other six men in her life goodbye, Jana drove with Jackson in his sports car through the National Mall.

Jackson looked dapper in his gray suit and indigo tie. "I'm so glad you're here, honey."

Jana squeezed his arm. "We thought you had given up on us."

"Never. We'll always be best buddies."

"Tell that to Brian."

"What do you mean?"

"I'll never admit saying this, but I think he's jealous of Adam."

Jackson did a double-take. "Brian is as straight as an arrow. Then again, thinking about Cupid in that little G-string. Maybe arrows aren't so straight."

Jana laughed.

"Tell your old chum what's going on with Brian."

"You must have noticed how our two guys scowl at one another."

"I thought it was because they don't know each other all that well."

"It's more than that, Jack. There's a kind of one-upmanship between them…like German Shepherds protecting their turf."

"But they're both so butch—and so cute," Jackson said with a wink.

"And they're both acting like children." Jana sighed. "As you know, Brian didn't have a very good relationship with his parents. I think it made him leery of other people."

"Adam usually plays well with others—especially me." He giggled. "His parents are terrific…his adoptive parents I mean. He never knew his birth parents."

"Does he care to find them?"

"Not particularly."

Jana looked out her window at the blur of buildings. "Has Adam mentioned why he doesn't like Brian?"

Jackson imitated Adam's deeper voice. "There's just something about the guy I don't like."

"Brian said the exact same thing about Adam." Jana shifted in her chair. "They'll be working and living together for a week. Let's hope they come to a meeting of the minds." *And not a meeting of the fists.*

"We love them, hon buns. They'll eventually learn to love each other."

"From your mouth to the Washington gods' ears."

Jackson drove up to the security gate of the US Capitol, gave their names to the militaristic guard, then parked the car.

They walked up the steps of the enormous Capitol building built in 1793, and Jana gasped with pride. She marveled at the 19th Century white neoclassical architecture, including the famous dome and countless columns. She smiled in remembrance of the country's forefathers and what they had sacrificed for freedom, liberty, and justice for all. "Jack, you get to work here every day!"

Jana entered the crowded building that smelled of disinfectant and age. She identified herself, and a stoic guard gave her an official looking badge to wear. Then she and Jackson walked up the stairs to the second floor, where Jackson directed her to the north wing— one of the newer wings. Jackson called out over his shoulder as he took off for the south wing, "Meet you back at the car at six. Enjoy your time with Senator Castle."

Jana walked through the center dome Rotunda and admired the one hundred and eighty foot ceiling as well as the paintings and sculptures of famous people and events in US history. Arriving at the north wing like a mouse in a maze, Jana turned corner after corner in search of her cheese—the office of Senator Cassandra Castle. Clicking her heels on the Georgia marble floor, Jana couldn't help thinking back to her nightmare about being chased down that same hallway.

Keep it together, girl. You don't want to come off like a flake when you meet your idol.

Jana asked a cleaning woman and a young page for directions. Turning a final corner, her heart leapt out of her jacket as she arrived at the office of Senator Cassandra Castle.

The office suite of junior senator Cassandra Castle was small and quite a distance from the Senate's main meeting room. A busy secretary quickly led Jana through the neat reception area into a cozy office with a French provincial desk and bookcase. Two maize-colored easy chairs faced the desk. The walls were adorned with various degrees and plaques of honor in appreciation of Senator Castle.

"Hello, Ms. Lane."

Jana was surprised the woman greeting her behind the desk was not Cassandra Castle.

The young woman's long blonde hair brushed against the shoulder pads of her emerald business suit. Her round aqua eyes, button nose, and thick lips gave her an everywoman persona, as did her melodious voice and friendly demeanor. "Obviously, I'm not Senator Castle." She rose to shake Jana's hand. "I'm Cassie's assistant." She offered a warm smile. "I'm also her sister, Lenore Castle."

Jana shook the woman's hand. "It's nice to meet you, Ms. Castle."

"Please, call me Lenore. May I call you Jana?"

"Of course."

"Good. Please, have a seat." She directed Jana to one of the chairs facing the desk then took the seat next to it. "Cassie is in a meeting, but she should be back shortly." Her dimples appeared. "I say *should* because some of Cassie's colleagues and constituents...how can I put this diplomatically?"

"Never stop talking?"

"That's about it."

The two women shared a laugh.

"Would you like coffee or tea?"

"No, thank you." Jana crossed her legs. "I hope I won't be too much of a bother this week."

"A bother!" Lenore swooned. "It's a pleasure to have you. I saw *His Obsession* three times."

No doubt to watch the scene with my leading man in the hot tub.

"You were robbed of that Oscar."

Jana smiled. "You're very kind."

"No, I'm not. You should have won." Lenore winked. "We'll have to correct that for *Madam Senator*."

"I really appreciate you and the senator taking your valuable time to speak with me."

Lenore laughed. "We're always going somewhere or doing something. I'm not sure how valuable it all is."

Jana slid to the edge of her seat. "I admired your father when he was the senior senator of Ohio. Samuel Castle was an amazing champion for *the little guy*."

"That he was. Cassie and I miss him a great deal." Lenore looked at a picture of her deceased father on the wall, and wiped moisture from the corner of her eye. "He was a wonderful father, an amazing statesman, and Cassie's role model."

"And how fitting it is that your sister has taken up the banner as junior senator."

Lenore nodded. "As one of only two female US senators, Cassie has her hands full—and not with cooking and sewing."

They laughed again.

The room seemed to glow as Senator Cassandra Castle walked into it.

She's even more youthful and beautiful than on television. And she's my age!

Jana rose and the senator took her hand as if Jana was the only person in the world. Their eyes met, and the senator said, "Jana Lane, what a pleasure."

"Agh, you, we, hello." Jana felt like a star-struck teenager. "Senator Cattle…I mean Tassel…Sassy Lassy…oh dear." *Why can't I stop talking?*

"Please, call me Cassie. I apologize for being late. I

was held up at an Energy and Natural Resources Committee meeting hearing reports on new power systems—sun and wind power." She smiled. "Mother Nature really does have all the answers."

"It seems like you are doing a fine job in helping her along." Jana giggled. "I can't believe I'm really here!"

"This may look impressive now, but after the week is out, you'll realize it's not all it's cracked up to be by the press. Tell me about *Madam Senator*."

"It's a terrific screenplay. I hope I can do it justice. I play a liberal female senator who is a champion for the disenfranchised, and on the rise to becoming vice president. While her career is golden, her personal life is tarnished by loving the wrong man."

Cassie sat behind her desk. "Sounds like a perfect Hollywood story."

"We're shooting in DC and in New York City."

"I know. Film production is good for DC's economy." Cassie glanced at her phone messages. "Anything urgent, Lenore?"

Lenore pointed to various piles of papers on the desk. "Sign these, call them, and meet with these at the time and place on your calendar."

"See, Jana, it's not all glamour and valor." Cassie signed papers as she spoke. "Have you met my sister?"

Jana nodded. "Lenore has been incredibly hospitable."

"She was the sweet one growing up," Cassie said.

Lenore replied, "I hid in Cassie's shadow. Our parents had me later in life."

"Which she never lets me forget," Cassie said, sharing a smile with Lenore.

Jana said, "As I mentioned to Lenore, I was quite a fan of your father's, and so sorry to hear of his passing from the heart attack…when was it…ten years ago?"

"Eleven," Cassie replied.

"Is your mother still alive?" Jana asked.

Cassie squeezed Lenore's hand. "Mom passed away twenty-two years ago, two years after Lenore was born. She had cancer."

"My mother died of cancer when I was thirteen. I know firsthand how difficult it can be."

Cassie nodded.

"Well, I'll leave you two alone." Lenore rested a hand on Jana's back. "Welcome to Washington, DC, Jana."

"Thank you again." Alone with Cassandra Castle, Jana gazed at the senator's twilight-blue satin jacket and skirt that matched the senator's eyes perfectly.

"What? The attire?" Cassie laughed. "I wore a pink satin gown to a Washington, DC fundraiser for MS and the press went wild. It caught on. So I wear satin whenever I can. It keeps the press happy—and it keeps my name in the newspapers." Cassie took a letter opener with her picture on it from inside her desk drawer and opened her mail. "I like to open my own mail. Call me old fashioned." She grinned. "Kudos on your fundraisers in New York for AIDS research, Jana."

Jana replied through a mouth drier than the Sahara Desert, "You *know* about those?"

"AIDS is one of my pet projects. Unfortunately with a Republican president and Senate majority, I've struck out each time at bat." She winked at Jana. "But I won't stop trying."

"You are quite a hero of mine."

Cassie seemed surprised. "Really?"

"Like your father, you are a tireless champion for the common person."

Cassie's eyes deepened in their sockets. "Yet people continue to act against their own best interests by electing conservatives who put large corporations before people."

"But they also continue to elect champions like *you*."

Cassie glanced at her open mail quickly then placed the letter opener on her desk. "You are a champion yourself, Jana." She ran a hand through her short, perfectly styled, blonde hair. "When I was a girl I was…different from the other little girls. Believe it or not, I never wore pink…or satin. I never even wore a dress. Dolls, toys, and games didn't interest me. I wanted to build things, solve problems, help my neighbors." She seemed miles away. "I had very few friends my own age. And adults looked at me like an outcast." She smiled. "Watching your movies got me through that difficult time. I'd sit in the movie theatre in my hometown in Oakwood, Ohio and become lost in a world where a young girl could rescue her father from pirates, ride bareback on a horse and save her little friend from bandits, be the first girl in outer space, and save a hospital from terrorists as a candy-striper." She pointed at Jana. "*You* are the reason I'm sitting here, Jana Lane."

Unable to speak, Jana blinked back tears. Finally finding her voice, she said, "I'm incredibly flattered." Jana added, "We were at Vassar College during the same time. We never spoke, but I was well aware of your debating awards and your work for social justice."

Lenore appeared at the door. "Cassie, your next appointment is here."

Jana swallowed the lump in her throat and rose. "Would you like me to leave?"

Waving her arms downward, Cassie said, "You wanted to shadow me. Sit and enjoy."

Jana retrieved a notepad from her purse.

A small, round man in a dark suit and horn-rimmed glasses entered the room. He carried a black briefcase larger than a piece of luggage, and looked at Cassie like a fisherman facing a fifty-pound tuna. "Senator Castle, thank you for seeing me again."

Cassie motioned him to the chair next to Jana's. "Please have a seat, Mr. Green. This is Jana Lane."

Jana smiled. "Hello, Mr. Green. I hope I'm not intruding."

"Not at all, Miss Lane." He sat and placed his briefcase on his lap.

Jana stifled a giggle as his comb-over parted and Mr. Green's bald head emerged like the Red Sea.

He said, "Senator Castle, as you know, I represent the Multitopower Conglomerate."

"I'm aware of that," Cassie replied.

He opened the briefcase and handed Cassie a series of brochures. "As I mentioned last time I was here, our affiliates manufacture numerous products as noted in our portfolio." He added, "Products for the safety of our country, created under strict guidelines, adding numerous jobs to the economy. We also support traditional family values in our hiring and business practices. I am here today to ask for your support in our various bids for government contracts."

"Mr. Green, as I said last time we met, I cannot offer you my support."

"Senator, we are a very large corporation with staggeringly high profits due to sound management principles."

"I'm well aware of that, but my answer has not changed."

He sneered. "Are you also *aware* that we are quite generous, and we consider it good business practice to support others—if they support *us*?"

Cassie tossed the brochures onto her desk. "Mr. Green, last night I did some research on your company."

Green loosened his collar. "You did?"

"I did," Cassie replied. "The *products* you manufacture are created in foreign countries without child labor laws. These children, some as young as six or seven years old, work twelve hour days in exchange for lunch. The workmanship is poor. The quality is worse. You talk your way into receiving government contracts with our armed services, homeland security, foreign affairs, space program, and agriculture offices only to lay off American workers and charge exorbitant amounts of money for faulty products that damage the environment."

"Now wait a moment, senator—"

"Your proclamation of family values is a code for anti-racial minority, anti-woman, and anti-gay business practices. That does not sound very *family-friendly* to me."

I can see why Cassandra Castle won awards in debating at Vassar College.

The lobbyist's face turned as blue as Cassie's

outfit. "Senator Castle, many of your colleagues in the senate are supporting our bid for government contracts—and not only your colleagues on the *right* side of the aisle."

Cassie replied, "And in exchange for my colleagues' support of massive tax breaks for your companies and the easing of environmental laws that pollute our water, air, and soil, you guarantee hefty donations to their next political campaigns."

Green scowled. "My company is completely reputable, senator."

"I disagree." Cassie threw the brochures into the wastebasket. "Please don't visit me again, Mr. Green."

"I believe you are making a huge mistake, senator."

"I agree. It was a mistake to see you again."

As if placing his Queen next to her Knight, Green said, "One of our chief supporters is Senator Maxmillion. Given your...*friendship* with the senior senator from your state, perhaps you will reconsider?"

As Jana wrote notes on her pad, a tall, thin, beautiful Native American young woman swept into the room with long, shiny black hair cascading behind her. The fire in the woman's dark eyes matched the crimson color of her business suit.

Lenore hurried into the room. "I'm sorry, Cassie, she ran right by me."

"That's all right, Lenore." As Lenore left the room, Cassie looked up at her newest visitor. "What can I do for you, Tamaya?"

"I was talking to Lenore and I overheard what Mr. Green just said," Tamaya replied with a sneer. "And I have a few things to say to the spokesman for the

Multitopower Conglomerate."

Green's spine stiffened.

Undaunted, Tamaya said, "Mr. Green, I am Tamaya Stormcloud of *Wake Up Washington*."

"I know who you are," Green replied with a sniff.

Tamaya's eyes bore into his. "What I heard just now sounded like a threat against my friend, Senator Castle."

Green closed his suitcase and stood. "No threat, Miss Stormcloud. I was simply stating the facts. As a journalist, you should know the statistics on reelection for senators who don't support the Conglomerate."

A cold draft entered the room. Tamaya clenched her fists. "Senator Castle is a fine senator who deserves to be reelected. Unleash your conglomerate fangs on someone else."

Green's jowls morphed into a knot. "Now *that* sounds like the threat."

"You want to hear a threat, Mr. Green? How about this?" Tamaya aimed and fired. "I've been doing a bit of research on your organization for an article I'm writing. It's still early in my investigation, but I've already uncovered quite a few interesting *tidbits*."

He grunted like a pig facing a butcher. "Senator Castle has already spouted her left wing fabrications about my company."

Tamaya came nose to nose with the lobbyist. "What *I've* uncovered goes *way* beyond using slave labor, not paying taxes, and damaging the environment."

Green looked like a bull in a tomato garden. "I would be very careful about what you print in your article, Miss Stormcloud. My conglomerate's staff lawyers are the finest in Washington." His eyes narrowed into slits. "And they are extremely *skilled*."

Tamaya's mouth watered at the prospect. "Don't worry, Mr. Green. I'll check every fact and figure, dot every i, and run it by *our* lawyers before going to print. But when I do, it will set Washington, DC on its ear, and the Multitopower Conglomerate on its ass."

Is that steam coming out of his ears?

Green turned to Cassie. "Please think about what I said, senator." He stormed out of the office.

Cassie said, "Well, Jana, you wanted to know what I do."

Tamaya took Green's seat, surprisingly not wiping it down first.

Cassie leaned back in her chair. "Tamaya, this is Jana Lane."

"I don't watch movies or television, but the reviewer on my newspaper liked *His Obsession*," Tamaya said to Jana.

"Thank you." *I think.*

"When do you start shooting *Madam Senator*?" Tamaya asked.

"Soon." *Too soon.*

Cassie smiled. "Jana is shadowing me this week to do research about the life of a female senator."

Tamaya took a large notebook out of her enormous bag. "That will make a good story."

A line appeared across Cassie's forehead. "Haven't you written enough about me, Tamaya?"

Tamaya seemed surprised. "What? The article about you and Max?"

"Yes, Tamaya, the article about me and Max."

"What was wrong with it?"

"What was *wrong*, very *wrong*, was that I told you about my relationship with Max off the record and in confidence—as a friend."

Tamaya let out a guttural laugh. "There is no such thing as off the record in journalism, Cassie."

Cassie seemed genuinely hurt. "Is there such a thing as *friendship*?"

I thought being kidnapped by a band of robbers in The Cowgirl and the Bandit was stressful. Jana rose from her chair. "Excuse me, I have to use the ladies' room."

As Jana walked out of the office, she heard Cassie say to Tamaya, "Thanks to your article, I've been dodging the press all of yesterday and today."

Jana shut the office door behind her.

Lenore rose from her desk and gave Jana a hug. "You looked like you needed that." The young woman sat Jana on a small loveseat near her desk then joined her. "The Capitol can be a capital nightmare at times."

So it seems. "Cassie was pretty upset—and rightfully so."

Lenore checked to make sure Cassie's secretary was deeply immersed in taking phone messages from reporters, then she leaned in and spoke softly. "Tamaya broke the story to the press about Cassie and Josiah Maxmillion dating."

"So I heard." Jana lifted her palms to the cracked ceiling. "Why is it such a big story? Cassie is single, and Senator Maxmillion is divorced—twice. Why does their dating have to be a secret?"

Lenore sighed. "Cassie and Max are from the same state, but they are very different politicians with quite disparate goals. When I came to work yesterday, I faced

44

a zoo of reporters clamoring for answers."

"You mean because he's a conservative and she's a liberal?"

"That and Max is old world, rich boys' club politics. Cassie is the wave of the future."

"How did they ever get together?"

"Good question."

The voices raised from inside Cassie's office.

Tamaya said, "I did it to boost your visibility, Cassie."

"You did it for your career, Tamaya."

"Don't push me, Cassie. I know a lot about you that I haven't printed."

The secretary hung up her phone and looked over at Jana and Lenore.

Jana turned to Lenore. "I need to stretch my legs. Do you think Cassie would mind if I took off for a bit?"

Lenore winked. "I don't blame you for wanting to escape before the start of round three."

"I also want to say hello to my husband. Brian is meeting with Senator Maxmillion about designing a new extension for the senators' offices."

Lenored clasped her hands. "God bless your hubby! We are in dire need of more space. Take your time. When Cassie is finished with Tamaya, I'll tell her where you've gone."

"Thanks. It seems like Cassie was finished with Tamaya when that article came out."

Jana left the office and walked down the hall to use the ladies' room. Continuing down the hallway, flashbacks of her dream caused her to stop and regain her bearings.

A young security officer asked, "May I help you

with something?"

Shocked back to reality, Jana asked, "Can you please direct me to the office of Senator Josiah Maxmillion?"

The serious young man replied, "Walk down the hall then make a left, a right, a right, and another left. It's the third door on the right."

Jana repeated the directions in her head as if learning lines for a film. Wishing she had breadcrumbs to help remember the way back, Jana embarked on her journey. Jana asked two more people for directions, and finally found herself in front of Senator Maxmillion's office. She noticed his secretary was not at her desk, so Jana entered the outer office and stood at the doorway to the inner office, where she heard two familiar voices.

"The new wing is totally doable and within the budget you've allotted," Brian said.

"The same goes for the construction of it," added Adam.

An unfamiliar, booming, older voice said, "Splendid, gentlemen. The senators will be quite happy to move to more modern and spacious quarters."

"Excuse me, senator." Brian's voice carried an unusually humble tone. "How did I get selected as the architect for this contract?"

Maxmillion replied, "I liked your sketches. And the malls you designed in Texas…and in my home state of Ohio were impressive. As for you, Mr. Stokes, I hear you are the best contractor in Washington, DC." He laughed. "And I liked your price quote. After meeting you two young gentlemen today, it's clear my instincts were correct. Holly—"

Maxmillion walked into his outer office before

Jana could escape. His charisma lit up the room like floodlights in a dark desert. Standing over six feet tall with wavy salt-and-pepper hair, strong features, a square jaw, and broad shoulders, the senator wore a form-fitting, navy-blue pinstriped suit and designer loafers. Though clearly past middle age, his tight skin glowed. "You aren't my secretary, Holly."

Jana felt her cheeks burn. "She must have stepped away from her desk."

He smiled like a king welcoming his favorite subject. "You are Jana Lane, Hollywood's sweetheart." His hand enveloped hers.

It felt warm and strong. "Senator Maxmillion, please forgive me for intruding."

"You aren't intruding at all. I know you've been visiting with Cassie about your upcoming movie. And I'm guessing that like most wives, including my two exes, you want to check up on your husband. Please come in. And call me, Max."

Jana followed the senator into his large office. In the center of the room stood an enormous cherry wood desk opposite a fireplace framed by a cherry wood mantel. Behind the desk was a large picture window overlooking a perfectly manicured lawn. Cherry wood bookcases lined the walls, and easy chairs were stationed in various meeting arrangements around the room. Max motioned for Jana to sit next to Brian, then he rejoined the group.

Jana explained, "I was stretching my legs. I didn't mean to crash your meeting."

"Jana Lane could never crash anything." Max winked at her. "Except through some pretty fierce waves in *Hawaiian Holiday*." He laughed. "I loved that old movie. You looked amazing in that grass skirt." He poked Brian's shoulder. "No offense, Brian."

"None taken." Brian forced a smile and then shifted his attention to Jana. "Is everything all right?"

Jana touched his arm. "Everything is fine." She rose. "I should let you gentlemen get back to work."

"Our meeting is over," Max said. "I'm quite pleased with your husband and with Adam. I'm looking forward to beginning the project immediately."

"Then I should—"

Max gently led Jana back to her seat. "Would anyone like a drink? Scotch? Bourbon?"

So that's where our tax dollars go. "No, thank you."

"I'm fine," said Brian.

"Me too," Adam added.

"Suit yourselves." Max poured Scotch into a crystal glass and sat across from Jana. "Tell me about your upcoming movie, Jana."

Jana cleared her throat. "It's about a successful female US senator who is unlucky in love."

Max smiled. "The price women paid when they left the home. I'm sure Cassie told you about some of her struggles."

I witnessed one—with a male lobbyist.

"And about how the press has been hounding her about dating me." Max's hazel eyes hardened. "Thanks to that damn Tamaya Stormcloud and her article in *Wake Up Washington*. I can't believe she printed that."

Adam said, "According to the article, Senator Castle is a Democrat, and you're a Republican. Does that cause a problem?"

Max sat back in his chair. "Not with my party

controlling the White House and Senate." He laughed. "The Democrats will eventually figure out that tax breaks for large corporations will have a trickle-down effect."

To raise C.E.O.'s salaries and the national deficit, lose jobs, and destroy the economy.

Adam said, "Senator Maxmillion—"

"Max, please."

Adam sat up tall. "Max, I read in the newspaper about your Protect the Children Act, which passed in committee. I understand you will be bringing it to the Senate floor for discussion and vote."

"Yes, it's a popular bill," Max said sipping his drink.

"Popular with whom?" Jana asked.

Max replied, "The fundamentalist base of my party, and the major stockholders of the Multitopower Conglomerate."

"How does your fundamentalist base feel about you dating a *female* senator—given what 1 Timothy 2:12 says about women not teaching or having authority over a man?"

"They're okay with it—if the woman is a Republican." Max laughed. "But kudos to you, Jana, for knowing your Bible."

"As a liberal Christian, I believe the Bible is inspirational not literal."

"I believe in traditional family values as outlined in the Bible."

Though you've been divorced twice.

"And Cassie and I both respect biblical traditional marriage."

One man with many women as his property?

"Cassie's only fault, like most liberals, is her bleeding heart. She'll talk to anyone, eat with anyone, listen to everyone's problems—the poor, the destitute, criminals, every minority group."

Just like Jesus.

Brian asked, "What do corporate moguls care about taking away children from gay parents and putting them in orphanages?"

Max answered, "They, like most of my constituents, believe a child should have a mother *and* a father."

"But in an orphanage the children will have neither," Adam said, clearly trying to remain calm and cordial.

Jana placed a hand on Brian's quivering knee. "Max, how do your supporters feel about heterosexual single parents raising children?"

"I assume they don't like it," Max replied.

"Yet you aren't proposing a bill to take away *their* children," Adam said through a clenched jaw.

Max rested his drink on a cherry wood end table. "I know what this is about." He turned to Adam. "You have custody of your twin sons. And you share a home with Congressman Mitchell, an acknowledged homosexual." He turned to Brian and Jana. "And Mitchell is your best friend."

Brian's eyes doubled in size. "You've done your research."

"I didn't get here by hiding my head under the concrete," Max said.

Adam said, "There are no federal equal rights laws including sexual orientation. Now that you know about me, you could fire me on the spot."

"I could. But I have no intentions of doing so." Max tented his fingers. "I couldn't care less if you share your bed with a woman, a man, or a kangaroo. All I care about is your work, and it's darn good." He leaned forward in his chair. "I'll be perfectly honest with you. This Protect the Children bill is needed right now. The base of my party can no longer quote the Bible against releasing slaves and interracial marriage, so they've moved on to the only minority group that is still hated and therefore vulnerable. Thanks to Tamaya Stormcloud's article, their attention is currently on my relationship with Cassie. But once the Protect the Children Act passes the full Senate, the base will be appeased. It will also satisfy our most powerful lobbyist group, the Multitopower Conglomerate, therefore ensuring my party keeps control of Congress in the next election."

"And you need both your party's base and the corporate lobbyists to get the Republican nomination for president," Brian said.

Max continued. "My bill will pass, a few children will be taken from their homes and moved into orphanages, and that will be that. The sharks will have been fed, and very little harm will have been done to anyone."

"Except for the children and their parents," Jana said.

Max locked eyes with Adam. "I promise you, no harm will come to *your* children. You have my word."

"I wonder if Hitler made that promise to any Jewish parents before World War II," Jana said.

"Jana, I thought you were shadowing *me*." Cassie Castle stood at the doorway with her hand on her hip.

Jana sprang from her chair. "I came in to say hello to my husband and our friend."

Extending a hand to Brian and Adam, Cassie said, "Cassie Castle. Pleasure to meet you."

Brian and Adam rose and shook the senator's hand.

Max also rose. "Brian and Adam are the architect and contractor designing and building our new extension."

"So I heard from Lenore." Cassie smiled at the two men.

"My pleasure," said Brian.

Not wanting to be overshadowed by Brian, Adam said, "My absolute pleasure."

Cassie said, "I'm heading over to the Senate Chamber, Jana. Would you like to join me?"

"Is that allowed?" Jana asked like a child in a petting zoo.

Cassie laughed. "Sure. As long as you can stay awake."

"Is Salloway still droning on about God only knows what?" Max asked, raising his eyes to the wall sconce.

Cassie replied, "I'm hoping he's stopped by now."

"It's doubtful." Max sighed. "And people wonder why we get so little done." Max looked at Cassie from head to toe. "You look beautiful as usual. Don't forget we're on for dinner tonight."

"Of course," Cassie said. "Jana?"

Jana followed Cassie out. Walking backwards, Jana said, "Thank you, Max. See you later, Brian and Adam."

Catching up with Cassie in the hallway, Jana bumped into Allan Green and accidentally sent his papers flying. "Excuse me, Mr. Green."

He looked at Jana and Cassie as if they were blisters, scooped up the papers, placed them back in a folder marked "Topower," then hurried into Max's outer office.

As they walked on, Jana said to Cassie, "I apologize for running off today."

"I'd run away, too, if I could."

"Senator Maxmillion is charismatic and charming."

"That he is. Unlike Mr. Green."

They shared a laugh.

Jana stopped at the end of the corridor. "Cassie, pardon me if this is none of my business, but can I ask you something personal?"

"Why not? Thanks to Tamaya my personal life is open season."

"It's just that…well, you and Max seem like an unlikely pair."

Cassie laughed. "You mean the age difference?"

"I was referring to your political philosophies." Feeling like a gossip columnist, Jana added, "Is it a case of opposites attracting?"

Cassie said as if a private joke to herself, "Maybe Max and I aren't all that different."

They continued walking and Jana said, "I don't believe that's true. For example, Max seems to be attached to the Multitopower Conglomerate, and I was in your office when you told Mr. Green you wanted nothing to do with them." Jana followed Cassie around a corner. "And I just asked Max about his Protect the Children proposal. I can't believe you support that."

Cassie stopped and Jana nearly bumped into her. "Jana, I find that bill the most despicable piece of legislative filth since McCarthy's witch hunts."

"Have you spoken to Max about it?"

"Many times."

"Isn't there anything you can do to stop it?"

A man's voice said, "Really, Tamaya? You want to have this discussion *here*?"

Jana and Cassie looked down the hall at Tamaya Stormcloud, her fists clenched to her sides, as she argued with a handsome Latino man wearing a stylish black suit and cherry-red tie.

Cassie said under her breath, "They're at it again."

"Isn't that Senator Ramirez from my state?" Jana asked.

"The one and only," Cassie replied.

"He's quite the heartthrob," Jana said.

Cassie laughed. "Yes, his biceps, dimples, and tight pants are on the news around the clock."

"His name is often mentioned as a possible Vice Presidential candidate on the Democratic ticket." *Why stop at your foot? Why not swallow your entire leg, Jana?* "I'm sorry, Cassie."

Cassie waved her manicured hands. "The press likes to speculate. Only the big boys in the back room know for sure."

"So that's *it*?" Tamaya waved a letter in Ramirez' face as if it was Exhibit A. "You tell me in a *letter*?"

Ramirez replied, "Can we talk about this later—in my office?"

Still waving the letter, Tamaya replied, "Clearly you can't *talk* about this at all!"

"Will you please lower your voice, Tamaya?"

Tamaya looked like a volcano about to erupt. "Are you afraid of a little *scandal*, Sancho?"

"I have to go into the chamber." He started to walk away.

Tamaya called after him. "After a year together, all I get is a *letter*?"

Ramirez turned back to face her. "Our relationship was toxic. I did us both a favor."

She threw the letter in his face. "You want to see toxic, Sancho. Wait until you and your *old sweetheart* read tomorrow's newspaper."

"This has nothing to do with her."

"Except that you dumped me the minute she floated into town."

Sancho gripped her arms. "Don't do anything you'll regret later, Tamaya."

She wrenched free. "The only thing I regret is ever falling for your con." Tamaya stormed off.

Senator Ramirez pounded his fists against his head, took in a few deep breaths to compose himself, then walked into the Senate Chamber.

Jana said to Cassie, "Tamaya Stormcloud doesn't seem to be having a good day."

"Neither does Sancho," Cassie said as she led Jana further down the hallway then into the chamber.

The senators debated spending millions of tax dollars to fund President Reagan's "Star Wars" plan to intercept nuclear missiles. The support seemed along party lines with the Republicans in favor and the Democrats against. Since voting appeared nowhere in sight, Cassie took Jana by the arm and led her to a quiet area in the back of the chamber.

Cassie whispered, "Visitors are supposed to sit and watch from upstairs, but you'll be fine here for a bit."

Jana felt like a tourist in Times Square. She

whispered back, "I can't believe I'm here."

Cassie explained, "This is where, among endless rhetoric, our laws are decided, cabinet members are installed, and judges are appointed for lifetime *sentences*."

"It's amazing," Jana said, unable to take her eyes off the action.

The Senate was called on a short break. To Jana's surprise, Sancho Ramirez approached her, exuding masculine charm and sensuality. "May I introduce myself, Ms. Lane? I'm Sancho Ramirez, your senator. I'm also a fan of your movies."

Jana shook his strong hand and her knees buckled underneath her. "It's an honor to meet you, Senator Ramirez."

"Please, call me Sancho." He unleashed a row of large pearly-white teeth. "May I speak with you after the session is over?"

"Of course."

Cassie cleared her throat. "Hello, Sancho."

"Cassie." He glanced over at his colleague like a wrestler checking out his opponent before a match.

"It sounded like you and Tamaya had a bit of a row." Cassie stuck the needle in all the way. "I wonder if *Wake Up Washington* will continue to give you all that glowing press?"

Sancho gritted his teeth. "Excuse me." He stormed out of the chamber.

Cassie looked around the vast room. "I don't see Max. I wonder if we will ever vote on Star Wars."

Maybe that's a good thing.

"I have time for a quick stop at the ladies' room. I'll be back shortly." Cassie was gone.

Jana felt goosebumps as she looked over at the dais for the presiding officer—a rotating senator elected by the majority/Republican party. Her eyes spanned the one hundred desks in a semicircle, where senators sat by order of seniority with the majority leader—Josiah Maxmillion—noticeably absent from his front seat.

The meeting resumed. Jana stood in awe and listened as senators took to the floor, yielding and accepting time to and from one another, making their cases for or against the vast expense of taxpayers' dollars.

After ten minutes had gone by, Jana realized she had left her notepad in Cassie's office. Wanting to write copious notes about her meeting with Max and about the senate debate, Jana hurried through hallways and around corridors. Again flashbacks from her nightmare plagued her, but she miraculously found her way back.

Jana entered Cassie's office and noticed Cassie's secretary and Lenore were not at their desks. *Probably on their lunch breaks.* Since Cassie's office door was open, Jana peeked her head inside and gasped at the sight of Tamaya Stormcloud, lying motionless on the Persian rug, surrounded by a pool of blood.

Chapter 3

A half hour later, Jana sat at a table in a small conference room down the hall from Cassie's taped off office. After finding Tamaya Stormcloud, Jana's screams brought a security guard who summoned the police. The two officers who arrived first ushered Jana into the small conference room, instructed her not to leave, and closed the door behind them.

Jana heard the door open and smelled the scent of grilled food. After a tin full of grilled chicken and vegetables over baby green lettuce and a bottle of water were placed down in front of her, Jana looked up at a familiar—and absolutely gorgeous—face.

"I'm Detective Bove." He stood at least six feet tall with straight black hair, piercing green eyes, a straight nose, full red lips, and a square jaw. To say he was muscular in stature was like saying Hercules was in pretty good shape. Bove's thick neck led down to strapping shoulders, mountainous pectoral muscles, and burly legs. He appeared close to Jana's age, and wore a black blazer, skin-tight white shirt, black tie, and black pants that barely contained his tree-trunk legs. He also looked incredibly familiar.

"Do I know you from somewhere?" she asked, trying to hide her attraction.

Bove replied in a deep, silky voice, "Please let me ask the questions, Mrs. Otley."

"Am I under arrest?"

"I thought *I* was going to ask the questions."

"You haven't asked any yet."

He raised a strong hand to the tin of food. "You should eat something."

"Is that a question?"

The detective sat next to Jana. She couldn't help noticing his abdominal muscles pressing against his shirt. When his large knee accidentally brushed against hers, shivers ran down her spine.

"Mrs. Otley, we aren't in New York or Hollywood. This is Washington, DC."

"I know where I am, detective. May I speak with my husband?" *Yeah, remember him?* "He may still be in a meeting with Senator Maxmillion."

"I prefer you didn't just yet."

"What would you *prefer* I do?"

"Eat some lunch, and answer my questions."

Jana ripped open a plastic pouch in front of her, picked up a plastic fork, and ate a mouthful of the salad. *Is he a chef or a detective? He can't be a chef. I've never seen a chef who looked like that. Actually, I've never seen a detective who looked like that.*

Bove took a notepad and pen from his inside jacket pocket and placed it on the conference table in front of him. "That smells really good."

She held out her fork. "Would you like a bite?"

He replied, "Don't tempt me." Bove scratched his muscular thigh. "Mrs. Otley—"

"Please call me Jana."

"No." He rolled his pen around his thick thumb and forefinger. "Mrs. Otley, tell me everything you can remember about what led up to you finding Tamaya

Stormcloud in Senator Castle's office."

"Where is Senator Castle now?"

"I thought we established that *I* am asking the questions. And you should drink something."

Jana took a sip of water.

"Now answer my question."

Yes, sir! "I am shadowing Senator Castle this week to research an upcoming film."

"But you weren't with Senator Castle when you found Ms. Stormcloud?"

"No, Cassie had left me in the Senate Chamber while she went to the ladies' room."

"How long were you alone in the Senate Chamber?"

"I wasn't alone. The senators were in there."

Bove took off his jacket and put it on the back of his chair. Jana couldn't help noticing his biceps and forearms nearly bursting through his shirt. "Let's try this again, Mrs. Otley. How long was Senator Castle in the ladies' room?"

"I don't know. I didn't follow her in there."

He looked at Jana like a parent with a rambunctious child. "Can you cut me some slack here, please?"

Their eyes met.

"Can you call me Jana?"

Bove looked at his notes—which were empty. "*Jana*, how long were you and Senator Castle separated prior to you finding Ms. Stormcloud?"

"About ten minutes."

As he wrote on his pad, Bove said, "Eat more lunch."

Jana obeyed.

"Was Senator Maxmillion in the Senate Chamber when you arrived or when you left?"

"No and no."

"Drink more water."

Jana did as she was told.

After more writing, Bove asked, "When you got to Senator Castle's office, was anyone in there?"

"Yes."

The detective looked at Jana as if her nose had grown three inches. "That's not what you told the police officer."

"Yes, it is."

He turned back pages on his notepad. "You told the police officer neither Senator Castle, her assistant, nor her secretary were in Castle's office."

"That's right."

"Then who was in Senator Castle's office?"

"Tamaya Stormcloud."

He ran a hand through his thick dark hair. "And you found Ms. Stormcloud where?"

"On the floor in front of Cassie's desk."

"Did you check her breathing or her pulse?"

"No. I knew she was dead."

"How?"

"She was surrounded in blood."

"Had you met Ms. Stormcloud prior to that time?"

"Yes."

"Where?"

"In the same room."

"When?"

"Earlier this morning. And later in the hallway near the Senate Chamber."

"Please tell me about those meetings."

Jana filled the detective in on Tamaya's arguments with the lobbyist from the Multitopower Conglomerate, Cassie Castle, and Senator Sancho Ramirez. Folding her hands in front of her, Jana said, "I'd ask Green, Cassie, Ramirez, and Maxmillion where *they* were during the time of the murder."

"The exact time hasn't been confirmed yet."

"She must have been murdered during the brief period after Tamaya and Ramirez argued in the hallway and when I found her dead."

He seemed to notice her for the first time. "You've been at the Capitol for only one day and you have a great deal of information."

Is that a compliment or a threat? "I also know Tamaya was stabbed in the chest."

"How?'

"When I found Tamaya, there was blood on her chest leading down to the floor."

Bove wrote on his notepad.

"Have you found the murder weapon?"

"Not yet."

"It was Cassie's letter opener."

His jaw dropped to his chest. "And how exactly do you know *that*?"

"When I was in Cassie's office earlier, she took her letter opener from inside her desk drawer. After she opened her mail, she left the opener on top of her desk. When I discovered Tamaya's body, I noticed everything in the room was as I had seen it earlier, except for the letter opener, which was no longer on top of the desk."

"Where was it?"

"My guess is wiped clean and returned to the desk

drawer."

"What makes you think that?"

"The same thing happened in my old film *School Spy* when I figured out my history teacher killed the principal. Do you have any other questions for me, detective?"

"Yes. Are you going to eat the rest of that salad?"

Jana shook her head no.

"Why not?"

"Thinking of finding Tamaya Stormcloud ruined my appetite."

Bove took the plastic spoon from the packet and reached for the salad. "The smell has been killing me."

"Enjoy, detective."

"You don't have to call me detective."

"What should I call you?"

"Bove."

"Is that your last name?"

"Who has a first name like Bove?"

"What's your first name?"

"Christopher, but I don't like it."

"Why don't you like your first name?"

"*I'm* asking the questions, remember?"

"And *I* was eating the salad."

Luscious dimples appeared in Bove's cheeks.

"Next question, Bove?"

He flipped his notepad closed. "We're finished…for now. How long do you plan on staying in town, Mrs.…Jana?"

"All this week."

"Where are you staying?"

"In the Southwest Waterfront area with my friend Congressman Jackson Mitchell." Jana offered him her water bottle.

Bove declined. "Have you been to Phillips Flagship restaurant?"

"No."

"Go there."

"Why?"

"The food is really good. And the Washington Marina is amazing at night."

"I'll check them out with my family." Jana rose.

Bove stood and placed a hand on her shoulder. Jana's heart raced as Bove said, "Go home with your husband. I need to talk to Senator Castle and her staff. But don't leave town."

You'd make a good drill sergeant. "I'm appearing here all week if you need me."

He smiled for the first time. "I may."

She cocked her head.

"I read about the murders you helped the police solve in New York."

"You *did*?"

He nodded. "And, *Girl Detective*, I remember your old movies very well."

"You *do*?"

"Every guy my age remembers Jana Lane movies. Your films got me through puberty. I saw them over and over again—except for the ballerina one."

Looking at his large shoulders, she said, "And here I thought surely you were into ballet."

He opened the door and looked her up and down. "I'm sure we will see one another again. I'll be in touch."

She looked at her wedding ring. *That's what I'm afraid of.*

Jana was relieved to find Brian and Adam waiting for her in the hallway outside the conference room. Since their meeting with Maxmillion was over, they had phoned Jackson to tell him they would drive Jana back to the house.

Upon arriving at Jackson and Adam's, Jana found Grace and the children in the kitchen. Grace hung up the telephone as the children joyously finished making oatmeal raisin cookies. After screams of "Welcome home," the four boys hugged Jana then raced outside to watch Adam cut wood for the fireplaces then play softball with Brian on the lawn near the lake.

Gloria removed a raisin from her hair and a cinnamon smudge from her sunken cheek. "The baby is having his nap upstairs. I just checked in on him, and he was fine." Looking at the egg splatter, honey, and oat flakes all over the kitchen, Grace said to Jana, "I know it looks like a tornado hit."

Jana smiled. "Maybe just a meteor."

They shared a laugh.

"I'll clean it up."

Jana put a hand on Grace's arm and felt like she was touching a twig. "Let's have tea and cookies first."

"You go ahead, Jana. I better get cracking, and I don't mean any more eggs."

Jana looked at Grace and realized the young woman's peach blouse and camel skirt were hanging off her body.

"Please, Grace, sit down a minute."

"I should clean—"

"I'll help you clean up later. Please, sit and talk to me."

The two women sat next to one another at the

natural wood kitchen counter.

"Is everything all right?" Grace asked, moving her dark hair behind her ears.

"It's been a rough day," Jana replied. "A reporter died at the Capitol."

"So I heard."

"How?"

"I guess...on the news."

Jana nodded. "I'd rather not let on to the children."

"Of course."

"And I'd also rather not talk about me. I'd like to talk about *you*."

"Me? Did I do something wrong? Aren't you and Brian happy with my work?"

Jana placed a reassuring arm around the girl. "Grace, your work is fine. The children adore you, and we couldn't ask for a more competent nanny."

"Thank goodness." Grace breathed a sigh of relief. "Can I make you some tea?"

"No, thank you. Grace, who were you talking to on the phone when I came in?"

Grace turned the color of her blouse. "My cousin in Westchester. She's been worried about me."

"I don't blame her."

"What do you mean?"

"I'm worried about you, too, Grace."

"Why?"

Jana took the girl's thin hand. "In the short time we've known you, I've noticed you don't eat much."

Grace sighed. "After Henry died, I lost my appetite."

"Henry passed away over two months ago. It's amazing how quickly you've bounced back. I admire you for that. I'd probably still be a basket case. But you have to eat, Grace, otherwise you won't have the strength to go on."

Grace looked down at her stomach. "Actually, I'm trying to take off a few pounds."

"Why?" *To play a skeleton for Halloween?*

"As you can see, I gained a little weight when I was living at my cousin's. All I did was sit around and cry—and eat. Jolanda is an amazing cook." Grace smiled. "Henry always kidded me that I was a 'chubet.' He often said I could eat him, or any man, under the table."

"Grace, Henry is gone, and it was a terrible tragedy, but not eating won't bring him back."

"I know that, Jana." Grace fidgeted in her chair.

Jana squeezed Grace's hand, hoping she wouldn't crack a bone. "Henry would want you to be healthy and happy and make a new life for yourself. You can't do that if you are starving yourself."

Grace laughed. "I'm hardly starving myself, Jana."

"What did you eat for breakfast today?"

Grace averted Jana's gaze. "I skipped breakfast."

"And for lunch?"

"A half a grapefruit I think."

"Grace, that's not enough food to keep you healthy."

"If you're worried about me taking care of the boys—"

"I'm worried about *you*."

Tears filled Grace's dark eyes. "I don't want to be fat, Jana."

"Fat? You're emaciated!"

Grace laughed. "My mirror tells me differently."

Jana slid forward in her chair. "Grace, do you know how Karen Carpenter died in February?"

Grace shook her head no.

"She had a disease called, anorexia nervosa."

"I'm not sick, Jana."

"Yes, I think you are sick, Grace."

Grace sighed and leaned back in her chair. "I didn't realize you had a medical degree."

"I don't, but I'm a woman, and I understand how negative comments about how we look can hurt...even comments made by those we love most."

"Jana, you're absolutely gorgeous with a perfect figure. What can you know about hurtful remarks about the way someone looks?"

"I'm an actress! Costumers, makeup people, directors, reporters, and audience members believe discussing my appearance is open season for all. I know how much it hurts, and I understand how it can distort reality." Jana took in a deep breath. "When you look in the mirror, you see a young woman who needs to lose weight, right?"

Grace nodded.

"But when everyone else looks at you, we see someone rail-thin who is starving herself due to fears of inferiority."

"I'm not starving myself, Jana."

"Yes you are. And you need help."

"You mean a psychiatrist?"

"Yes. Someone who can work with you, and help you to get better."

The circles under Grace's eyes darkened. "What is this disease again?"

Jana repeated it. "You are not the only woman

suffering from it. Please, won't you get some help?"

Grace looked away. "I don't know, Jana."

"Grace, you went through a terrible ordeal. You must be an incredibly strong young woman to have come through it. Now is the time to understand the toll that loss took on you, and to find your way back to being the strong and resilient woman you are inside."

"I'll think about it, Jana."

"Do you promise?"

Grace nodded then asked, "Why are you doing this for me?"

"Because you deserve it."

The boys and men came inside, washed, and put on chino pants and sweaters. Jana changed into a tangerine jacket and slacks with a tight white bodice blouse. Grace stayed home with B.J., while Adam drove everyone else to the Smithsonian Museums.

Upon arrival, the boys raced past the signs pointing to the zoo and the various art, history, and science museums; and they headed straight for the air and space museum. After being transported into space by the numerous interactive exhibits on space travel, all four boys decided they wanted to be astronauts.

The next stop was the Jefferson Memorial. Though the cherry blossoms were no longer in season, the famous site looked beautiful, surrounded by still, inky water, emerald-green trees, Kelly-green grass, and a periwinkle sky. The children ran ahead with their fathers racing after them, and Jana stared at the huge historic structure, taking in the white marble dome and columns. Jana was breathless as she entered the memorial and came face to face with the enormous statue of the third president of the United States. She thought about the author of the Declaration of Independence who believed, "All men are created equal." Her state of reverence was broken when she noticed Devon and Ed climbing up Jefferson's leg with Tyler and Topher at their heels.

Realizing space travel and monument travel build quite an appetite, Jana took Detective Bove's suggestion and recommended Phillips Flagship restaurant for dinner. The group enjoyed mouthwatering fish dinners, then they went for a walk along the Washington Marina. The sky was a tapestry of scarlet, ruby, amethyst, and indigo, which reflected on the white sailboats and motorboats resting in the calm water.

The children pointed to boat after boat screaming, "Can we have one?" Their fathers responded by reminding them of the rowboat in the lake back home.

Walking hand in hand, Brian said to Jana, "I'm sorry you had such a rough day, babe."

She eyed the children. "Tell me about *your* day, Brian." She smiled at Adam. "With Adam."

Brian opened his mouth but Adam beat him to it. "Maxmillion wasn't the monster I expected."

"You saw a monster today, Daddy?" Topher screeched in hopeful anticipation.

"No," Adam replied. "We had a business meeting with a senator."

"Does the senator tell the astronauts where to fly?" asked Devon.

Brian replied, "No, but he chairs the Armed Services Committee."

"He pretends to be a chair?" asked Tyler.

Adam put his arm around his son. "Not exactly,

pal."

"Then what does he *do*?" asked Topher.

"For one thing, he wants to meet you two guys," Adam said.

Not to be left out, Brian said to Devon and Ed, "And you two guys as well."

"Yeah! We're going to meet a senator!"

"Can we ask him about the space program?" Topher exclaimed.

Adam laughed. "Sure. Just don't ask him if you can ride a spacecraft."

"Can we ride a spacecraft?" Ed asked.

"No," said Brian, messing Ed's hair playfully.

While the boys walked ahead to plan their strategy for their time with the senator, Brian said to Adam, "I wish you hadn't told them that."

Adam replied, "What? Not to ask if they can ride in a spacecraft?"

"About Max's invitation," Brian said with a sneer.

With one eye on the children and the other on his partner, Jackson asked, "Maxmillion asked you to bring the kids to his office tomorrow?"

Adam nodded. "We're showing Max the plans for the new wing." He glanced over at Brian. "If Brian has them ready."

"They'll be ready," Brian said like a child being reminded to do his homework on a Friday night.

Jana closed her jacket against the June evening air. "Why does Senator Maxmillion want to meet our children?" *To throw them in the oven of his gingerbread house?*

Adam answered, "He's a family man."

Just ask his two ex-wives.

"Max doesn't have kids of his own," Adam explained. "He wants to get to know the families of the people he's working with."

"Some family man," Brian said through a clenched jaw. "He wants to take away the children of gay people."

"Did you ask him about his Protect the Children law?" Jackson inquired with the words coming out of his mouth like sour milk.

Adam nodded. "Max said it's just a ploy to get the Republican nomination for president…and so the press will get off his back about his relationship with Senator Castle."

"Do you believe him?" Jackson asked Adam.

"*I* don't," Brian replied.

Jana said, "Though I disagree with Max politically, he seemed nice enough when I met him. Now that the kids are all off from school, it might be a good experience for them to visit his office."

Brian looked like a tiger facing a cobra. "You actually *want* our kids to meet that creep?"

"*You're* the one working for him," Jana replied.

"I agree with Jana," Adam said. "How many kids get to meet the majority leader of the Senate?"

Jackson weighed in. "I'm with Brian. I don't trust that guy and his homophobic supporters."

Feeling like a hostage negotiator, Jana said, "Since we're *all* going to the Capitol tomorrow, how about the kids come along to meet Max *and* Cassie."

"Sounds good to me," Adam said.

Brian stared Adam down. "I don't like it." Brian turned his wrath on Jana. "And I can't believe you are taking *his* side."

"There aren't any *sides*, Brian," Jana said removing her hand from his.

"It seems there are," Adam said glaring at Brian.

Noticing the tears brimming in Jana's eyes, Jackson put his arm around Brian. "Maybe they're right. I've taken Topher and Tyler to the House to meet other members of Congress. They enjoyed it. You and Adam will watch the kids when they're with Maxmillion. Speaking of the kids…" Jackson rushed ahead and pulled the children off a dock.

When Jackson returned and the children were walking at a safe distance ahead, Brian said to Jana, "You want to bring the kids to Castle's office after that reporter was murdered in it?"

Take a deep breath. Holding up the white flag, Jana said, "All right, you and Adam can bring the children to meet Max then go home. They won't be out of your sight for a moment."

Jackson said, "You said Tamaya Stormcloud was killed, but you didn't give us the particulars. The kids are out of earshot. So spill the murder beans, hon."

Jana filled them in on her day in the Senate. "So as I see it, there are four suspects for the murder."

"Sell it, *Girl Detective*," Jackson said pinching her arm.

Ignoring him, Jana said, "Cassie Castle could have done it to silence Tamaya."

"Silence her from saying what?" Jackson asked like a gossip columnist.

Jana shrugged her padded shoulders. "I was in the outer office with Cassie's sister, Lenore, so I couldn't hear everything they said, but it sounded like Tamaya threatened Cassie about something."

Jackson nodded. "And since Cassie wants the Democratic VP nod, this would not be a good time for a scandal Washington, DC style."

"Maxmillion seemed angry with Tamaya for releasing the story about his relationship with Cassie," Jana said.

"You think he took revenge?" Adam asked.

"It wouldn't be the first time that happened in Washington," Jackson said, squeezing Adam's hand.

Jana continued, "I overheard Tamaya threaten our Senator Sancho Ramirez about something she had on *him*."

"What is it?" Jackson asked like a soap opera fanatic during a commercial break.

"Evidently there's a woman from his past…back in Sancho's life, which didn't make Tamaya very happy," Jana explained.

"Who's your fourth suspect?" Jackson asked.

Jana replied, "A lobbyist, Mr. Green…or his boss, Benjamin Topower."

"How does Topower fit in?" Brian and Adam asked in unison before sharing angry looks.

Jackson said, "Topower fits into everything…probably because he *owns* everything."

"The Multitopower Conglomerate seems to be pulling Max's and many other senators' strings," Jana explained. "Cassie wants no part of it. Tamaya was investigating them."

Still licking his wounds, Brian asked Jana, "Are you *investigating* Tamaya Stormcloud's murder?"

Don't start a fight with the children nearby. "I was questioned by the detective. He looked familiar." *And absolutely gorgeous.* "But I couldn't place him."

74

"What's his name?" Jackson asked.

"Detective Christopher Bove," Jana replied too quickly.

Adam and Brian lit up like sparklers at New Year's Eve.

"Bove was a professional quarterback," Brian said.

That explains his amazing physique.

Adam said, "Bove had a shoulder injury and retired from football."

That explains his grouchy personality.

"And evidently he became a detective," Jackson said. "Since you found the body, honey, I'll bet you'll be hearing from him again."

Jana thought about Bove's handsome face, rough demeanor, and insistence about her eating the salad. "I guess I will."

When they arrived back at the house, Jana read the boys a bedtime story—about an astronaut. Then she gently kissed her sleeping baby, wished Jackson, Adam, and Grace a goodnight, and retired to the guest bedroom, where Brian was already in bed. She changed into a maroon satin nightgown, then pulled down the hand-sewn patchwork quilt and climbed into bed.

"I wasn't taking Adam's side," Jana said to Brian's back.

"You could have fooled me," Brian replied.

"I really think the kids will enjoy seeing the Capitol."

"Only if aliens take it over."

She hooked her finger into the waistband of his boxers. "Why do you dislike Adam so much? He's our best friend's partner, a good father, a hardworking contractor—"

"And a know-it-all." Brian turned to face her. "The guy acts like there's nothing he doesn't know, including what I'm thinking."

I should take lessons from Adam. "What do you mean?"

Brian sat up in the huge, carved, Maplewood four-poster. "Like tonight at the marina. He made that comment about me not finishing the plans for the new wing."

"Are they finished?"

"I'll put a few last minute touches on them in the morning before we leave."

So Adam was right.

"Adam isn't the architect, *I* am. And how did he know I was stressing about being ready for tomorrow's meeting?"

"Isn't it a good thing for a business partner to know what the other partner is thinking?"

"No, because he was *also* thinking how much he can't stand *me*."

"How do you know?"

"I just know, okay?"

Jana lay back on her overstuffed pillow. "I think Adam behaves that way with you because he thinks *you* don't like *him*."

"Well, he's right about that. He acts like the kids when they play a game...always trying to win at all costs."

"Maybe Adam is trying to keep you on your toes."

"So much for you not being on Adam's side." Brian turned his back to her again and rested his head on his pillow.

"Regardless of whether or not I agree with Adam,

there's no excuse for biting my head off—at the marina or now." When Brian didn't reply, Jana said, "I know you're faking sleep, Brian. I'm an actress, remember? Let's finish this discussion."

Brian cocked his head back to face her. "Okay, you want to finish this. Here's how it's finished. I can't stand Adam, and I wish we'd never come here." Like a child pulling a temper tantrum, Brian squeezed his eyes shut and pulled the sheet over his face.

I didn't realize I was raising four boys.

Jana lay on her back with her eyes closed, thinking about her harrowing day at the Senate. Visions of Tamaya Stormcloud lying on Cassie's office floor surrounded by a pool of blood swam in front of her. Her body finally gave into the thick, soft sheets, and Jana was transported into a hallway leading to offices in the north wing of the Capitol.

Hearing heavy breathing behind her, Jana walked faster down the hallway, turned a corner then another. The sound of menacing footsteps permeated her ears. She ran. More footsteps. More breathing. Jana ran faster until her heart pounded in her ears like a bass drum. Her breathing became labored. Her legs weakened. She couldn't breathe. As she turned around the next corner, Jana's heel skidded on the marble floor, and she tripped, landing in the strong arms of Detective Christopher Bove.

Chapter 4

The next morning, the house was a flurry of activity getting ready for the visit to the Capitol. Everyone was washed, dressed, fed, checked, and rechecked, then the two cars drove off with shouts of "goodbye!" to Grace and B.J.

They entered the Capitol building and were outfitted with the appropriate badges, then Jackson made his way to the south wing; and Brian, Adam, and the four boys walked with Jana to the north wing.

Arriving at Senator Maxmillion's office suite, Jana accompanied her guys into Max's outer office to give the boys a final check for cowlicks, visible shirttails, scuffed shoes, or lint on jackets. Before Max's secretary or assistant were able to announce them, Max ventured into his outer office. The senior senator from Ohio looked patriotic in a navy-blue suit, white shirt, and red tie.

"Well, who do we have here?" Max bent down to address the children.

"I'm Devon, and this is Ed," Devon said, looking adorable in his little sky-blue suit.

Ed added, "I'm Devon's brother."

"He's younger," Devon said to set the record straight.

Max smiled and shook their hands. "It's a good thing having a brother. Don't you think?"

"Sometimes," said Devon.

Jana felt her face turn the color of her coral business suit. She played with her pearl drop necklace. "They're good boys."

Ed grimaced. "Except when we have to take baths."

Everyone laughed.

Max shook more hands. "Hello again, Brian, Adam, and lovely Jana." He spotted Tyler and Topher. "And who do we have here? More businessmen scheduled to meet with me?"

Tyler explained, "We're not men. We're just kids."

Topher added for clarification, "We're only ten years old."

"Going on fifty," Adam said with a pat to their backs.

Max said, "It's a pleasure meeting all of you."

"My daddy brought plans to show you," Ed said. "The picture looks like a space station."

Devon added, "Dad just finished drawing them before we left."

Brian placed a hand over Devon's mouth. "I'm ratted out by my own son."

Having inherited the competition gene from his father, Topher said to Devon, "My daddy is going to build the plans for real."

"I can hardly wait to see them," Max said with a wink.

Lenore Castle appeared at the doorway, looking like a martini in an off-white blouse and skirt with an olive sweater. "Jana, I thought you might be here."

Max stood up straight. "Lenore, it's nice to see you in this neck of the woods. And don't you look lovely today."

"Hello, Max." She offered a shy smile. "Forgive the intrusion. I need to speak with Jana."

"Of course," Max said. "I haven't seen Cassie yet today. Tell her to come visit me this afternoon."

"Cassie has a meeting with the machine workers' union," Lenore said.

Max put his arm around Lenore. "Then come visit me yourself. Cassie's birthday is coming up next month. Let's put our heads together and come up with a good gift idea."

"I'll call you later." Lenore turned to Jana. "Are you ready, Jana?"

"Of course." Jana kissed her boys. "Have a good day. See you soon." She patted Topher and Tyler's heads. "You, too, guys." *Don't let Max put you in an orphanage.*

Max put his arms around the boys. "While your fathers let me have a look at the plans in my office, I've arranged for my assistant Danny to give you a tour of the Capitol. Would you boys like that?"

"Are there any spaceships in the Capitol?" Topher asked.

"No, but there are plenty of people around here who act like they're from outer space," Danny replied as he rose from his desk. Ushering the boys out, Danny said, "Come on, fellas, the tour is starting." And they took off.

Jana gratefully followed Lenore down the hallway and around the corridors. "Is something wrong, Lenore?"

"I'm sorry if I seem a bit flustered." Lenore fidgeted with the ruffles of her blouse and the gold brooch on her jacket lapel. "We're in a bit of a tailspin over what happened yesterday."

"Is Cassie's office still taped off as a crime scene?"

"No, thank goodness. The detective ordered those off this morning."

"Is Cassie in her office?"

"She's at her Nutrition and Forestry Committee meeting." Lenore moved a stray blonde hair behind her ear. "She'll be tied up there for quite a while."

Jana did a double-take. "Then why did you come looking for me?"

"I asked to see you." Detective Christopher Bove stood at the door to Cassie's outer office looking fetching in black chino slacks, a black leather jacket, and a tight forest-green dress shirt that matched his eyes.

Lenore asked, "Would you like to use Cassie's office for your interrogation, detective?"

"Am I being interrogated?" Jana asked.

"Follow me." Bove led Jana into Cassie's office. Then he shut the door, sat on the desk, and motioned for Jana to take a seat on the opposite chair. "Have you eaten breakfast?"

Is he a detective or a caterer? "Yes. Why?"

"My parents own a restaurant. I was brought up hearing about food."

Which reminds me. "We tried the restaurant you recommended."

"What did you order?"

"The flounder."

"Good choice. Did you have the crab cake appetizer?"

"No."

"Have that next time."

As hard as she tried, Jana was unable to divert her gaze from his muscular thighs. "Is there anything else you want to ask me?"

He flipped open his notepad. "Good thing you did that *School Sprite* movie."

"*School Spy.*" She smiled. "I thought you said you watched my old movies."

"I did. But I didn't pay attention to the titles...or the plots." His dark hair fell over one eye. "You were right about the letter opener being the murder weapon."

"Are there any prints on it?"

He shook his handsome head no. "Wiped clean."

"Any trace of blood?"

"Yup. We're testing it to see if it's Tamaya Stormcloud's, but we're pretty sure it is." Bove placed his pad on the desk then tented his fingers. "Is there anything else you can remember about yesterday?"

Jana caught a glimpse of his biceps bulging out of his jacket like ripe cantaloupes waiting to be picked. *I don't know if I can remember five minutes ago.* "I told you everything I know, detective."

"Call me, Bove."

"Why don't you like your first name?"

"It's a long story."

"I have all morning. Evidently, Senator Castle is tied up in a committee meeting."

He took in a deep breath and his pectoral muscles nearly tore his shirt open. "Can we stick to the investigation?"

"Of course." *Until noon when you'll ask me if I ate lunch.*

"I've talked to the security guard and maintenance

worker in this wing. I also spoke with Ms. Stormcloud's mother." He flipped through pages of notes. "Not much there." He leaned back on the desk and Jana stared at his thick neck and strong shoulders. "I want to interview Senator Castle, Lenore Castle, Senator Maxmillion, and Senator Ramirez."

"Sounds like a good plan."

"And Benjamin Topower."

"The CEO of the Multitopower Conglomerate?"

"The one and the same."

"Does he talk to people?"

"I'm hoping he'll talk to us."

"*Us*?"

He nodded. "I want you to help me."

"*Help* you? Me? Why?"

He smiled and two luscious dimples appeared. "Because you were *The Girl Detective*."

"Detective…Chris…Bove." Jana sighed in frustration. "It's really hard for me to call someone by his last name."

He sat in the chair next to hers and filled her nose with the tantalizing scent of pine. "I don't like my first name because it's what my fiancée used to call me…before she left me at the altar for my brother."

She must be insane. "Ouch."

"Yeah. It left me feeling not very good about women."

"I'll keep that in mind."

"Don't be sarcastic."

"Was your fiancée sarcastic?"

"Yes, among other things." He unclenched his jaw. "Will you help me do the interviews?"

"Is that allowed?"

"Having you in the room when I interview someone?"

She nodded.

"Why not?"

"I assumed it might be against a law or a policy."

"I'm not arresting anyone. Is there a law or a policy against talking to people?"

"*Now* who's being sarcastic? And how do you know I didn't kill Tamaya Stormcloud then scream for help?"

He said as if he could see inside her soul, "I know."

Jana sighed. "But why do you want *my* help?"

"I told you yesterday. I did my homework. I know about how you solved those murders in New York."

She narrowed her eyes to slits. "And *I* know something about *your* past."

"What?"

"You were a professional quarterback before you retired."

"It doesn't take an ace investigative reporter to find out about that. I was pretty famous."

"Yet, I'd never heard of you."

He grinned like a boy pulling a girl's ponytail. "That's because I wasn't as famous as *The Pirate Princess.*"

She sat back in her chair. "After you solve this case, you just might be."

"All the more reason to help me with the interviews—for my future fame."

They shared a smile.

Bove said, "Sometimes people open up more to someone like you than to someone like me."

"Are we that different?"

He leaned in, his breath warm and sweet on her face. "You'll have to find out. You in the game?"

Jana regrouped. "Okay, Bove." *Until my husband explodes.*

"Good." Bove rose and opened the office door. "Ms. Castle, can you join us?"

Lenore looked like she'd been summoned to testify at a grand jury hearing. "What is it, detective?"

"He wants us to call him, Bove," Jana explained.

Bove led Lenore to the seat next to Jana's. "Do you mind if Jana stays while I ask you a few questions?"

"Of course not," Lenore said as she crossed then uncrossed her ankles. "What do you want to know, Detective Bove?"

He sat on the desk again.

Hey, Lenore, want to play tic-tac-toe on his abdominal muscles?

Bove asked with pen and notepad in hand, "Ms. Castle, can you tell me what you did yesterday afternoon between the hours of one and two?"

Lenore replied, "At one o'clock, Cassie was in the Senate Chamber. Tamaya Stormcloud came into the office quite upset."

"Where was the secretary?"

"Out to lunch with a group of other secretaries."

"Which restaurant?"

Oh for goodness sake.

Lenore replied, "I'm not sure."

"Go on," Bove said.

"Tamaya asked if she could use Cassie's phone to call her editor. I told her she could."

Bove crossed his calf over his knee. "Then what happened?"

Lenore cleared her throat. "I went to lunch."

"Where?"

"It was a nice day, so I took a walk outside."

He wrote a note. "Did you speak with anyone?"

"No."

"What did you eat?"

Here we go again.

"I brought a sandwich from home."

"What kind?"

Really, Bove?

"Ham and cheese."

Before Bove asked what kind of cheese was in Lenore's sandwich and if the ham was smoked, Jana said, "Lenore, you were so kind and helpful to me yesterday."

Lenore looked down at her lap. "Thank you. It was my pleasure."

"Cassie was as well. Were you and Cassie close growing up?" Jana asked with a warm smile.

Lenore's shoulders dropped, and she seemed to relax. "Cassie is quite a bit older than me. Of course our father was busy here most of the time. He literally devoted his life to his constituents, working day and night to make their lives better. I admired him so much for that."

"But he wasn't home a great deal?"

Lenore nodded. "Since our mother died when I was a toddler, Cassie took care of me."

"And now as Cassie's assistant, you take care of *her*."

Lenore fiddled with the hem on her skirt. "I like to think so."

Jana replied, "After only one day of shadowing

Cassie, I can tell that's the case."

Lenore squeezed Jana's hand.

"Before Cassie and Max began dating, did Cassie ever mention being interested in him?" Jana asked.

"No."

"Why do you think that is? Because they are so different?"

"Yes, and because Cassie always seems more interested in her job…like our father."

Jana asked, "Before they got together, had Max ever mentioned *his* interest in Cassie?"

"Not to me."

Jana continued, "As you know, Cassie and Max were both upset about Tamaya's article about their relationship. Did Cassie discuss it with you?"

"Cassie is so busy. We rarely get the chance to talk, here or at home."

"But you hear a great deal from her office," Jana said.

Lenore nodded.

"Do you think Tamaya knew something else about Cassie or Max? Something she had over them?" Jana asked.

"I wouldn't be surprised. Tamaya was a good investigative reporter."

Bove slid to the edge of the desk. "Could your sister have killed Tamaya Stormcloud for revenge over Stormcloud publishing that story?"

"Absolutely not! My sister would *never* hurt anyone." Tears filled Lenore's eyes. "Nobody knows Cassie better than me. She was always there for me growing up. And not only for me. Like my father, she has devoted her life to the people back home in Ohio, and to making the country a better place." Lenore turned to Jana. "Besides, Cassie and Tamaya were close friends." Lenore said almost to herself, "As close as friends can be in Washington, DC."

"How about Maxmillion? Could he have sought revenge for Tamaya's story?" Bove asked.

"I strongly doubt it," Lenore replied. "Max may be a political lion, but he's a pussycat inside."

Senator Sancho Ramirez, wearing a designer gray pinstriped suit and gold tie, peeked his head into the office. "Excuse me. Kelly was not at her desk."

"She's out today," Lenore said. "And Cassie's at a committee meeting."

"Actually, I was hoping to speak with Ms. Lane."

"With *me*?" Jana said like a girl being asked to dance by the cutest boy in school.

Ramirez explained, "There's a gentleman in my office who would like to meet you."

"Does he want an autograph?" Jana asked, fishing for a pen in her purse.

"Not exactly."

Bove rose. "Senator Ramirez, I'm Detective Bove. Since you are here, may I ask you a few questions about the death of Tamaya Stormcloud?"

"Of course, detective."

The phone rang.

"May I be excused?" Lenore asked.

"Yes," Bove replied.

Jana added, "Thank you, Lenore."

Lenore left for the outer office and shut the door behind her.

Bove motioned for Ramirez to take Lenore's seat. "Senator, were you and Ms. Stormcloud a couple?"

Ramirez nodded and his perfectly styled black hair remained in place. "We were together for a year."

"You don't look very broken up about her death," Bove said.

"We split up."

"When?"

"Yesterday."

"Why?"

Ramirez slumped his broad shoulders. "We argued a lot."

Bove wrote on his notepad. "Who broke up with whom?"

"It was mutual."

That's very gentlemanly.

Bove laughed bitterly. "It's never *mutual*. Who broke things off?"

Ramirez sighed. "I did. And Tamaya wasn't happy about it."

"I can relate," Bove said with a sneer. "Did you two argue?"

"We had words."

That's for sure.

"What kind of words?" Bove asked.

"Pretty unpleasant ones," Ramirez said looking down at his European designer black loafers.

Bove paced behind the desk. "What time did you two share these *unpleasant* words?"

The senator's black eyes narrowed and the lines between them deepened. "About one-thirty, I guess."

"Then what happened?"

"I went into the Senate Chamber."

"For how long?"

"Just a few minutes."

"How come?"

Ramirez ran a strong hand through his hair and not one follicle moved. "I forgot something in my office."

"What?

"My notes. So I went to get them."

"How long did you stay in your office?"

"About a half hour."

"That's a long time to retrieve notes."

"I was reading messages and reports."

"Did anyone see you?" Bove asked with a suspicious look.

The senator thought about it. "No."

"What about your assistant and your secretary?"

"My assistant was in the Senate Chamber, and my secretary was out to lunch." Ramirez looked at his gold watch. "Are we through, detective? I left someone in my office."

Jana looked at Bove. He nodded to the door.

Ramirez said, "Thank you, detective. Ms. Lane?"

Jana rose and followed Ramirez out the door.

When they were in the hallway, Ramirez said, "I apologize for taking you away."

Jana replied, "I was going to say the same thing to you. I'm sure you have better things to do than fetch me for a fan."

They turned a corner. "Ms. Lane—"

"Please, call me Jana, senator."

"Please call me Sancho, Jana." Two delectable dimples appeared on each of his olive-colored cheeks. "I think you'll want to speak with my visitor."

Jana stopped at the entrance to Sancho's office. *Bove asked me to help with the investigation, so here goes.* "Sancho, Cassie and I overheard you in the hallway when you broke things off with Tamaya."

He blushed. "I'm sorry you had to hear that."

"Tamaya mentioned something about your new girlfriend who was an *old girlfriend*."

He nodded. "Someone from my past recently came back into my life. I'm interested in pursuing it further."

"Why didn't you tell Bove about it?"

"The lady wants to keep our relationship a secret...at least for now."

Jana touched his forearm. "Sancho, Tamaya threatened you...something about printing your *secret*."

"Tamaya was an angry, vindictive woman who delighted in lauding her role as a journalist over everyone around her to make them obey her every wish."

"Yet you stayed with her for a year."

"I was a man in love."

Or in fear.

"Tamaya threatened Cassie in the same way."

Jana asked, "What did Tamaya have over Cassie?"

He shrugged. "Beats me. Tamaya played her cards close to her chest."

So do you, senator. "Do you know of anyone who would want Tamaya dead?" *Besides you.*

"Tamaya wrote other tell-all articles about people in Washington, DC. I assume they weren't too thrilled."

"Any recently?"

Sancho nodded. "She wrote one about your congressman, Jackson Mitchell."

Really? Jana followed Ramirez though his outer office into his main office. The room was so full of papers, books, photographs, and journals, Jana could barely see the young, thin, bald man sitting opposite

Sancho's desk. The senator moved a stack of files off his chair and sat behind his desk. "Jana Lane, this is Jake Sawyer from our home state."

The man stood up slowly, lightly gasping for air.

Those are karposi sarcoma marks under his beard. "Please don't get up, Mr. Sawyer." Jana moved a stack of reports and sat in the chair next to him.

Sancho said, "Mr. Sawyer has been visiting me over the last few months in hopes of obtaining funding for AIDS research and patient care." He sighed. "The Republicans won't see him. The Democrats listen but thus far have produced no results—myself included."

Jake coughed then cleared his throat. "Miss Lane—"

She took Jake's hand in hers. It was cold and damp. "Please call me Jana."

"Jana, when Senator Ramirez mentioned you were here, I asked him if I could meet you. You're my hero."

"I'm no hero," Jana said.

Jake shook his head weakly. "Yes, you are. The two fundraisers you held in upstate New York raised a great deal of money, and called attention to the fact that countless numbers of people are dying." He added sadly, "Countless because the medical community had no funding to count them."

"And we haven't gotten much farther since," Sancho added.

Jake lightly squeezed Jana's hand. "When I was in the hospital, I watched your old movies on television. Every time you told your little friend Timmy you would be his friend forever, no matter what he'd done, or how badly he felt, I pretended you were talking to me. In *The Cutest Scientist* when you visited Timmy home sick in bed…and you brought him that medicine you concocted from the plants in your aunt's garden…and when he felt better, I felt better, too." He let out a sad laugh. "Your medicine probably would have worked better than what they gave me in the hospital." Tears filled his red eyes. "I want you to know how much your movies mean to me, and how much I appreciate your work for people like me. But even more than that, I want you to know how much it means to me that somebody cares. *Somebody* cares about *me*."

He wept on Jana's shoulder. She patted the back of his head like she did with her children when they weren't feeling well. "Jake, the people living with this plague…people like *you*…are the heroes. As hard as it is, you have to keep fighting. We *all* have to keep fighting until we finally lick this dreaded disease."

Tears ran down Jake's sunken cheeks. His dry lips cracked as he looked at her and smiled. "Thank you, Jana Lane. Thank you from the bottom of my broken heart." He lifted the cane next to his chair, rose carefully, and slowly walked out of the room.

Jana wiped her eyes with a tissue. "We have to do something."

Sancho rested back in his chair. "I proposed bill after bill for funding, and each time the majority voted it down. And now I'm fighting Maxmillion's Protect the Children Act. But it's a losing battle. Even some members of my own party like Cassie disagree with Max, but are afraid to take up the sword against it." He placed his head in his hands. "The Spanish Inquisition, the Crusades, burning witches at Salem, the Holocaust, McCarthyism, Jim Crow laws, the military's gay witch hunts, and now this. When will we learn? Why don't people see that persecuting one minority group persecutes *all* of us?"

"I've got it!"

Jana's slap on his desk caused Sancho to jump from his seat.

She said, "If Congress won't fund AIDS research, development, and healthcare…and if our *representatives* in Congress won't stop Max and his ilk from passing the so-called Protect the Children Act, that doesn't mean I have to sit back and take it."

"What are you going to do?"

"Fight them," Jana said with renewed energy.

"With what ammunition?"

She smiled. "I'm the *Pirate Princess*, remember."

Sancho left her in his office and headed for his committee meeting. Jana searched the office for a phone book. Upon finding one under his desk lamp, she sat behind Sancho's cluttered desk, located the phone under a constituent's letter, and called the Ford Theatre. Having heard the historic theatre occasionally booked performances and events, Jana breathed a sigh of relief when her booking was accepted—thanks to the Jana Lane fan who answered the phone. Next, she phoned the local newspaper offices to secure advertisement, and scheduled local radio and television interviews. Finally, she called a familiar number.

"Simon."

"Baby doll! How are things in Washington, DC? Did they make you president yet?"

"Hardly." Jana rested her feet on a stack of law books. "I need your help."

Simon's aging voice cracked. "Is there a problem with your research for the film? Did the producers contact you to try to talk you into accepting less money, your name under the title, a reduction in the number of your scenes?"

She smiled. "No, Simon, everything is fine. Cassie Castle is being quite accommodating." *When I get to see her.*

He breathed a sigh of relief. "Are you learning about what a senator does each day?"

I've gotten a pretty good idea. "Yes, Simon."

"Are you working on your character for the film?"

"Simon, everything is fine regarding my research."

"Thank goodness. Have you solved the murder mystery yet?"

Jana laughed. "You read about Tamaya Stormcloud?"

"Of course I read about Tamaya Stormcloud. You're in Washington, DC. What other news would I read about?"

"Detective Bove asked me to help him speak with some people."

Simon let out a guttural laugh. "Meaning you'll figure out who done it in no time." He gasped. "Wait a minute. By Detective Bove, do you mean the ex-quarterback with the face like a male model and a body like a Greek statue?"

She giggled. "You follow football now?"

"No, but I follow guys who look like Chris Bove. And I'm guessing you are *following* him, too."

"Simon, shame on you. I'm married."

"But it's Chris Bove! And don't tell Cornelius I said that."

"Your secret is safe with me, Simon—if you do me a favor."

"I'd do anything for you, baby doll, you know that. Does Chris Bove need an escort for your movie premiere?" He laughed naughtily.

Jana got down to business. "I want you and Cornelius to come to DC and produce a show...a fundraiser for AIDS and money to fight Senator Josiah Maxmillion's Protect the Children Act."

Simon grunted. "The Protect the Children Act is vermin, just like Maxmillion and his motley crew."

"Then you'll do it?"

"Sure. I can make some calls and get some people to perform. When do you want to have the show?"

"This Saturday night."

"What!"

"At the Ford Theatre."

"Has your hair rinse reached your brain?"

Jana placed the phone away from her ear as Simon ranted and raved. When he was finished, she said, "I know you can do this, Simon. Pull every string you have." She giggled. "And pull Cornelius' string, too. Let me know which hotel you'll be staying in, and give me a call at Jackson's the minute you get here."

"Why can't I ever say no to you?"

"Because I'm Jana Lane."

Jana hung up the phone and noticed the corner of a yellow Post-It on the desk sporting the words, "Love, Tamaya." She dislodged the paper from its stack and realized it was a newspaper clipping. After quickly reading the article, Jana glanced up at the picture and caption.

"My mother was right. I need to be a lot neater." Sancho Ramirez entered his office. "I'm on a break from my committee meeting. I thought I'd catch up on phone calls."

Jana let the article slip out of her hand. "I apologize. I didn't mean to look at your personal things."

"But you did. And now you know what Tamaya had over me."

They switched places and Sancho sat behind his desk.

Jana asked, "When did she find this?"

He sank into his chair. "Months ago."

"Is that why you continued dating her?"

He nodded like a little boy caught telling on a bully.

"But you broke up with Tamaya yesterday."

The expression on his face turned from sadness to joy like the two drama masks. "I have a shot at someone from my past…who I really like." He smiled. "Who I really *love*. I think I always have."

Hoping not to sound too nosey, Jana asked, "Why weren't you and she together?"

"We were neighbors when we were younger. I always had a crush on her." His dimples appeared. "She liked me, too." He sighed. "But I was ten years older. Another guy came in and swept her off her feet."

"Where is he now?"

"Out of the picture.'

"So the coast is clear?"

"Right."

Jana sat on the chair opposite the desk. "Does she know about…?" She pointed to the article.

He looked at the picture. "She knows, and she doesn't care. It was fifteen years ago when I needed money for law school." He stared at the picture. "With all that long hair and the mustache, most people wouldn't recognize me."

"But Tamaya did."

"And so did you."

"And now that you're a senator, you don't want your constituents to know you were a member of The Hunk Squad."

Sancho grimaced. "Dancing around the stage half naked with women putting dollar bills in my G-string is not a noble activity for a senator."

"But you weren't a senator at the time. Surely people would understand."

"*Some* people." He laughed morosely. "But others like Maxmillion would have a field day refuting my *family values*. It would kill my chances of getting the Democratic nomination for vice president." Sancho looked like a kid asking for candy. "Can I count on you to keep my secret, Jana?"

"I have to tell Bove, but I'll ask him to keep it quiet."

His pearly white teeth emerged. "What can I do to say thanks?"

"What are you doing this Saturday night?"

"Wow, this picture really got to you."

Jana smiled. "I'd like you to attend a variety show benefit to raise money to combat AIDS and the so-called Protect the Children Act."

"I'll come, but my stripping days are over."

"Deal."

Jana left Sancho's office, then checked in with Lenore who told her Cassie was at another committee meeting. With time to kill, Jana walked to Max's office to check in on her family and friends. She stopped just outside the doorway to Max's outer office at the sight of a famous philanthropist speaking with Topher and Tyler.

Benjamin Topower sat on a loveseat wearing a designer cerulean suit and brick-red tie with a matching pocket handkerchief. Though clearly a senior citizen, his hair was jet black and his face wrinkle free, no doubt thanks to his beautician and plastic surgeon. His chiseled features and steel blue eyes gave him a robotic quality. Having finished their tour of the Capitol, Topher and Tyler stood near Topower, waiting for their father to finish his meeting with Brian in Max's inner office.

"My daddy is in there with Max," Topher said to Topower.

"He's my daddy, too," added Tyler.

Topower smiled and his face didn't crack. "I am meeting with Max when your father leaves."

"I like your suit," Tyler said.

"Why, thank you. I like your suits, too," replied Topower revealing large white laminates.

Topher said, "What are you and Max meeting about?"

"I'm helping Max with his campaign for president."

"Is Max going to be the next president?" Topher asked.

"Would you like that?" Topower replied.

The boys nodded.

"Can we help him become president, too?" Tyler asked.

Topower laughed. "Let's say you two sit with me, and we put our heads together about that."

Tyler sat on one side of Topower and Topher sat on the other.

"I'm Tyler."

"And I'm Topher."

Topower smiled. "It is very nice to meet you boys. My name is Ben."

"Hi, Ben!"

"You two young men look quite dapper," Topower said. "My wife helps me groom and get dressed in the morning. Does your mother help you?"

Tyler replied, "Our mother is gone. Our daddy and papa take care of us."

Topower's spine stiffened. "What is your father meeting with Max about?"

"Our daddy is building a wing for Max," explained Tyler.

"He means a wing for this building," Topher added.

Topower put his arms around the boys. "That's a good thing, don't you think?"

The boys nodded.

"Where are you two young lads from?"

"Hyde Park."

"That's in New York," Tyler added.

"How long will you be visiting Washington, DC?" Topower asked.

"We live on the Southwest Waterfront," Tyler said.

"Why is that?" asked Topower, squeezing the boys' shoulders.

Tyler replied, "Our papa is a congressman."

"That would be Congressman Mitchell?" Topower said.

Topher nodded. "Papa stays in our Hyde Park

house for a week, every three weeks."

"I miss him," Tyler announced.

"I miss him, too," Topher added. "But we're all together in the summer. It's better that way."

"Papa makes the best chili," Tyler proclaimed.

"And Daddy is the most fun in the shower," Topher added.

Topower raised a dyed eyebrow. "You take a shower with your father, Topher?"

"Only when we won't wash," Topher answered.

Topower moved a strand of hair behind Topher's ear. "But Topher, wouldn't it be better to have a mother?"

"Ew! I wouldn't take a shower with a girl," Topher said.

"We had a mother, but she went away. We like it better with Daddy and Papa," Tyler explained.

Topher nodded his agreement.

Tyler asked, "Where do you live, Ben?"

"As a matter of fact, one of my houses is not very far from here," Topower replied.

"How many houses do you have?" Tyler asked.

Topower thought a moment. "Six at present."

"We only have two," Topher said.

"Do you have a swimming pool?" Tyler asked.

Topower replied, "Our house in DC has an outdoor swimming pool, an indoor swimming pool, a tennis court, and a rifle range. With our children grown and gone, and with me traveling so much, they remain idle most of the time."

"Can we visit sometime?" Topher asked.

Topower laughed. "That would be very nice, Topher."

"Do you have a spaceship?" Topher asked.

"Will a boat and a jet do?"

The boys nodded.

Topower rested a hand on each boy's knee. "You two boys are absolutely delightful."

Speaking of delightful children, where are mine? Jana entered the waiting room and asked the secretary, "Do you know where my children have gone?"

The young woman replied, "After their tour, they wanted to see you. So Danny took them to Cassie's office."

Jana replied, "Thank you. I'll catch up with them."

As Jana turned from the secretary, Tyler and Topher jumped off the loveseat and ran to either side of her. "Jana! We had a great tour. Daddy and Brian are still talking to Max. Devon and Ed went with Danny to find you."

She gave each boy a hug. "Thank you for letting me know. I'm glad you are having a good day."

Topower rose and joined them. "Pardon me, these two delightful boys have been keeping me company while I wait for Senator Maxmillion. I'm Benjamin Topower."

"I know who you are," Jana replied.

"And I know who *you* are." Topower smiled. "My children loved your old movies."

"Thank you."

"But my wife and I were not very much taken with your latest film, *His Obsession*," Topower added. "It was a bit too racy for us."

Jana, as always, was gracious. "I hope you enjoy my next film, *Madam Senator*."

"Ah, that's why you are in DC," Topower said.

"Jana's a shadow!" Tyler explained.

She squeezed Tyler's chin. "I'm shadowing Senator Castle."

Topower replied, "Can't say I share her politics."

"Yet, you are meeting with Cassie's companion," Jana said.

Topower announced, "Max is a good man…and a good senator. He deserves the right to be majority leader of the Senate, and our next president."

And your funding of his campaign will enable you to make every decision for him after he's elected.

"I have to go to the bathroom," Tyler announced.

"Me, too," Tyler added.

"It's right down the hall," Max's secretary replied.

Topower said, "I'll take you two boys."

"We're old enough to go by ourselves," Topher explained.

"That's right, Ben," Tyler added.

Once they were gone, Topower said, "They are absolutely adorable."

"Yes," Jana said. *We can agree on that.*

"What a tragedy that they lost their mother."

"She was institutionalized."

"I'm sorry to hear that. I am also sorry to hear they are being brought up in a home without a mother."

Jana glared at him. "I am staying in their home, and it is a fine one."

"I'm sure a woman's presence is quite welcome." Topower added with a thin smile, "But it doesn't take the place of a mother."

"Many well-adjusted children were brought up by single parents, or by parents of the same gender, Mr. Topower."

"There are many unnatural things imposed upon unfortunate children."

Yes, like your hair—and mine.

"One of the things I will be speaking with Max about today is his Protect the Children bill."

"His bill or yours?" *Or is there any difference?*

Topower chortled. "Max is quite good about carrying out the will of his constituents."

As long as they are rich and powerful.

Topower said, "I believe the bill will move quickly through Congress, and the president will sign it."

Jana put her hand on her hip. "Mr. Topower, tell me something. Why do you care if gay couples raise children?"

"Everyone should care. Children are our lifeblood, our hope, our future. Our children mean everything to me. I will do everything in my power to protect them."

Jana felt her face flush. "Children are very important to me, too, including my friends' children. So, I am doing everything in my power to squash your hateful, bigoted, disgusting bill."

Topower unleashed a frigid grin. "Careful, Miss Lane, this isn't Hollywood. You aren't the *Littlest Farmer* or the *Jungle Girl* here. This is Washington, DC, a place with rules."

"And I plan to follow every one."

"Careful, you don't slip up and get hurt."

"Is that a threat, Mr. Topower?"

He laughed. "I don't threaten anyone to get what I want, Miss Lane." He smirked. "I generally don't have to."

Time for a little probing. "I met your lobbyist, Mr. Green, yesterday. He was quite upset over Tamaya

Stormcloud's investigation of your conglomerate."

"So he told me."

"Where were you yesterday afternoon between one and two in the afternoon, Mr. Topower?"

He laughed. "Are you playing *The Little Detective* again?"

"I'm not playing, Mr. Topower. I'm assisting Detective Bove in his investigation."

"All right. I was at home...in my sauna."

"Alone?"

"Yes."

"And how about Mr. Green?"

"I have no idea."

"I believe Detective Bove will be contacting him directly."

"Fine." Topower straightened his tie. "My conglomerate owned a large percentage of Bove's football team." He smirked. "And of course we donate generously to various police fundraisers."

"That won't make any difference to Bove."

Topower laughed. "You are as naïve as your old friend Timmy. As a businessman, I've learned *everyone* has a price."

Chapter 5

Jana found her children in Cassie Castle's outer office playing a card game with Lenore.

"Mommy!" The boys abandoned their game and rushed into Jana's arms.

"How are my two favorite boys?" Jana asked.

"There aren't any spaceships in the Capitol," Devon said.

"But it was a cool tour anyway," Ed said. "I liked the tall ceiling."

"That's the rotunda," Lenore said from her desk.

Jana put a hand on Lenore's shoulder. "Thank you for keeping them company."

"My pleasure." Lenore smiled. "It beats scheduling appointments with veterans, religious leaders, and lobbyists."

"Each of whom I have to speak to this afternoon." Cassie entered the office wearing a lavender satin dress and matching scarf. She carried a large bag full of books and notes. Noticing Jana's sons, she remarked, "And they seem to be getting younger each year."

Jana motioned for her boys to stand up straight. "Senator Castle, these are my sons, Devon and Ed."

"It's a pleasure to meet you, gentlemen," Cassie said.

"We're not gentlemen," Ed explained. "Devon's eleven, and I'm only seven."

Cassie and Jana shared a laugh.

"And you are already more of a gentleman than some of my colleagues." Cassie shook Devon's hand. "Hello, Devon." She moved on to his brother. "Hi, Ed."

As they shook hands, Ed looked at Cassie's forearm before the sleeve of her dress dropped back into place. "What's that purple mark on your arm? Is that a mole like I have on my stomach?"

"Ed!"

Cassie shushed Jana. "I banged my arm getting out of my car this morning. Do you ever do that, Ed?"

"No," Ed replied. "But I bang my leg a lot."

Cassie grinned. "Then I guess we have something in common." She asked Jana, "How's my shadow today?"

"Ready for duty," Jana said followed by a salute.

"Can we shadow box with you, Mommy?" Devon asked.

Jana said, "Excuse me, Cassie. Let me take my boys back to their father. He's meeting with Max again about the new wing."

Lenore popped up like a piece of toast. "I'll take them back."

Cassie said, "I have to dictate a letter to you, Lenore."

Jana gathered the boys. "No problem. I'll take them back." Jana led her sons through the hallways to Max's office, where they found Brian and Adam in the outer office.

"How did your meeting go?" Jana asked.

"Max loved the plans," Brian said proudly.

Adam countered with, "There were a few problems in the design, but I can fix them in construction." He bent down to the four boys. "Did you guys like the tour?"

"Yes! We want to do it again!"

Jana whispered to Brian, "You look in better spirits than you did last night and this morning."

Brian whispered back, "I was—until Adam made that remark about my design."

"Is Max meeting with Benjamin Topower?" Jana asked.

"*That's* who that was," Brian said slapping his forehead. "I thought he looked familiar."

"Who's Benjamin Topower?" Adam asked, standing beside Brian.

"You don't know who Benjamin Topower is?" Brian asked as if Adam had said he hadn't heard of peas and carrots.

Adam raised his eyes to the cracked ceiling. "I wouldn't have asked you if I knew."

Brian said like a teacher holding a number chart, "Benjamin Topower is the CEO of the Multitopower Conglomerate. He owns most of the big companies and most of the press in the US."

"And most of the conservative politicians." Jana added, "He's also an advocate of the Protect the Children law."

Adam's chest puffed out. "I'm going to give him a piece of mind."

Jana held him in place. "I wouldn't burst in there. I don't think anything you say will change Topower's mind."

"So, we just do nothing, and let him try to take my kids away from me?" Adam asked.

"Not exactly." Jana filled them in on her talk with

Topower, and her plans for the Ford Theatre show and fundraiser.

Adam smiled and put his arm around her. "You're still Jana Lane, every kid's best friend."

Brian pulled Jana toward him. "And my amazing wife."

With the kids playing tag in the hallway, Adam said, "Come on, Brian. Let's take the kids home then take another look at your drawings. I'd like to point out some places that don't work."

"Adam, when did you get a degree in architecture?" Brian asked.

Jana patted Brian's arm. "You're an amazing architect, Brian, but look at the gorgeous home Adam built. I'd hear him out."

Brian looked at her as if she had spouted pea soup from her mouth. "Thanks for the vote of confidence, babe."

"Brian—"

The children threw themselves into Jana's arms for goodbye hugs then followed their fathers out.

I'll deal with Brian later.

"I don't think that's a very good idea, Ben."

"Max, it's just for one afternoon."

Jana couldn't help overhearing the two men talking in Max's office. With Max's secretary and assistant both away from their desks, Jana stood at Max's door and continued to listen.

"It's too risky, Ben."

"I have been very generous with you, Max."

"And I appreciate it. But, think about what you are asking me to do."

"I'm not accustomed to being told no, Max."

Joe Cosentino

"And I'm not saying no. I'm simply saying we have to start this thing slowly, and build up the momentum without attracting any red flags."

"I thought you were on board with this, Max. I am counting on you to push the law through the Senate."

"And I will. Ben, you may own most of the media, but you don't own all of it. Tamaya Stormcloud is proof of that. Let's not give the liberal media any fodder for their dissent. Why not wait until after the law passes? And why begin with these two? Why right now?"

"Max, let me make myself clear. I want you to do this for me. And I want this done now." After a pause, Ben added, "Do you understand me, *Mr. President Elect?*"

Jana ducked away from the door as Ben left the office in a huff and stormed down the hallway. She peeked into Max's inner office and found Max sitting at his enormous desk with his head in his hands. Feeling a strong presence next to her, Jana turned to find Bove knocking on the fancy molding around the doorway.

"Senator, I'm Detective Bove."

"Yes," Max said as if waking from a bad dream.

"We'd like to ask you a few questions," Bove explained.

We'd?

Max looked at his watch. "I'm due in the Senate Chamber shortly."

"It shouldn't take long," Bove said. "Is it all right if Ms. Lane joins us?"

Max smiled at Jana. "The more the merrier." Max motioned for Bove and Jana to sit in the large, comfortable chairs near his desk.

Bove readied his notepad and pen. "Senator, where

110

were you yesterday afternoon between one and two?"

"My meeting with Jana's husband and Adam Stokes, a local contractor, had ended." Max sat behind his desk. "I'm afraid this is a bit embarrassing."

"I'm sure Detective Bove will be discreet," Jana said in her role as *good cop*.

Max scratched his neck. "I was getting ready to head over to the Senate Chamber. Given some of my more...loquacious colleagues, I knew we wouldn't be voting for quite a while. I hadn't gotten much sleep the night before, and that loveseat over there looked mighty inviting."

"So you took a nap?" Jana asked.

Max nodded like a child caught at the cookie jar.

"Did anyone see you?" Bove asked.

Max chortled. "I shut the door, detective."

Bove's biceps bulged as he jotted down a note. "Senator, were you angry when Tamaya Stormcloud printed the article about your relationship with Senator Castle?"

"It certainly put this office into damage control," Max replied.

"That's not what I asked," Bove said with penetrating eyes.

Max sighed. "Of course I was angry. For many in my party I became a turncoat or a traitor."

"Did you speak to Ms. Stormcloud about it?" Bove asked.

"I tried, but she wouldn't take my calls," Max responded.

Jana slid to the edge of her seat, "Max, in the short time I've been doing research for my film, I've grown to admire both you and Cassie."

The politician produced a winning smile. "Thank you, Jana. We have enjoyed getting to know you—and your husband."

"But I must admit, I find you and Cassie an...unlikely couple," Jana added.

"Strange bedfellows?" Max laughed. "Jana, those of us on opposite sides of the aisle have very different priorities, views, backers, and voters, but many of us are good friends who respect and admire one another when our work day is done." He leaned back in his huge leather chair. "I had my eye on Cassie for some time. She is a beautiful woman who is smart as a whip—no pun intended. And, like her father before her, and like me, Cassie is incredibly devoted to serving her country."

"Senator Castle is also nearly ten years younger than you," Bove said.

"Age is just a number," Max replied with a wink.

Jana crossed her legs. "Max, I'm sure you've heard the speculations that you will be the Republican nominee for president, and Cassie has a good shot as the Democrats' vice presidential nominee. Won't that put an incredible strain on your relationship?"

Max stared out into space as if watching the movie of his life. "Perhaps. But when I want something, I go after it. Whether it's a political office, a table at a restaurant, or a woman." He refocused on Jana. "And I usually get it."

Jana checked her watch and rose from her seat. "I'm supposed to be shadowing Cassie now. Will you two gentlemen excuse me?"

Max was at her heels like a nipping dog. "I'll walk with you, Jana."

Bove stood up. "I need to check in with my office."

"Please feel free to use my secretary's phone in the outer office," Max said.

Bove gazed at Jana. "I'll catch up with you later."

Sounds tempting.

Jana and Max walked to Cassie's outer office, where Max rested a hand on Lenore's shoulder. "Lenore, always hard at work. And so lovely as usual."

Lenore looked up from her desk and smiled. "I'll bet you say that to all the assistants."

"Not to my assistant, Danny," Max replied with a wink.

Cassie appeared at the doorway of her inner office. "Max, shouldn't we be in the Senate Chamber?"

"We have a little time to kill." Max put his arm around Cassie.

Did she wince?

Max said, "I want to spend a few minutes with the most enticing woman in Washington, DC." He pointed to Lenore. "And her equally enticing sister."

Cassie replied, "Lenore has work to do."

Max said, "Is your boss overworking you, Lenore?"

"Terribly." Lenore laughed. "That's what sisters are for."

Cassie took Max's hand. "Let's step into my office."

I feel like the shadow in Peter Pan. "I'll wait out here, Cassie?"

"Please join us, Jana."

They entered the office and Cassie sat behind her desk. Jana took a chair opposite. Max stood behind Cassie rubbing her shoulders.

"You seem tense, love," Max said.

Cassie replied, "I'm concerned about the discussion leading to the vote for your Protect the Children proposal."

Max announced, "I've spoken to the members of my party. The vote will go along party lines as usual. So it will pass."

"I'll be speaking against it," Cassie said.

Max replied, "Fine. It will win you some points with your party."

"Sancho said he will speak against it as well," Jana offered.

"I'm not surprised." Cassie scowled.

"Careful, love. Your shoulders just got tighter," Max said.

"You're committing political suicide, Max." Cassie added, "It's a stupid, vicious bill akin to segregation. Please, won't you reconsider?"

"Cassie's shadow agrees," Jana echoed.

Max threw up his hands. "We've been over this a dozen times, Cass. I promised Ben I would propose the bill. Like everything else in Washington, it will make a big splash then dissipate quickly."

Jana spoke up. "Speaking of the proposal, I would like to invite you both to a fundraiser benefit performance I am hosting this Saturday evening at the Ford Theatre. My agent is arranging for musical and comedy acts to perform."

"What are you raising funds *for*?" Max asked with an arched eyebrow.

Jana replied, "AIDS research and treatment…and for advertising funds against the Protect the Children Act."

"We're not going," said Max.

Cassie replied, "Please don't speak for me, Max."

Jana took her aim. "Sancho Ramirez is going."

"I'll attend," Cassie said.

Max and Cassie locked eyes.

"I don't think that's very wise, Cassie."

"Why is *that*, Max?" Cassie asked.

Max replied, "Thanks to Tamaya Stormcloud, everyone knows we are dating. They'll wonder why you are supporting a fundraiser attempting to vilify *me*."

Jana explained, "We're not trying to vilify anyone. We simply want children to be able to stay with their parents."

"Drop the bill, Max," Cassie said with a no-nonsense look.

"I told you I can't do that," he replied, meeting her glare.

"Then I'm going to the benefit without you." Cassie leafed through messages on her desk.

"All right." Max plopped into the empty seat opposite the desk. "Maybe Lenore will take pity on lonely me and join me for dinner Saturday night."

Cassie dropped the messages on her desk. "Lenore will come with *me*."

Jana rested a hand on Max's shoulder. "Please come, Max. It will show you are a good sport who is bipartisan and open to hearing from the other side."

After a pause, Max rose. "Cassie and I will discuss it tonight."

"I have to work late." Cassie held up a binder. "Committee reports to read."

"You'll read them at my house," he replied.

"But Max—"

He rested his hands on her desk. "I will pick you up here at six tonight." His gaze bore into hers. "See you in the Senate Chamber."

After Max left the office, Jana noticed Cassie's hands quivering. "Are you all right?"

Cassie unleashed a tense smile. "I'm fine." She sighed. "I guess all couples have their disagreements."

How to be tactful? "Cassie, I hope you don't think I'm speaking out of place, but you and Max don't seem much like a couple to me."

"What do you mean?"

You asked for it. "I know you are dating, but there's a tension between the two of you. You are polar opposites with completely divergent ideals. You seem like a different person when Max enters the room…as if you are…frightened of him."

Cassie laughed. "That's ridiculous.

Good thing she's a politician and not an actress. "I like you very much. You and Lenore have been so accommodating, kind, and friendly to me. But I'm sorry, I don't believe you about Max."

Cassie leaned back in her chair. "Then what *do* you believe?"

"I think Max has something over you."

"That's ridiculous." Cassie read a report—upside down.

Jana noticed a purple mark on Cassie's neck. "And why do you have those marks on your skin?"

Cassie covered the mark with her scarf. "I told you I bumped into something."

Lenore stood at the doorway. "Cassie, Detective Bove is here to see you." Lenore turned to Bove like a teacher confronting a bully in the schoolyard. "My sister would never hurt anyone, including Tamaya Stormcloud. Our father taught us to respect and serve our fellow man."

"I appreciate the vote of confidence, Lenore, but you're my sister. I'm sure what you think about me doesn't matter to Detective Bove." Cassie gazed at the tall, muscular, and handsome ex-football star. "What can I do for you, detective?"

"Do you mind if I ask you a few questions?" He sat in the empty chair and placed a large paper bag at his feet.

His scent makes me want to run barefoot through the woods with him.

"I'm due in the Senate Chamber soon," Cassie replied.

"This won't take long."

"Ms. Lane is assisting me with my investigation," Bove replied with a nod in Jana's direction.

"Do you mind, Cassie?" Jana asked.

"Of course not. You're my shadow, aren't you?" Cassie answered with a wink.

Bove readied his notepad and pen. "Senator Castle, where were you between one and two yesterday afternoon?"

"In the Senate Chamber."

Jana said, "But you left about that time."

Cassie tilted her head. "That's right. Something I ate for lunch didn't agree with me." She blushed. "I'm afraid I spent most of that time in the ladies' room."

"Did anyone see you?" Bove asked.

Cassie replied with a smirk, "The stall accommodated only me."

He looks so adorable when he's caught off guard.

Bove said, "Senator, I understand you and Tamaya Stormcloud had quite a row in your office yesterday morning."

Cassie leaned back in her chair. "Tamaya and I are old friends. She defended me in a meeting with a lobbyist. After he left, I let her have it for publishing her article about Max and me."

"Because Cassie told Tamaya about her relationship with Max in confidence," Jana explained.

"And what was Tamaya's response?" Bove asked Cassie.

"She basically told me, any publicity is good publicity," Cassie replied.

"But you and Tamaya continued to argue," Jana said. "Lenore and I heard you from the outer office."

Cassie laughed. "Jana, you're doing a great job shadowing me." She looked up at Bove. "Detective, sometimes friends know how to hit a raw nerve in one another, and they argue. It was over shortly after it began."

Jana said, "Cassie, as Tamaya's friend, do you have any idea who killed her?"

"Especially given the fact that she was murdered in your office," Bove added.

A crease formed between Cassie's perfectly tweezed eyebrows. "Don't you have a murder weapon, detective, or fingerprints, fibers, or whatever you people do to solve murders?"

Bove offered Cassie an officious-looking smile. "We have the murder weapon—your letter opener...wiped clean of prints. The rug had many different clothing fibers, which is not unusual for a senator's office with a great deal of traffic."

Cassie looked at her designer gold watch. "I'm due in the Senate Chamber." She rose. "You're welcome to join me, Jana, but I fear you'll be bored senseless."

Bove stood with his wide back facing Jana.

Will those massive shoulders rip a hole in his leather jacket?

Bove said, "I'm taking Jana to lunch."

That's news to me.

"Is it all right if we use your office a bit longer?" Bove asked.

Cassie stood at the doorway. "Stay as long as you like." She smiled at Lenore. "If any of my constituents have a problem, please send them right into my office."

Lenore and Cassie shared a laugh.

"When will you be back?" Lenore asked.

Cassie replied, "When I've had enough of listening to my colleagues debate the Protect the Children Act."

Jana hurried to the doorway. "Will you speak out against it?"

"You bet I will." As she left, Cassie said, "Don't work late tonight, Lenore. Go home and get some rest."

"I will," Lenore said before Bove closed the inner office door.

Bove walked back to his seat and opened the paper bag. The smell of grilled salmon and dill filled the office. He placed two containers, plastic utensil packets, and napkins on the edge of Cassie's desk, and motioned for Jana to take the seat next to him. "Have some lunch."

"Here I thought you were taking me to a restaurant."

"I am. It's from my parents' restaurant."

119

Jana opened the cover and took in the pleasing presentation of the grilled salmon with creamy dill sauce drizzled over grilled asparagus, broccoli, baby tomatoes, and leaf spinach. "This looks wonderful."

Bove speared a huge piece of salmon. "I know."

"Did you and your ex-fiancée eat at your folks' restaurant a lot?"

He dropped the fork into the container.

"I'm sorry if I brought back bad memories."

"Don't talk about Allison, okay?"

"*You* brought her up yesterday."

Bove looked at Jana like an abused puppy. "Allison and I went to my parents' restaurant every Saturday night for dinner. That's where she met my brother. He was the chef."

"Was?"

"I guess he still is. They have a replacement chef while Mike and Allison are on their…" His eyes filled with moisture.

"How long were you dating?"

"Two years. Stop asking about Allison."

"Did you date someone before her?"

"I had lots of women on the road when I was a football player, but I wouldn't call that *dating*."

Jana took a bite of her lunch. "This is absolutely delicious, as was yesterday's lunch." *The little I got to eat of it.* "Thank you for bringing it."

Bove said more to himself than to Jana, "I can go into the restaurant, see my parents, order takeout, but I can't sit at a table."

Jana rested her hand on his. "I understand."

"No, you don't." He ate his lunch.

"Just because I'm married that doesn't mean I

haven't experienced disappointment in my life."

Bove's biceps pressed against his leather jacket as he wiped his mouth with his napkin. "What *disappointment* has Jana Lane *experienced*?"

Her eyes narrowed. "You more than most people should know fame does not always bring fulfillment."

"Weren't you *fulfilled* as a child star?" He smirked. "I was certainly fulfilled watching your movies."

Between bites Jana replied, "Actually, I was quite fulfilled as a child...until I left Hollywood at eighteen."

"Why?"

"I was attacked at the studio."

"Did they catch your attacker?"

She nodded, still feeling the pain. "Three years ago...after I lost most of my family. It was the same person you read about in the newspaper."

He looked at her as if for the first time. "I'm sorry you lost some family members."

"I'm sorry you lost Allison."

They ate in silence.

Bove said, "From what I've read and seen, murder seems to follow you."

She bit into a succulent broccoli spear. "Does anyone else in your office know I'm involved in this case?"

"No. And they won't. You got it?"

She saluted. "Yes, sir."

He swallowed a mouthful of salmon. "I know I can be gruff. It's how I am. I don't mean anything by it."

"I'm married. I've had a bit of experience in the gruffness area."

"Problems with hubby?" He continued eating his lunch.

She sighed. "Brian and I have been down this dark road before. We'll get back into the sunshine."

His muscular thigh brushed against her leg as he took two bottles of water out of the paper bag.

Bove handed her a bottle.

Drink some water and calm down, girl.

"What's the problem at home?" he asked.

Jana stammered, "I…don't…think—"

"Hey, I showed you mine." His wiped some dill sauce off his chiseled jaw then took a swig of water.

Jana leaned back in her chair. "As I mentioned yesterday, our best friend, Jackson Mitchell—"

"The congressman."

She nodded. "—invited us to stay with him…and his partner…and his partner's…now *their* two children."

"Relax. I'm not homophobic. My best friend on my team was gay. He had to keep it hidden. Hopefully someday that will change."

"I hope so, too."

"Go on." Bove finished his lunch.

"Jackson's partner Adam and my husband Brian were hired by Senator Maxmillion to be the architect and contractor to build the new wing of senate offices."

"Which is which?"

"Excuse me?"

"Who's the architect and who's the contractor?"

"Why does it matter?"

"Why don't you want to answer my question?"

Jana exhaled loudly. "Brian is the architect and Adam is the contractor."

He nodded. "What's the problem?"

"Brian didn't think it was a good idea to get

involved with Max due to Max's proposal of the Protect the Children Act."

"And Adam *did*?"

"Not at first, but he came around."

"Money talks." Finished with his lunch, Bove threw his napkin into the container. "Where do you and Jackson weigh in?"

"At first we agreed with Brian."

"Then you moved over to Adam's side, and now Brian feels you betrayed him."

Jana did a double-take. "How did you know?"

"I figured it out." He stretched his massive back. "And I wasn't even *The Girl Detective*."

She drank water, deliberating whether or not to pour the rest over his head. "Brian and Adam don't get along."

"Why is that?"

"Jackson and I think it's because they are so much alike."

He thought about it. "Could be, or maybe they're jealous."

"Jealous of what?"

"How much attention their spouses pay to their friends…and not to them."

She laughed. "Are you a detective or a psychiatrist?"

"Sometimes I don't know the difference."

Finished with her lunch, Jana turned toward Bove and again marveled at his breathtakingly good looks and powerful physique. "I'm surprised you didn't go into acting."

"I'll let Fred Dryer do that for me—for now." He put the empty lunch things back into the bag. "How did the meeting go with Max, Brian, and Adam?"

"Fine. They seem to like Max. And so do the kids."

"Max hasn't locked them in an orphanage yet?"

Jana replied, "Max says it's pure politics—pandering to his base to get the Republican nomination for president."

"Do you believe him?"

She ran a hand through her teased blonde locks. "I don't know what to believe—including about my friend Jackson."

"What do you mean?" Bove was back in detective mode with readied notepad and pen.

"Senator Ramirez mentioned to me that Tamaya Stormcloud wrote an article about Jackson. Evidently, Jack wasn't too happy about it."

Bove shrugged. "Mitchell has been out of the closet since he came to DC. What did Stormcloud write about that upset him?"

"I don't know, but I intend to find out—tonight."

Bove jotted down a note, then he handed Jana his card. "Call me when you find out." He rifled through his notepad. "In the meantime, let's compare notes on suspects."

"I'm totally in the clear?" Jana asked.

He pinched her cheek. His fingers felt warm and thick against her skin. "*The Littlest Farmer* would never murder anyone."

She looked down at her wedding ring. "We spoke with Max and Cassie together. Sleeping and using the bathroom aren't exactly strong alibis."

"And they were both pretty ticked off about Tamaya's story." Bove leaned in closer to her. "You said you talked to Ramirez?"

Jana nodded, trying not to stare at the pectoral muscles nearly bursting out of his dress shirt. "As you know Ramirez said he was in his office alone during the time we think Tamaya was murdered. But that's not all. Tamaya was blackmailing Sancho...until he finally broke things off with her."

"When was that?"

"The day she was murdered."

"What did she have on him?"

"Confidentially, his past as a male stripper for The Hunk Squad."

Bove grinned. "After I retired from football, they asked me to join their ranks."

I'm not surprised.

"I went the detective route."

"You made the right decision."

He laughed. "You think I couldn't fill the dancing shoes...or the G-string?"

"No. I think you'd fill...I mean you'd be a terrific...women...and probably some men, too, would love..." *Is there a muzzle in that paper bag?*

Bove stood and his knee brushed against hers. Jana fanned herself with her napkin.

"You warm?" he asked.

"I'm fine." *Why couldn't I have been born a lesbian?* "Can we talk about other suspects?"

"I don't know. *Can* we?"

Focus—and not on his sexy smile! "I also spoke with Benjamin Topower, the CEO of the Multitopower Conglomerate. He was home alone during the time of the murder."

"So was his lobbyist lackey Allan Green who I talked to."

Jana exclaimed, "And neither one of them would be happy about Tamaya's threat to research and report on the shenanigans going on in the Conglomerate."

"What shenanigans are those?"

Jana scratched her chin. "I don't know, but I want to find out."

Bove snapped closed his notepad. "Anything else?"

Jana rose and stood near the bookcase. "Isn't that enough for one day?"

"It's never enough—until we catch the killer."

Jana avoided his gaze. "Of course. That was foolish of me. Just like it was foolish of me to bring up Allison."

"Which you just did again."

"Agh, I'm sorry!"

He leaned in toward her. "Jana, stop being sorry." Bove rested his hand on the bookcase. "You're not foolish." He leaned in closer with their chests nearly touching. "I appreciate your help." Their lips were inches apart. "And I appreciate *you*."

Jana's knees dipped.

Cassie opened the door, threw her bag on the floor, and plopped down behind her desk. "The Protect the Children Act passed!"

Chapter 6

Jana spent the afternoon watching Cassie speak with school groups, scouts, teamsters, and religious leaders. It was difficult for Jana to pay attention to any of it, since she was seething about the passage of the Protect the Children Act in the Senate.

When Jackson drove her back to his house, Jana took the opportunity to ask her best friend and congressman about Tamaya Stormcloud's article. With Donna Summer crooning "She Works Hard for the Money" on the car radio, Jana said, "It seems Cassie and Max aren't the only politicians featured in one of Tamaya Stormcloud's articles."

"What do you mean, hon?" Jackson asked as he stared straight ahead at the road.

"Senator Ramirez mentioned Tamaya wrote an article about *you*. What was it about?"

Jackson took off his tie with one hand and steered with the other. "Am I a suspect? Will you visit me in jail with a nail file in a cake? And don't forget to bring Adam for conjugal visits." He giggled. "Or Brian."

"Just answer my question, Jack."

"Actually the article wasn't about me. It was about Adam."

Jana did a double-take. "What *about* Adam?"

"It was a vicious article about how a new congressman—me—was 'setting up house' with a contractor—Adam—whose wife had gone insane when he came out of the closet."

"But Adam's wife had psychiatric problems for years."

"And wouldn't you know Tamaya Stormcloud *conveniently* left that out of her article."

"Did Topher and Tyler see it?"

"No, but some kids at their school did." He wiped his eyes with the sleeve of his suit jacket. "Thankfully, Topher and Tyler are strong kids."

"Adam must have been fit to be tied."

"Like a bull in a rose garden." Jackson turned a corner. "He ranted and raved about that article for months."

How can I put this delicately? "Jack, did Adam mention what he did after he and Brian left Max's office on the day Tamaya was killed?"

"He and Brian had another tiff, so Adam went for a walk inside the Capitol to blow off some steam. Why?"

"No reason."

"Even *you* aren't that good an actress, hon buns. I know what you're thinking."

"I'm not thinking anything."

"Jana Lane is always thinking about murder suspects. And this time, you're thinking wrong."

Back home everyone ate dinner in the dining room and played board games. Then the adults told the children to take baths or showers, or a combination, and tucked them into bed. While Adam and Brian argued over which one of them won the board games with Jackson failing as referee, Jana looked in on Grace and B.J.

Jana entered the bedroom, and Grace hung up the

phone. Then Jana sat on B.J.'s bed, kissed his adorable cheeks, told him how much she loved him, and covered her youngest child with the bedsheet.

"Who were you talking to?" Jana asked Grace.

Grace's robe hung off her thin body like a coat on a skeleton. She rose from the rocking chair near the phone. "A guy I know from back in New York."

"New Yaaaa," B.J. echoed.

Jana asked Grace, "Are you dating him?"

Grace grimaced. "He'd like to. But I can't date anyone."

"Why not?"

"You know why not."

B.J.'s eyes grew heavy. Once he had fallen asleep, Jana motioned for Grace to join her in the hallway outside the bedroom. They sat together on a wood-carved, overstuffed loveseat next to a carved end table with a Tiffany lamp on top of it.

"Would you like some hot chocolate?" Jana asked.

"No, thank you," Grace replied.

"Have you eaten anything today?"

"I had some yogurt."

"That's it? All day?" *Bove would have a field day feeding you.*

"My husband used to say I had enough fat on me to fill a butcher shop."

Jana took her hand. It felt like a popsicle stick. "Grace, is that why you think you can't date anyone? Because of your husband?"

Grace nodded then pushed her dark hair behind her ears.

"Don't you think your husband would want you to grieve his loss then move on with your life? Wouldn't

Joe Cosentino

he want you to find happiness, and not to be alone?"

"Of course. But why would anyone want to date *me*?"

"Why *wouldn't* someone want to date you?"

Grace looked down at her stomach. "I obviously have a weight problem, Jana."

"Yes, you do. You are severely *underweight*."

Grace laughed. "You're just being nice."

Jana took the girl by her pebble-sized shoulders. "I'm concerned about your health."

"I'm healthy enough to take care of B.J."

"This isn't about B.J. It's about *you*. Grace, please, won't you see someone? I'll pay for it. I'll drive you."

"I can handle this, Jana."

"Obviously you *can't*." Jana rubbed her forehead. "Have you looked at yourself in the mirror lately?"

"I tried once. It's too painful. I hate being fat."

"What about this young man from New York? Can you talk to him on the phone about this?"

Grace shook her head no. "He remembers me from before I put on the weight." Tears filled Grace's eyes. "He's in Washington, DC now, but I don't want him to see me like this."

I don't blame you. "Invite him here."

"I can't do that."

"Why not?"

Grace paced the hallway. "I've enjoyed talking to him on the phone. He's a terrific guy. We get along really well. But if he sees me so overweight, he'll never want to talk to me again."

"What's his name?"

"Please don't call him, Jana. You'll ruin everything. Talking to him is the only thing that makes

130

me happy."

"Grace, you have a choice. I contact the phone company to trace who you have been talking to and invite him here myself, or you invite him. Which will it be?"

"Why are you doing this, Jana?"

"Because I care about you." Jana sat Grace back down on the loveseat. "Won't it be nice to see him and talk to him in person?"

Grace nodded and tears fell onto her robe. "I'd love to see him, Jana. And I know he wants to see me. He's told me so many times."

"Then invite him for dinner tomorrow night at seven. We'll be expecting him."

Grace fidgeted with the belt of her robe. "I hope I'm doing the right thing."

"You are." Jana walked Grace back into the bedroom. "Now get some sleep. Tomorrow is going to be a big day."

Jana walked down the stairs and into the large sitting room, where she found Adam and Brian standing in front of the huge picture window with a view of the lake. They were in the heat of battle.

Instead of jeans and sweatshirts, they might as well be wearing armor.

Jackson stood next to the stone fireplace as referee.

"*You* were the one who wanted to work with Max," Brian shouted. "The wheels are in motion; you can't back out now. You understand my designs perfectly, and you'd better build them!" Brian grimaced like a child eating liver. "And the changes you made on them really work."

Adam replied through gritted teeth, "I thought

you'd be happy I want out of the new wing. It's no secret that you can't stand me."

Jackson, the lawyer and politician, spoke up. "You're a great contractor, Adam. Brian's plans are terrific. You complement one another professionally."

"Even though personally you're a pain in my butt," Brian said to Adam.

Jana stood in front of them. "Can you please lower your voices? You'll wake up the children."

Adam threw his arms up in the arm. "They'll hear a lot more noise when they're in an orphanage."

"Nobody is taking our kids to an orphanage," Jackson said.

Adam responded, "They reported on the radio that Max's Protect the Children Act passed the Senate, and the president was quoted as saying he will sign it."

"But it has to pass the House first," Jana explained. "Jackson won't let that happen."

Jackson lowered his head and slid down onto the sectional sofa. The others sat around him.

Jana said, "The Democrats control the House. There's no way it will pass." She added with desperation, "Right, Jackson?"

"I think the Republicans have the votes to do it."

"Jack, you..." Adam was too choked up to continue.

Brian added, "...can't be serious!"

"Unfortunately, I'm dead serious." Jackson swallowed hard. "I'll fight like a tiger, and I know many of the other Democrats will join me. The problem is Democrats from the less liberal districts are afraid about not getting enough funding and votes for their reelection," Jackson explained. "We have to run every two years in the House. Thanks to the fundamentalists and their tax-exempt religious TV networks, gay still means pedophile to many voters."

Adam took Jackson's hand. "Can't you talk to them, honey?"

Jackson squeezed Adam's hand. "I'm a resident of Sodom and Gomorrah to some voters."

The story of Sodom and Gomorrah was about rape and greed, not sexual orientation.

Brian explained to Jackson, "Adam means, can you talk to your colleagues before the vote?"

Adam looked at Brian like a judge facing a serial killer. "How do *you* know what I meant?"

"Was I wrong?" Brian asked.

Adam looked down at his work boots. "No. But you don't have to gloat about it."

"Who's gloating?" Brian replied with a grin.

The phone rang. Jackson walked over to the phone table. "Yes?" His jaw dropped. "Hello, Max."

Adam rose. "Give me that phone."

Brian held Adam back.

"What can I do for you, Max?" Jackson asked. "Yes, we were just talking about that."

Adam shouted, "Tell him he can stick his new law down his bigoted throat!"

Jackson waved his arm for Adam to be silent then said into the phone, "Yes, I heard construction on the new wing begins next week."

"And I'm burying Max under the concrete foundation!" Adam said in a rage.

Jackson continued, "I don't know, Max. I'll have to ask Adam."

"Ask me what? When I'll be able to visit my kids

in the orphanage?" Adam cried.

Brian placed his hand over Adam's mouth.

Jackson said, "This isn't a good time for Adam to come to the phone, Max."

Assuming you want to keep your hearing.

"A guided tour of Washington with you tomorrow?"

"I'll throw him in the Potomic!" said Adam, freeing himself of Brian.

Jana leapt up and took the phone. "Max, this is Jana."

"What are you doing?" Jackson asked her.

Jana shushed him. "It's nice speaking with you, too, Max."

"Has she lost her mind?" Jackson asked Brian who replied with a shrug.

"I'd like to make a deal with you," Jana said into the phone.

Jackson said, "She's in Washington, DC two days and she's already a dealmaker."

Jana continued into the phone. "I'll talk Adam and Brian into going with you tomorrow…if you'll come to my fundraiser show at the Ford Theatre Saturday evening."

Adam and Brian looked at one another as if entering an alternate universe.

"Do we have a deal?" She unleashed the famous Jana Lane smile. "It's a pleasure doing business with you, Max."

Jackson stood in front of the sectional like a stand-up comic facing a drunk audience. "Since the plans for the new wing are in such good shape, and building doesn't start until next week, to show his appreciation,

Max would like to take Brian, Adam, and the four kids on a sightseeing trip around Washington, DC then out to dinner tomorrow."

Jana stood next to Jackson. "And I just told him you will go."

"You must have hit your head on one of the columns in front of the Capitol," Adam said.

Brian hit Adam's shoulder. "Don't talk to my wife like that." Then Brian asked Jackson, "Did Max mention the bill passing the Senate?"

Jackson nodded. "He said it's pure politics."

"And you're stupid enough to believe him?" Brian said.

Adam pushed Brian's shoulder. "Don't talk to my partner like that."

"He was *my* best friend before he was *your* partner," Brian said.

"Will you two stop acting like children?" Jana said like the mother who lived in the shoe.

Adam and Brian pointed to one another. "*He* started it!"

Jackson said, "Max promised no harm would come to Topher and Tyler."

"A sightseeing trip then out to dinner? I wouldn't walk across the street with that creep," Adam said.

Brian replied, "We wouldn't be walking. He'll have a car...probably a limo."

"Then I wouldn't *ride* with him across the street," Adam said. "Is that better, Brian?"

"Shut up, Adam."

"*You* shut up, Brian."

"You should go," Jana said.

"There must be something in the water at the

Capitol," Adam and Brian said in unison, followed by dagger eyes at one another.

"Hear me out." Jana took in a deep breath. "In my old movie, *Young Mermaid*, my father, the king of the mermen, was at war with the king of the fishmen. When my father was sleeping…in a giant clamshell, I made my way to the fish king and swam around the ocean with him, looking at the amazingly beautiful species of fish. As we toured his part of the ocean, we got to know one another. He opened up to me and I did the same to him. So, when the human fishermen attacked the mermen, the fishmen army and mermen army joined forces against the fishermen and won."

"What a fishy story," Jackson said.

Jana replied, "Fishy or not, it makes sense."

"Not to me," Adam said turning his back on her.

"Not to me either," Brian replied, agreeing with Adam for the first time since they arrived in DC.

Jana rested a hand on each of their shoulders. "Don't you see? Better the devil you know." She stood between them. "Go with Max. The children will enjoy it. You'll like it, too."

"No I won't," Adam and Brian replied in unison, followed by, "Stop doing that!"

Jana continued, "I think you will. And more importantly, you can get to know what makes Max tick—and maybe how to win him over to *our* side."

"He'll never be won over to our side," Jackson said.

"Then Brian and Adam might at least be able to get some useful information from him," Jana said. "That's why I invited Max to my fundraiser at the Ford Theatre on Saturday night."

Jackson asked, "Yeah, about that. You invited Max to a fundraiser against his own bill?"

"And he's coming?" Adam and Brian said in union, followed by raised fists.

Jana nodded. "Can you imagine the press picture of Senator Maxmillion at my benefit to raise money to fight his Protect the Children Act?"

****

The arguments continued as each couple went up to bed. Lying in their huge wood-carved four-poster with the homemade quilt at their feet, Jana and Brian could hear Jackson and Adam arguing in the next bedroom.

Brian said to Jana, "Can you believe the nerve of that guy?"

"Which guy?" Jana asked, adjusting her silk tangerine nighty.

In his T-shirt and shorts, Brian replied, "Adam. He talks me into meeting with Max then he wants to back out of building the new wing. How am I supposed to start all over with a new contractor who won't understand my plans?"

Jana cuddled against her husband. "Brian?"

"What?" He put his arms around her.

She rested her head on Brian's chest. "I think you like Adam."

"What?" Brian jerked up, nearly giving Jana whiplash.

Jana sat up and rested her sore head on his shoulder. "And I think Adam likes you, too."

Brian laughed loudly. "You must have had too much wine at dinner."

Curling her legs around his, Jana said, "And I think

you know I'm right." Jana leaned in for a kiss.

"You're wrong. I can't stand Adam." Brian lay on his side. "As my wife, you should know that. It seems like Adam knows me better than *you* do."

Jana said to Brian's back, "In *The Pirate Princess*—"

Brian's snoring drowned out the story. Jana slid down, closed her eyes, and joined her husband in agitated slumber.

****

In Jana's nightmares, she was chased down the hallway of the Senate building by Max, Cassie, Lenore, Ben, Sancho, and Adam. She woke alone in the bed, assuming it was morning, then groaned when the clock on her night table displayed the time of 1:28am.

Hearing familiar voices from downstairs, Jana put on her silk tangerine robe and ventured out into the upstairs hallway.

Adam shouted from the kitchen below, "You put down everything I say and do, Brian."

"That's because you act like you know everything," Brian answered.

"I know what I know," Adam replied.

"Which to you is everything," Brian shouted.

Adam continued his rant. "And you contradict everything I say."

"No I don't."

"See?"

Jackson appeared next to Jana wearing a violet nightshirt. He rubbed his Afro. "Men!"

"They sound like an old married couple," Jana said.

"Should we be worried?"

Jana playfully hit Jackson's backside.

"Ooow, that felt good. Do it again," Jackson said with a giggle.

She laughed in spite of herself.

Adam asked Brian, "What are you doing down here anyway?"

"I can't sleep. Hot chocolate usually helps. What are *you* doing downstairs?"

"I was going to make hot chocolate, too, but now I'm changing the recipe to hot arsenic—for you."

"Very funny."

Banging pots, Adam said, "Why couldn't you sleep?"

Brian answered, "I was thinking about tomorrow."

"Me too."

"I like honey instead of sugar," Brian said.

"Me too," Adam echoed.

"What do you think we should do?" Brian asked.

"What do *you* think we should do?"

Brian said, "Let's drink this and figure it out."

"You drink first."

Jana and Jackson shared a smile then returned to their beds.

****

Jana woke the next morning, looked out her bedroom window, and found Brian, Adam, and the four boys out in the boat on the lake, no doubt in the heat of blissful battle and one-upmanship. Since Cassie was tied up in business meetings all morning, Jana slipped into a canary dress with matching shoes and eye shadow then asked Jackson to drop her off at a restaurant in downtown Washington, DC.

Finding Simon and Cornelius to be fashionably late

for their breakfast meeting, Jana sat in a ruby-red booth and perused the menu. As the Eurythmics' "Sweet Dreams Are Made of These" played over the sound system, a middle-aged woman with very teased hair approached her.

"Excuse me." The woman pushed her thick black glasses up her thick nose. "You must get this all the time, but you look a little like Jana Lane. You know who I mean?" The woman played with the pink plastic necklace hovering over her pea-green kimono. "She did all those movies as a kid then we didn't hear from her for a while. I thought she was dead." She poked Jana's shoulder and laughed. "But she resurfaced like the second-coming with that terrible movie *His Obsession*."

Simon Huckby entered the restaurant with a flourish. "It was not terrible! That movie was sheer magic. Hence the Academy Award nomination for its star. And she didn't *resurface*. Jana Lane was, is, and always will be the greatest star in the galaxy!" Wearing a fuchsia and magenta spandex jumpsuit with a chartreuse scarf and waist pouch, Simon kissed the air around Jana's cheeks and sat next to her. Then he glared at the woman like a tiger ready to pounce on his prey. "And, madam, you are looking at her!"

The woman gasped as if she'd seen a ghost. "Oh my God!" She fetched a pad and pen from her purse. "Can I have your autograph, Miss Lane? Please make it out to Pierina Pecatollapia."

"Of course." Jana signed the pad.

"Thank you, Miss Lane." The woman walked backwards out of the restaurant. "I'm sure your next movie will be better than the last one."

Cornelius Chamberlain joined Simon and Jana at

the table. Nearly twice as tall and thin as his partner, Cornelius was clad in a lemon shirt with aqua slacks, suspenders, and bowtie. Though as old as Simon, and an avid musician and motorcyclist, Cornelius had a youthful quality that made him seem lighter than air. "You're still tops in my book, Jana." He blew her a kiss.

"And tops in the hearts of all *true* Americans," Simon added.

Jana said, "It's so good to see you both."

"You know I'm never far away from you, baby doll," Simon said.

"How was your train ride?" Jana asked.

"Like riding over a mountain in a stage coach," Simon said.

"You should know, love," Cornelius said with a wink at Jana.

Jana asked, "And your hotel?"

Simon replied with a grimace, "Like a flophouse in Korea during World War II."

Cornelius raised an eyebrow. "Stay in many of those, did you, Simon?"

"That's not the point." Simon drank his water.

"What is the point, love?" Cornelius asked stifling a grin.

Simon replied, "The point is that I would ride on a donkey with fleas, and sleep in an alley full of muggers with tuberculosis for my baby girl."

"Then breakfast is on me," Jana said.

"If you insist," Simon said magnanimously. After the waitress served them juice, took their orders, and left, Simon asked Jana, "So tell Mama, how are things going with Senator Castle?"

"Fine," Jana replied. "I've certainly learned a great deal about being a senator." *For better or worse.*

"Good." Simon drank his juice.

Cornelius said, "Jana, you will be proud of us. I've lined up the musicians for the benefit."

"And I've lined up the talent," Simon added. Simon ran through the litany of singers, comics, magicians, and ventriloquists for the benefit.

Jana said, "That's wonderful! You two are amazing!"

"Yes, we are," Simon said.

Cornelius pinched Simon's knee under the table and they shared a knowing giggle.

Simon cleared his throat. "But isn't the Ford Theatre a national historic site run by the National Park Service? How did you book it, baby doll?"

Jana nodded. "It is also rented out on occasion for events like ours. I've put ads in the local newspapers, and I'm scheduled to do radio interviews tomorrow morning and Friday morning."

"We'll be a sell-out at two hundred dollars a ticket!" Simon said snatching and eating a piece of toast as the waitress placed them on the table. "And not a moment too soon since the Senate passed that horrendous, so-called Protect the Children Act."

"Luckily, we don't have children, Simon," Cornelius said.

Reaching for two more pieces of toast, Simon said, "Jana Lane is my child. Not by birth, but by love and devotion."

And by ten percent of my salary. Jana squeezed Simon's hand and heard a crack.

The waitress served their breakfasts—oatmeal and

fruit for Jana, an omelet for Cornelius, and three waffles, two sausages, three eggs, and three pancakes for Simon. Before the waitress left, Simon asked, "And can you please bring us some toast—with extra butter and jam?" Then Simon turned to Jana, "That vicious Senator Maxmillion should be shot at dawn in front of the Capitol. He should try persecuting any other minority group. He'd never get away with it. Somebody should stop him!"

"He'll be at the benefit," Jana said scooping up her oatmeal with her spoon.

Simon dropped his fork and held his hand to his heart. "Why? To spy on the enemy?"

Jana ate the warm oatmeal covered with cinnamon. "I'm sure you've read Maxmillion is dating Senator Castle."

"That's like the devil dating an angel," Cornelius said, licking egg off his lips.

"They're both expected to attend the benefit," Jana said. "As is Cassie's sister. I'm also expecting many of the Democrats in the House and Senate, including Senator Ramirez from New York, and of course my friend Congressman Mitchell and his partner, Adam."

Simon said with various breakfast foods sticking out of his mouth, "Are they all the suspects for the murder case?"

Jana replied, "At present. Detective Bove has things well in hand."

"And his hands are pretty *well*—as is the rest of him," Simon said with a snicker.

"Should I be jealous?" Cornelius asked with a wide grin.

Simon waved his partner away. "Bove wouldn't be

interested in me." He looked at Jana. "My beautiful baby doll no doubt has his attention."

"Bove has been busy interviewing suspects," Jana said. *And making me swoon.*

Simon poured more syrup on his pancakes. "Tell me about the suspects and their motives."

"You'll meet everyone at the benefit."

Simon clapped his tiny hands together like a child at a birthday party. "Gathering all the suspects in one place for the sleuth to solve the case. What fun!"

Once they finished breakfast, Jana, Simon, and Cornelius took a taxi to the Roosevelt Memorial. As Hudson Valley, New York residents, they enjoyed comparing the site in DC to the FDR mansion and museum back in Hyde Park, New York. They marveled at the fascinating pictures, artifacts, and stories about the great Democrat who as president created the New Deal.

Jana dropped Simon and Cornelius off at their hotel, then asked the taxi driver to take her to the nearest public library.

Reaching the library's information desk, Jana asked for Tamaya Stormcloud's article on Congressman Jackson Montgomery, and for every article they had on the Multitopower Conglomerate.

A few minutes later, Jana sat at a small desk in the corner of the library surrounded by stacks of newspapers, magazines, and microfilm dispensers. Tamaya's article on Jackson was exactly as he had stated, an exposé on Adam's wife, including her medical history and mental breakdown. Jana read copious information about the numerous businesses housed within the Conglomerate, their charitable donations, and their financial support of various conservative political candidates.

Feeling frustrated by her inability to uncover new information, Jana left the library and took a taxi to the Department of Commerce. Upon entry, she asked the receptionist where to file a Freedom of Information Act request. When she finally found the appropriate office, Jana filled out a lengthy form then sat on a lumpy gray sofa for a half hour until a tired-looking African American woman plopped a stack of folders down in front of her.

Jana sat on a creaky chair at a long table and examined various documents referencing the Multitopower Conglomerate, including certificates of incorporation, list of officers, board members, shareholders reports, and other legal information. While examining the biographies of the officers, including the CEO Benjamin Topower, Jana noticed each board member was a married male of great wealth who belonged to something called the H.A. Organization. With eyes blurred from reading so much fine print, and a nose itchy from the dust on the pages, Jana returned the folders.

Next, Jana stepped into a phone booth, checked in with the box office manager at the Ford Theatre, then took a taxi to the Capitol.

In the hallway outside of Cassie's office, Jana ran into Cassie coming from a committee meeting. The senator looked beautiful as usual in a cerise satin dress with matching earrings.

"Perfect timing," Cassie said. "You can watch me answer letters from constituents." She grinned. "How'd you like to respond to the people who want me to take care of their parking tickets?"

Cassie's grin disappeared as they entered her outer office and found Max and Lenore on the loveseat whispering and giggling together. "Lenore, please go into my office and wait for me. I have some letters to dictate," Cassie said.

"Of course, Cassie."

Once Lenore was gone, Max put his arm around Cassie. "How are you today, my love?"

Cassie replied, "Incredibly busy. Imagine that, the taxpayers want me to work for my salary." She headed for her office but stopped at the doorway, "Weren't you going sightseeing today?"

"With my husband, Brian's business associate, and our children," Jana offered.

Max smiled like a wise, old owl. "My driver is waiting for me as we speak." He started to leave.

Jana stood in front of him. "Thank you for agreeing to come to my benefit show Saturday night."

"Then you *are* coming?" Cassie asked Max.

Max nodded. "How could I miss such wonderful entertainment?" He blew a kiss to Cassie. "And such amazing company. Tell Lenore to come with us. My treat."

Jana said, "You'd better act fast. The box office manager at the Ford Theatre told me ticket sales are going very well."

"Many people love Jana Lane," Max said with a hand on her shoulder.

Jana replied with a frozen smile, "And many people, including me, can't stand by quietly while a destructive law moves through Congress to take children away from their parents."

"The President will sign it and the bill will soon be forgotten." He walked to the door. "Enjoy shadowing my honey, Jana. She's the best senator we have." He winked. "Except for me." And he was gone.

"Isn't there anything you can do to stop this bill?" Jana asked Cassie.

"I tried," Cassie replied. "I spoke as long as I could on the Senate floor. And I discussed the bill with many of my colleagues privately—on both sides of the aisle—prior to the vote." She sighed. "I'm tired of arguing with Max about it." Cassie walked into her office and sat behind her desk opposite Lenore.

Jana took the seat next to Lenore and looked up at the picture of their father on the wall above the desk. She marveled at the strong resemblance between the great senator and his daughters. "I'm sure your father would be proud to see you both working in the Senate," Jana said.

"He instilled in us a love for our country and for service to others," Lenore said. "There was and never will be anyone like him."

Cassie smiled at her sister. "We're doing a pretty good job, Lenore."

Lenore returned the smile.

Cassie rolled up her sleeves. "All right, let's get to this stack of letters."

Is that a welt on her arm?

Cassie dictated responses to Lenore, and Jana's mind wandered to her research on the Multitopower Conglomerate. *Why are all the members of the Conglomerate members of the H.A. Organization? And what does H.A. stand for?*

At the end of the day, since Jackson had to work

late, Jana took a taxi back to the house. She checked in with Grace who was changing upstairs, then Jana prepared dinner in the large, rustic kitchen. With the men and boys out sightseeing with Max, the house seemed oddly quiet and still. When the turkey tetrazzini was in the oven, the salad washed, cut, and arranged, and the bread heated, the doorbell rang.

Jana shouted upstairs, "I'll get it, Grace," then opened the door. "Sancho, what are you doing here?"

Sancho, looking handsome in a Kelly-green pin-striped suit and emerald tie with his black hair slicked back, stopped in the tracks of his black Italian loafers. "Did I come on the wrong night?"

"I didn't mean to be rude, but I wasn't expecting you," Jana said.

"Grace invited me."

"*You're* the…you and *Grace…years* ago…in *New York*?" *Spit it out, girl.* "Sancho, forgive me. I didn't know you are Grace's friend from her past."

"Obviously. May I come in?"

"Of course!" Jana walked Sancho into the living room.

Sancho looked out at the lake. "What a nice view."

"Yes. My best friend Congressman Jackson Mitchell and his partner Adam Stokes live here with their children."

"I remember Tamaya's article about that."

"Please take a seat."

He sat on the sectional near the fireplace.

"The article wasn't very fair," Jana said.

"That's Tamaya for you. Nobody knows that better than I do."

Would you like a drink?"

"A glass of wine would be great."

Jana poured a glass of white wine in the kitchen. "Please accept my apologies again, Sancho. I had no idea you were Grace's old friend." Jana served Sancho his drink then sat next to him on the sectional.

Sancho took a sip of wine, then said, "I told you about Grace when we were at the Capitol. I didn't know at the time you were the woman she worked for."

"And *I* didn't know you were her *man that got away.*"

Sancho sat back on the sofa. "I think I fell in love with Grace the first minute I saw her." He smiled nostalgically. "I remember she came to my door to raise money for some charity. She was only eighteen. I was living with my parents, studying for law school. I invited her in and we talked for hours. Whatever makes people connect—we had it *big time*. She was such a delight to be around—even with all her problems. Hearing about them made me want to protect and take care of her."

Jana leaned forward. "Her *problems*?"

Pain exploded across his face. "Hasn't Grace told you about it?"

"No, she hasn't. And her background check came through fine before we hired her."

"It would."

"That's awfully cryptic."

Sancho put his glass on a wood-carved end table. "Sorry, but I don't feel it's my place to talk about it. By the time I passed my bar exams, Grace was married and gone."

"And now that her husband is deceased—"

"I'm hoping we can make up for lost time."

"And Tamaya Stormcloud can no longer stop you."

Sancho looked down at the wood floor. "I won't lie and say I miss Tamaya. I don't."

"But you *did* miss, Grace. Over all these years."

"I never stopped thinking about her." He looked like a little boy telling a secret. "And when she called to tell me about her husband, I'm embarrassed to admit, I nearly hit the ceiling with joy. We've been talking on the phone every day since." His dimples appeared. "And when Grace told me her employee was taking her to DC for a week, I was on cloud nine."

"But Grace's husband passed away two months ago. Why didn't you visit Grace at her cousin's house in Westchester, or at my house in Hyde Park once she'd been hired as our nanny?"

"I remember Grace's cousin, Jolanda, before Jolanda got married...when she lived next door to Grace. She was a nice girl. The two of them were really close."

"It seems like they still are."

Sancho nodded. "When Grace moved in with Jolanda, I begged Grace to let me see her. I even called Jolanda, but Grace wouldn't let me visit. I kept trying in vain when Grace moved to Hyde Park. I was surprised when Grace told me on the phone that *her employer* invited me over tonight."

Jana walked to the window. "I think I know why Grace didn't want to see you."

He followed her like a hawk. "Please tell me. Grace mentioned something about gaining weight. But she can't think I'd care about *that*."

Get ready, Sancho. You're in for a big surprise. Jana walked to the staircase and called up the stairs,

"Grace, Sancho is here." When she received no response, she called louder, "Dinner will be ready soon." Hearing nothing from upstairs, Jana said to Sancho, "Please excuse me. Make yourself comfortable. Have another glass of wine if you like."

While Sancho paced below, Jana mounted the stairs. When she came to Grace's room, she knocked on the door. "Grace?" Receiving no answer, Jana opened the door and found Grace lying on the rug.

Chapter 7

Grace lay on the floor of her bedroom with a new twilight-blue dress hanging off her emaciated body. Jana's scream brought Grace's date racing up the stairs. With Jana kneeling on one side of her, and Sancho at the other, Grace finally opened her eyes. "What happened?"

Jana took Grace's ice-cold hand. "You must have fainted."

At the sight of Sancho, tears filled Grace's eyes. "You're here."

He ran his finger across her cheek. "I'm here. And I'm not going anywhere." Sancho helped Grace to sit up, then he rested her head on his chest.

"I feel better now," Grace said.

"Grace all better!" B.J. said happily from his bed.

While Jana went to B.J., Sancho kissed the top of Grace's head. "What's happened to you, Grace?"

She replied, "I know. I'm sorry. I've let myself go."

Sancho carefully helped Grace to her feet. "What do you mean?"

"I try not to eat much, right Jana?"

Jana nodded sadly.

"But I can't take the weight off," Grace explained.

Sancho and Jana shared a knowing look.

"Weight off!" B.J. said.

As Jana tucked B.J. back into bed, Sancho pulled Grace into him for a long kiss then he said, "I'm going to take care of you, Grace."

"I like the sound of that," Grace said.

"But you have to help," he said. "I'm going to drive you to the hospital."

"Is that necessary?" Grace asked.

"Yes, I'm afraid it is," Sancho replied.

"But why?"

"They'll be able to help you. We'll *all* help you get your strength back. But you have to do what the doctors say. You have to eat what they tell you to eat. Okay, Grace?"

"I don't think that's a very good idea, Sancho," Grace said.

"Do you trust me, Grace?"

"Of course."

"Then please do what I'm telling you. Do what the doctors tell you. Do you promise?"

They kissed again.

She replied, "I promise."

Sancho led Grace out of the room with his arm around her bony back and her head on his shoulder.

"I'm so glad you're here, Sancho."

"Me too." Sancho called out over his shoulder, "Jana, I'll call you when Grace is settled in."

With B.J. nearly asleep, Jana followed them to the upstairs hallway.

"What about B.J.?" Grace asked.

Jana answered, "B.J., and all of us, will be fine. Just get well then come back to us, Grace."

"Thanks, Jana." As Sancho walked her slowly down the stairs, Grace said, "I'm sorry, Sancho. I've made so many mistakes in my life. What I did in the old neighborhood, marrying my husband, and not letting you visit me."

As they went out the front door, Sancho said, "I know all about past mistakes. But all that matters is the future. And the future is you and me finally together."

Once B.J. was asleep, Jana went down to the kitchen, and in honor of Grace, she ate her dinner then wrapped the leftovers. Shortly afterward, Sancho phoned to report Grace was on IV fluids and resting comfortably in the hospital—with Sancho at her side. Grace had also spoken to a therapist and a dietician, and thanks to some coaxing from Sancho, she agreed to follow the prescribed diet. Sancho would be spending the night in the hospital to make sure she followed orders. An appointment with a psychiatrist was scheduled for first thing the next morning.

Jana washed and put away the dishes, then sat on the sectional and looked out at the cobalt sky hovering over the gray still water. She enjoyed the peaceful solitude until the four boys exploded into the living room like cannons.

"Mommy! We rode in a big black car like a spaceship!"

"We had a great day! Max is really cool!"

"Jana! You missed everything!"

"Don't worry, we'll tell you all about it!"

The boys jumped around Jana like natives encircling their prey.

Ed screeched, "We saw Mount Vermin!"

"Mount Vernon!" Devon shouted to his younger brother.

Topher cried, "We saw the Revolutionary War!"

"It was the encampment reenactment," Brian explained from the kitchen.

"And we saw a Christmas!" screamed Ed.

"He means a Gristmill," Brian said, pouring himself a glass of cranberry apple juice.

"And a blackmouth!" Tyler giggled.

"That's a blacksmith, Tyler," Adam said while pouring himself a glass of juice. "Brian, you should close the top of the juice container fully."

Brian looked like a branded horse. "I *did* close it tightly, Adam."

"It was pretty loose when I opened it," Adam said.

"Maybe that's because you are soooo much stronger than I am," Brian said.

"That must be it." Adam laughed triumphantly.

Brian growled. "I'll get you next time."

"No you won't."

"We'll see, Adam."

"Yes, we will, Brian."

Who should I tend to first, the children in the living room or the children in the kitchen? "It sounds like you had a wonderful day, boys."

"We did!"

"And we went to the National Zoo," Devon said.

"We saw a zebra and a *cantaloupe*," Ed added.

"Antelope," Brian and Adam said in unison.

Topher said, "And we saw an ostrich, a bear, and baby monkeys."

"And two elephants!" Tyler said.

"Oh, my goodness," Jana exclaimed.

"Max also took us to the Naval Heritage Center," Brian the ex-Navy man said.

Jackson came out of the bathroom. "I couldn't

enjoy the naval exhibits. I kept thinking about how gay people are thrown out of the armed forces."

"That'll change one day," Brian said as he poured then handed Jackson a glass of juice before Adam could get to it.

"I hope I live to see it," Jackson replied.

Me too, my friend. "Did you have a nice dinner?"

That started the kids screaming and jumping again.

Wrong question.

"I ate a big piece of steak, Mommy!" Devon said.

"Me, too!" Ed added.

"Mine was bigger," Devon said.

"*Mine* was bigger!" shouted Topher and Tyler.

Jackson said, "You kids want some juice?"

"Yeah!"

After the boys had juice and cookies, they went upstairs to wash and dress for bed. The adults read them an intergalactic bedtime story about a space colony infiltrated by worm-eating aliens, and somehow the children fell asleep.

Jana stood and faced the other adults sitting on the sectional couch in the living room rubbing their tired feet. "How did things go with Max? Clearly he was a hit with the boys."

Adam ran a hand through his chestnut hair. "It's the strangest thing. I want so much to hate him for what he did in the Senate. But the truth is, I like the guy."

"But surely you were able to tell him what you think of his bill," Jana said.

Jackson replied, "Each one of us got a crack at him, but Max didn't waver."

"He kept insisting the boys were safe," Adam said. "Since Max is our employer, we couldn't go too far."

But Max didn't go too far when he proposed a bill to put Tyler and Topher in an orphanage?

Jackson said, "I detest Max's politics, but I tried to separate the person from the problem."

"You're a bigger man than I," Jana said.

Jackson rose to his feet. "You can say that again."

She slapped his thigh.

"Max showed us and the kids a terrific time," Brian said. "And he gave us an incredible contract at the Senate. The guy is dangerous politically, but he's not all bad."

I wonder if they said that about Hitler.

Jana filled the men in on what happened with Grace. They agreed to tell the children Grace was on a short vacation with Sancho and would return home soon. Then they all walked upstairs.

On the upstairs landing, Adam asked Brian, "How do you like the king size bed? I carved it myself."

"My butch woodsman!" Jackson giggled.

"It's beautiful," Jana said. "And very comfortable."

"Did you quilt the comforter and the curtains, too, Adam?" Brian asked with a smirk.

Adam replied, "Yes, and I'm going to wrap you in them and throw you out the window right after you fall asleep."

Brian fought hard to stifle a laugh. "Try it, Adam."

"Maybe I will." Adam pinched Brian's cheek. "Sleep well, Brian."

Once Brian and Jana were in bed, Jana rested her head on her husband's wide chest. "I'm glad Grace is finally getting help."

Brian wrapped his arms around her and hugged her tightly. "That's amazing about Grace and Sancho

Ramirez."

"Evidently, they've had a long history together as *the one that got away*."

"I'm glad you weren't the one that got away," Brian said looking at her adoringly.

"Me too."

They shared a long, passionate kiss. Then another. And another.

With her arms around her husband's strong back, Jana said, "I'm still not a Max convert, and I'm doing my best to bring down his bill, but I'm happy you and the boys had a good time sightseeing today."

"Thanks."

After another warm, moist kiss that tasted like cranberries, Jana said, "I did a little sightseeing myself today with Simon and Cornelius after our meeting about the benefit."

"Where'd you go?"

"To the Roosevelt museum."

He kissed her neck. "That reminds me of home."

She squeezed his abdominal muscle and Brian wrapped his leg over hers.

"I think what you're doing with the benefit is terrific." Brian rested Jana on her back and looked down at her. "I love how much you care about other people."

She looked up. "I love how much you care about me and the kids." After another kiss, Jana said, "It looks like you and Adam are getting along better."

Brian released her. "Talk about stifling the mood. Why did you have to bring up Adam?"

She rolled onto her side and rested her head in her palm. "Because you two didn't get along, but now things seem…better."

Brian collapsed into his pillow. "Yeah, they're better. But not great."

Jana laughed.

"What's so funny?"

"I'm not one to say I told you so."

"Since when?"

"But I told you so."

He caught her giggles.

"Can you two stop having so much fun in there?" Jackson shouted from the next room.

"Don't make me wrap you in that comforter, Brian," Adam said.

Brian answered, "Only if you and Jack come in it with me."

"Hey, what about me?" Jana said.

Jana and Brian laughed, made love, then fell asleep. Jackson and Adam did the same.

****

Jana Lane ran down the winding hallway of Senate offices. She could feel her heart pounding in her throat. Who was chasing her and why? Where could she hide? A hand touched her arm. She screamed. Something fell on her chest. A toy block?

"Mommy play blocks!"

Jana opened her eyes to B.J. sitting next to her on the bed, building blocks on her stomach.

Your daddy is the architect, not me.

Jana built then knocked down a number of architectural wonders. Then she threw on her silk turquoise robe, bathed, changed, and dressed B.J., then raced down the stairs after him to get his breakfast.

She knew that Jackson had already left to prepare

for the big debate in the House on the Protect the Children Act before the vote on Monday. Jana walked past seven empty breakfast bowls on the kitchen table to the screened-in porch at the back of the house, where she saw Brian and Adam on the grassy knoll near the lake arguing over various home construction techniques while the boys swam in the lake.

Jana called out, "Brian, I have to leave. Please come inside and take B.J."

"Daddy take B.J.!" B.J. echoed while running circles around his mother.

"Be right in," Brian answered.

Adam shouted, "Don't believe him, Jana. He likes me too much to leave my side."

"You're asking for it, Adam," Brian said.

"And who's gonna give it to me, Brian?"

Jana placed her hand on her hip. "Brian, I can't be late for this radio interview."

Adam said, "Yeah, listen to your wife, Brian. Nobody wants to interview *Mr. Jana Lane*."

"Or Mrs. Jackson Mitchell," Brian replied.

B.J. watched his father and Adam wrestle into laugher. "Daddy silly."

That's for sure. "Brian, are you coming inside?"

"Go inside, Brian. The *guys* will stay out here," Adam said.

Brian headed inside. "Just wait until I get back out here."

"I'm shaking," Adam replied with a laugh.

Jana changed into an apricot business suit with a rope chain gold necklace and earrings, kissed Brian and B.J. goodbye, then went by taxi to the radio station. Since she had given interviews for most of her life, Jana was a pro at avoiding pitfalls like talking about other celebrities or her family. Despite the usual inane questions from the interviewers about her weight, taste in men, and personal life as a child star, Jana always made sure to get in the information she wanted before her time on the air was up.

The assistant producer greeted her and brought her to the sound studio, where she sat opposite the host. The middle-aged man nodded to her from across the table, adjusted his headset then said, "Good morning, Washington, DC! It's Marky Mango in the Morning with ex-child star, current actress, and *liberal* activist Jana Lane. Good morning, Jana."

Jana adjusted her microphone. "Hello, Mark."

With a sneer on his face, Mark said, "Jana, tell us the truth. When you were a child star, was the little hula girl and sweet candy striper hooked on drugs like so many child stars nowadays? Were you a sweet little virgin on screen, but a sexual siren off screen?"

Jana took in a deep breath. "My work schedule didn't leave time for those things."

He unleashed a snide laugh. "Come on, Jana. Fess up. You never had a fling with your little co-star Timmy Timlin?"

"No."

"And how about a roll in the Hollywood hay with your hunky co-star on *His Obsession*, or your leading man in your upcoming *Madam Senator* flick?"

"My marriage is quite solid. Actually, my husband is the architect for the new wing being added to the Senate offices in the Capitol."

Marky Mango chortled. "And how is *that* working out with your husband who was hired by Senator

Maxmillion, the majority leader of the Senate? The very same Senator Maxmillion who proposed and championed the Protect the Children Act, which *you* are fundraising to fight?"

Jana struggled to keep the pitch of her voice steady. "My husband is not involved in politics."

"But it seems, like so many *liberal* actors, *you are*! How has it been going head to head with the probable Republican candidate for president?" Mark took a sip of water and wiped his forehead with a handkerchief.

Jana replied, "I bear no ill will against Senator Maxmillion. The purpose of the benefit is for top singers, musicians, comedians, magicians, and ventriloquists to share their talents free of charge in an effort to raise money for AIDS research and funding, since our representatives in Washington, DC have been seriously delinquent in this regard. We are also raising money and awareness to combat the Protect the Children Act, which passed in the Senate and is being voted on in the House on Monday. At the benefit, I will make a pitch for every concerned citizen to phone his or her member of congress and ask him or her to vote no on this bill." Before Marky could cut her off, Jana gave the phone number to call at the Ford Theatre to purchase tickets.

The talk show host glanced at the clock on the studio wall. "Jana, tell us why America's sweetheart cares about AIDS and the Protect the Children Act."

Jana replied, "We *all* should care. Our family members, neighbors, and co-workers are dying of a terrible disease for which there is no cure, and very little research is underway to find one."

"But since AIDS is contracted sexually, didn't

those *so-called victims* get what they deserved?"

"If everyone who had sex got a terminal disease, there would be very few people left on the planet."

"But in the case of AIDS, we are talking primarily about homosexuals."

"In this country at this time that is true."

"I was brought up to believe homosexuality is wrong."

"I was brought up to believe people are people."

Marky laughed. "That's right. You were brought up in a show business household, which explains a lot."

Jana answered, "I don't believe one needs to be brought up in a show business household to care about others. Which is why everyone should be against the so-called Protect the Children Act."

"And why is that?"

"Because children belong with their families. Government has no right to infringe on that right."

With a snide laugh, Marky Mango said, "But isn't that what Senator Maxmillion and his cohorts are fighting for? The right for birth parents to raise their children?"

Jana tried to remain calm. "No. The bill that passed the Senate will take children *away* from their parents—if the parents are gay or lesbian."

"But how can their parents be homosexuals?" He laughed. "The way I understand the mechanics, that's just not possible, Jana."

"A parent is a parent whether his or her children are biologically conceived or gotten through adoption."

He chortled. "But isn't that what the radical homosexual activists want us to believe? That a mother and father are no longer necessary to raise a child?"

Jana bit her lip. "As a mother, I am certainly not lessening the role of mothers in our society. However, the reality is that in some cases a child can have one mother, one father, two mothers, or two fathers. If the parents love their child, the child is far better off than in an orphanage."

Marky crooned into the microphone, "And there you have it, ladies and gentlemen. The last word from Hollywood's liberal elite trying to change the definition of family and take away *your* family's traditional values."

Jana interceded. "Excuse me, Mark, can you explain how a gay couple raising a child would take rights away from a straight couple raising a child?"

"And that's all the time we have—"

"Wouldn't having more families strengthen the family dynamic in our society?"

"Until next time, stay well, stay happy, stay close to God, and stay America."

The moment they were off the air, Marky leaped from his chair and headed out of the studio, which happened to be owned by the Multitopower Conglomerate.

The assistant producer thanked her for coming, then Jana used the public phone in the hallway to call Simon at his hotel for a quick check-in about the benefit. Simon assured Jana that she was "sheer perfection" on the live radio telecast, then explained that he and Cornelius had checked in with the free talent—and everything was a go. Finally, Jana phoned the Ford Theatre. Due to the frenzy of ticket sales after her radio interview, Jana was put on hold a number of times before receiving the good news that ticket sales were nearly at capacity.

Since she knew Cassie was in committee meetings all morning, Jana taxied to the Washington Memorial, Washington, DC's oldest and most famous monument. As Jana stared up at the over five-hundred-foot stone testament to the commander of the Continental Army and the first president of the United States, she thought about those so-called rebels living in the thirteen colonies fighting against wealth and power to live in freedom. She couldn't help but compare their struggle to gay people in America seeking the right to live, work, and raise families without persecution.

Jana couldn't resist taking the elevator up to the vast observation deck, where she marveled at the stunning panoramic views of Washington, DC, Maryland, and Virginia, including many historic buildings, waterways, parks, and shrines.

Next, Jana visited the Lincoln Memorial, where the sixteenth president of the United States sat high in his chair, immortalized by marble, behind stone columns as a symbol of unity, strength, and wisdom. As Jana stared at the thoughtful look on the great man's face and recalled his work for equality, she wondered what he would think of the Multitopower Conglomerate.

Finally, Jana walked to the adjoining long pool of water designed by Henry Bacon. Depending on Jana's position, the pool reflected the Washington Monument, the Lincoln Memorial, the surrounding trees, or the crystal-blue sky. When her feet hurt from walking, she sat on a bench and enjoyed the warm weather. Like the pool in front of her, Jana reflected, but her reflections centered on the murder of Tamaya Stormcloud. The newspaper reporter certainly made enemies after she

Joe Cosentino

printed the exposé on Adam, released the story about Cassie and Max, and threatened to write about Sancho's secret past life and the Multitopower Conglomerate.

Jana spent the afternoon in Cassie's office watching the junior senator from Ohio patiently listen to various pitches, complaints, suggestions, demands, and requests from numerous groups and individuals. As Jana looked up at the framed picture of Cassie's father on the wall then down to Cassie sitting at her desk beneath it, Jana realized Cassie Castle was definitely Samuel Castle's daughter.

Since debate on the Protect the Children Act was still going on in the House when Jana left the Capitol, she took a taxi home. Jana entered the house and found a note on the kitchen counter stating Brian, Adam, and the boys went out to dinner at a diner then to a drive-in science fiction movie.

I assume Brian and Adam will argue over the plot of the movie, the four boys will be riveted to the action, and Brian Jr. will fall asleep at the opening credits.

Remembering she hadn't told Bove her latest news about the case, Jana sat at the kitchen counter, slipped off her shoes, found Bove's card in the drawer, and phoned him.

"Bove. What?"

"You don't sound too happy," Jana said.

"It's Thursday night," he replied.

"What's wrong with Thursday nights?" Jana asked.

"It was my dance night with Allison." He added sarcastically, "Thanks for asking about it."

Jana couldn't hold back a laugh. "You *danced*?"

"Every Thursday night. Is there something wrong with dancing?"

166

"No." She continued to chuckle.

"I remember you as The Pink Ballerina."

"You do *ballet*?"

"We did ballroom…and more recently disco."

"Is that why you sound so grouchy? Because you miss dancing?"

"That…and I haven't eaten…or solved the case. The letter opener tested positive for Tamaya Stormcloud's blood, by the way."

"Bove, I have some news about the investigation."

"Have you eaten yet?"

"No. My family and friends have abandoned me for dinner out and a drive-in movie."

"Do you like to dance?"

"I was The Pink Ballerina, remember?"

"Give me your address."

Jana obliged.

"I'll pick you up in twenty minutes."

"Where are we going?"

"Aren't you following? Out for dinner and dancing."

Jana hung up the phone, grabbed her shoes, and rushed upstairs to change into a cherry-colored bodice blouse with matching jacket, black lace gloves, and black heels. Just as she finished freshening her makeup and re-teasing her hair, the doorbell rang. She hurried down the stairs, and her jaw dropped nearly to her cherry and lemon print skirt at the sight of Bove in white parachute pants and blazer, a baby-blue T-shirt, and white loafers. Standing in the doorway, he asked, "What's wrong?"

Jana somehow found her voice. "I wasn't expecting you to look so…casual."

"Did you expect me to go dancing in a dark suit? Let's go."

Aye Aye, captain.

Bove led Jana to his convertible, and they took off.

Before she knew it, Jana sat opposite Bove in an upscale dance club at a table for two near a huge polished wood dance floor and seasoned orchestra. Bove ordered white wine and veal osso buco for him and veal scaloppini in lemon cream sauce for her. Jana sat back and admired the gorgeous club with its ivory walls, fancy gold molding, and enormous crystal chandeliers.

Once the waiter had served the wine, Jana took a sip then said, "This place is beautiful."

"It was Allison's favorite." Bove wiped a tear from his eye. "She's a great dancer."

The orchestra played David Bowie's "Last Dance."

Jana rose and took Bove's hand.

"What are you doing?"

"As the song says, let's dance."

"You don't have to—"

"I want to."

Jana led Bove to the dance floor, where they showed off their disco moves, including Bove twirling her around like a top.

She said, "You're a good dancer, detective."

"Don't look so surprised." As he lowered her for a back bend, Bove said, "You're pretty good yourself."

"When I was a kid, I took dance lessons at the studio."

"The Pink Ballerina never danced like this."

They continued their gyrations until the music changed to Sergio Mendez's "Never Gonna Let You

Go."

Bove held Jana in his arms and they danced to the slow, romantic ballad.

"You're beautiful," Bove said, looking deeply into her eyes.

I was thinking the same thing about you.

He explained, "Sometimes you see an actress on the screen, and she's mesmerizing. Then when you meet her in real life, you realize it's all makeup and special lighting. Not you."

"Have you met many actresses?" Jana asked.

"A couple…on other cases."

They continued dancing.

"Is Allison an actress?" Jana asked.

"Yeah, in real life." He grimaced. "She was…is a travel agent. I'm sure she and my brother are having one hell of a honeymoon."

"Allison's loss is my gain."

Bove bent down and wrapped his muscular arms around her. His kiss was forceful, but soft, warm, and gentle.

Jana pulled away.

"I'm sorry. That was out of line." Bove released her and walked back to their table.

She followed him.

"Let's go," Bove said.

"Bove."

"I know what you're thinking."

"Bove."

"You don't have to say anything or stay here with me."

"Bove! Sit down!"

They resumed their seats.

Now it's my turn to be blunt. "Take a sip of your wine."

He obeyed.

She continued. "I enjoyed the kiss as much as you did."

Leaning forward in his seat, Bove's eyes lit up like shooting stars.

"*But* I'm happily married." *Happily when Brian and I aren't arguing.* "So, as tempted as I am, nothing can happen between us."

"Something definitely happened between us," he said with a smirk.

"You're right. I felt it, too. But it can't happen again. Do you understand?"

His head hung to his plate. "I don't blame you for not being interested in me, Jana."

"Boy, Allison really did a number on you."

"You think?" He blinked back tears.

"Bove, what Allison did to you was horrible, but don't let her keep doing it. You have too much going for you to wallow in pain and resentment."

His handsome face hardened. "I'll never forgive them."

She squeezed his strong hand. "Then forgive yourself."

"Did you play a girl psychiatrist in an old movie, too?"

"No, smart aleck. I learned that from living." She smiled. "Now, can we enjoy our dinner—as friends and cohorts?"

"Sure." He returned her smile. "Jana Lane really is every guy's best friend."

Once their dinners were served, Jana salivated at

the tantalizing scents making their way from her plate to her nose. As the flavors melted on her tongue, she said, "I have some information for you."

"As long as it's not about Allison, I'm all ears."

Jana swallowed her food and filled in Bove on Tamaya Stormcloud's article about Adam's wife.

"Ouch."

"Exactly."

"And like each of our other suspects, Adam was at the Capitol and has no alibi for the time of Tamaya's murder." *Sorry Adam.* Jana washed down her food with a sip of wine. "And Cassie Castle has marks on her body."

"You mean birthmarks?"

"No, purple spots."

"Maybe she has weak blood vessels."

Jana shook her head no. "They're attack marks. I know what they look like from *The Sweet Candy Striper*. The makeup artist had to recreate them for the scene where the hospital administrator attacked me."

He grinned. "Jana Lane really does know everything."

She leaned in and whispered, "Cassie Castle stiffens like a board whenever Max is around, especially when he talks to Lenore."

"Which of your movies taught you that?"

She hit his shoulder and he barely flinched. "Bove, if Cassie isn't happy with Max, why is she dating him?"

Bove swallowed a piece of veal. "And why is she risking her political career?"

Jana speared a pearl onion. "I did some research on Benjamin Topower's Multitopower Conglomerate."

"What did you find?"

"They're very rich and very powerful."

"Everyone knows that…especially Maxmillion."

"But everyone may not know that each member of the Congomerate's board of directors is also a member of a group called the H.A. Organization."

"I've never heard of it."

"Neither have I. But what if Tamaya Stormcloud did, and she was about to enlighten her readers before she was killed?"

Bove wiped his mouth with his napkin. "We've got a lot of questions."

"And no answers—yet." She started on her potatoes. "All of our suspects are coming to my benefit show at the Ford Theatre Saturday night. Maybe we'll get lucky and one of them will slip up."

He took another sip of wine. "You were terrific on the radio by the way."

"You were listening?"

"Of course."

Jana cringed. "Don't tell me you're a fan of Marky in the Morning?"

"No, I'm a fan of Jana Lane." He winked.

"Are you coming to the fundraiser?"

"I wouldn't miss it. Need a dance partner?"

"I'll let the professionals take care of the dancing."

"I don't know. We were pretty good together." He smiled. "We make a great team."

Jana returned Bove's smile. "As they say, timing is everything."

Chapter 8

The next morning, Jackson, wearing a plum-colored suit, drove Jana to her second radio interview on his way to the Capitol. After complimenting her harlequin-green pants suit and gold snake necklace, Jackson tied his gold tie as he drove.

"You got in as late as we did last night, honey," Jackson said.

Jana looked out the window so Jackson couldn't see the guilty look on her face. "I had a meeting with Detective Bove about Tamaya Stormcloud's murder."

"At his office?"

Jana said casually, "Since I was alone last night, Bove and I went out to dinner."

"Where?"

Jana mumbled, "A dance club."

"Did you two *dance*?"

"Isn't that what people do in a dance club?"

"Did he come on to you?"

"Of course not."

"Look at me, Jana Lane Otley!"

Jana's eyes met his. "All right, he flirted a little."

"I knew it!" Jackson said like a matchmaker at a wedding.

Jana said, "Bove's wounds haven't healed yet from a break-up."

"Does he know you're married?"

"Of course he does. It was just a little kiss."

"A *kiss*! He *kissed* you?" Jackson nearly swerved off the road.

"I didn't kiss him back. Not really. Maybe a little bit."

Jackson regained control of the wheel. "Does *Brian* know?"

"He knows Bove and I went out to dinner."

"But not about the dancing and the kiss?"

"I'll tell Brian…soon." She glared at Jackson. "So please don't say anything to him."

"My lips are sealed, hon buns." He giggled. "Unlike yours with that gorgeous hunk of football player."

She hit Jackson's knee. "He's not a football player anymore. And I'm helping him with his investigation."

"I'm sure he's been doing a great deal of *investigating* with you."

"Can we change the subject?"

"Sure," Jackson said with feigned innocence. "What would you like to talk about? Plays in football?"

Jana answered like a school principal at a lockdown. "Very funny, Jack." *Speaking of my husband.* "Brian and Adam seem to be getting along better."

"Yesterday they played a game of *football* in the back of the house."

Jana gazed at the cloudy sky. "How did the debate go yesterday in the House on the Protect the Children Act?"

Jackson's grin turned to a groan. "I, and a number of other Democrats, spoke against it, but the Republicans have enough votes to pass it."

"That's insane!"

"That's Congress."

"It's not over yet." Jana clutched the sides of her seat. "I can't wait for the benefit."

A half hour later, Jana sat in another radio studio. This time Allan Green, lobbyist for the Multitopower Conglomerate, sat next to her, wearing a drab dark suit. Jana noticed the overhead lighting reflecting on his bald head.

The middle-aged female host sitting across from them, wore a tight pink dress, plastic multicolored jewelry, high-teased bleached-blonde hair, and layers of makeup in an obvious effort to take off twenty years. Unfortunately, it had the reverse effect and added twenty.

The talk show host whispered into the microphone, "This is Carolyn Morninglow spreading glow into your morning. My guests this morning are ex-child star and current *controversial* celebrity Jana Lane, and Mr. Allan Green representing the prestigious Multitopower Conglomerate."

Who no doubt own this studio, too.

"Thank you both for coming." Carolyn smiled at Jana. "You are sponsoring a fundraiser Saturday night at the Ford Theatre, Jana, to raise money for AIDS research and to, in your words, raise money to defeat the Protect the Children Act that passed the Senate and is up for a vote in the House on Monday. I have to tell you, Jana, as a Christian, I feel your actions are discriminating against me."

Jana's head reeled from the woman's backwards logic. "I am a Christian as well, Carolyn, but the stories I read about in the New Testament are of a loving savior who heals the sick, ministers to the disenfranchised, eats with everyone, and welcomes all families."

"The Bible condemns homosexuality," the woman replied with a sneer.

Jana replied, "As it condemns women wearing jewelry and makeup, not lying out in the field during menstruation, marrying when not a virgin, and speaking in church." Jana adjusted her headset. "There are also different translations of the original Greek and Hebrew, which have been rewritten over the centuries. So no one can be certain of the exact intent of the men who wrote the beloved books that make up the Bible."

Carolyn sipped her soft drink, which smelled of rum. "I know what my minister teaches me, Jana."

"But your minister's beliefs are not civil law." *At least not yet.*

Glancing at the clock on the wall, Carolyn said, "Let's move on to Mr. Green. Do you feel that the Multipower Conglomerate is under attack by the powerful Hollywood lobby led by Jana Lane?"

Allan Green squirmed in his chair, and replied in a nasal voice, "Our conglomerate is made up of highly successful, family-friendly companies who donate a great deal of money to charity."

Carolyn cooed, "And your CEO, Benjamin Topower, is a family man who supports the Protect the Children Act."

"That's correct."

Carolyn turned to Jana. "Jana, would passage of this bill take audiences away from all the Hollywood movies and television programs about single parents?"

Jana replied, "The Protect the Children Act, if

passed in the House and signed by the president, will not target heterosexual parents, single-parents, or heterosexual couples who adopt. It discriminates against only one group of people—gays and lesbians and their children. That's why I am hosting the benefit." Jana quickly gave the phone number for tickets.

Allan Green said, "The Multitopower Conglomerate does not target or discriminate against anyone." He added with a smug look on his chubby face, "Our founder is being discriminated against for in this day and age daring to believe in traditional family values."

Carolyn said, "Thank you Allan Green from the family-friendly Multitopower Conglomerate, and Jana Lane from the world of make believe. Viewers, we will return after this break from our sponsor."

No doubt the Multitopower Conglomerate.

Carolyn shook their hands and thanked them for being on the show. Mr. Green scurried out of the studio like a mouse with a piece of cheese. As Jana was leaving, Carolyn said, "Just so you know. This is personal for me. My daughter is a lesbian. She and her partner want to adopt a child. I want my daughter to be happy." She smiled. "And I'd love to be a grandmother. But I need to hold on to my beliefs."

And your job. "Why not believe in your daughter?"

Carolyn held Jana's arm. "I believe in family values."

"Then value your family, Carolyn."

"That's easy for you to say."

"And it will be easy for you to do. Just give it a try. Choose love, Carolyn."

"I don't know if I can."

"Have faith, Carolyn."

Back in the lobby of the radio station, Jana phoned the box office at the Ford Theatre, and received the good news that the benefit was sold out.

She took a taxi to the Capitol, and arrived at Cassie's office to find it empty.

Lenore said from her desk in the outer office, "Cassie's at a press interview about a women's healthcare bill she is sponsoring." Lenore sighed. "Which has no chance of passing with the Republicans controlling the Senate."

Jana sat on the loveseat across from Lenore's desk. "Does Max support it?"

"I'm afraid not."

"Lenore, I've tried, but I just can't understand why Cassie and Max are together."

Lenore joined Jana on the loveseat. "Max is a very attractive, wealthy, and charismatic man."

"But Cassie doesn't care about those things. She's a champion for the common worker, the environment, education, healthcare, equal rights."

Lenore nodded. "Just like my father."

"Then why are Cassie and Max a couple? It just doesn't make sense."

Lenore shrugged. Adjusting the shoulder pads of her ivory suit, she said, "As they say, love is blind." She walked back to her desk. "And sometimes love hurts."

Jana was at her side in a flash. "Are you as concerned as I am about the marks on Cassie's body?"

"Cassie insists they are a result of her clumsiness," Lenore said obviously not buying it.

"Have you noticed Cassie bumping into things at home or at work?"

"Not that I ever saw, but I can't imagine Max would hurt Cassie...or any woman." Lenore looked away. "I wonder if..."

The phone rang. "Lenore Castle." She nodded. "Yes, Danny, she's here." Lenore looked at Jana. "I'll tell her." After she hung up the phone, Lenore said, "Max would like to see you in his office." Lenore looked at her watch. "He must have gotten back early from his Armed Services Committee meeting, and he wants to see you before his meeting with Benjamin Topower."

Jana headed for the door. "Please tell Cassie I will see her tomorrow at the benefit."

"Will do."

"Are you coming tomorrow night?"

Lenore looked like a debutante before the cotillion. "Max is picking us up."

"See you there."

Lenore added to Jana's back, "Tell Max I said hello."

When Jana entered Max's outer office, she noticed his secretary was out, so she made her way to the assistant's desk. "Hello, I'm—"

The middle-aged, thin, balding man with a mustache leapt from his seat as if a mouse had jumped onto his lap. "Jana Lane! I love your old movies! I ditched Little League practice every Saturday afternoon as a kid to go to the movie matinee. When my parents found out, they beat me with my baseball bat."

"I'm sorry."

He grabbed her arm and sat her next to him on the

nearby sofa. "It was worth it. I used to pretend I was your little friend, Timmy. That you and I were best friends. I imagined we went through all those adventures together." He clutched at his yellow sweater vest, nearly knocking off his clip-on bowtie. "As a teenager, I faked having mono so I could stay home and watch a movie marathon of your early movies on TV. I watched *Daddy's Girl* at three in the morning and cried so loud I woke my parents."

"Thank you." *I think.*

"I'm Danny, Max's assistant. I heard you were shadowing Cassie for your new movie. I met your kids when they were here with your husband. They were so well behaved…quiet as mice."

"Thank you." *My children?*

"Max is still at his committee meeting, and the secretary is out to lunch. Can I talk to you…privately?"

"Of course."

Danny shut the door then resumed his seat next to Jana on the sofa. He whispered like a spy sharing an international secret, "I hope this doesn't shock you." He inhaled deeply then blurted out, "I am not heterosexual."

And the shocking news is?

"Do you promise not to tell anyone?"

"If you promise not to tell anyone I'm not homosexual."

He laughed then breathed a sigh of relief. "Thank you. I knew you would understand."

"Danny, why are you telling *me*?"

He looked both ways then said softly, "I heard about your upcoming fundraiser at the Ford Theatre."

"Are you coming?"

"I can't. I'd lose my job."

"But Max is coming."

"Only to scope out the enemy camp."

Jana tented her fingers. "Why do you work for Senator Maxmillion?"

"For the same reason your husband works for him. I need the job."

"Danny, what is it you'd like me to do?"

"Jana, my friend…" Obviously throwing caution to the wind, Danny said, "My *partner* and I have lived together for twenty years. Seven years ago I adopted a baby girl, Sonja. She's absolutely adorable, and Tony and I love her so much." He rubbed his hands against his brown corduroy slacks. "Max's Protect the Children Act is wrong. You have to stop it."

"That's what the benefit show at the Ford Theatre is all about—raising money to educate the public, and to hire a lawyer to fight it in court if necessary."

He wrung his hands. "We don't have time. Something needs to be done *now*."

Jana smiled. "Max didn't ask you to call me over here, did he?"

"No, he didn't." Danny spoke like someone talking to a hard of hearing foreign-born visitor. "Jana, I am *leaving* the office now. And I won't be back for a while. So *nobody* will be here." He mimed the words as he spoke them. "So you can feel free to wait in Max's office for him. But please *don't touch* any of his things, especially his *files*." He pointed inside Max's office. "Particularly the file in his *top right* drawer, which is usually locked, but happens to be *open*. And whatever you do, don't open the file marked, *Multitopower Conglomerate*."

If you lose your job, don't take up acting.

"Do you understand?"

Should I repeat the secret code? "I understand."

"Good." Danny hurried to the door. "Good luck, Jana Lane." Then he left, closing the door behind him.

Jana walked into Max's office, sat behind his desk, pulled open the top right drawer, took out the folder marked, "Confidential: Multitopower Conglomerate," and placed it on top of the desk. Quickly opening it and reading various financial and business data, Jana found a letter from Ben promising to fund Max's campaign for president in exchange for Max's support of various tax breaks, easing of environmental regulations, and the Protect the Children Act. When she got to the bottom of the folder, Jana picked up a sheet of paper with the words, "Historical Apprentice Organization Charter" on top of it.

The H.A. Organization!

Jana read, "The Historical Apprentice Organization celebrates our rich cultural heritage, whereby wealthy, landowning men with a trade took in a young male apprentice and shared the man's knowledge and expertise with the youth." The document went on to give information about meetings, dues, and other rules and regulations for the organization, including that members must be of a certain age, income bracket, own property in the US, be politically conservative, and legally married. It also explained how members of the organization would use their wealth to build and visit orphanages, where they would share their business expertise with young, male, orphan apprentices in the spirit of our historical ancestors. Finally, it included a strict confidentiality clause for all members.

"Max, where is your office staff?" Benjamin Topower asked.

Max replied from the outer office, "I'm sure Danny will be back soon."

Jana closed the folder and quickly put it back into the drawer. Then she reenacted a scene in *Daddy's Girl*, where young Jana Lane eavesdropped on her father's talk with his doctor. She leapt into the closet, hid behind boxes of office supplies, and closed the door behind her—leaving it open a crack.

Max opened his office door and plopped down behind his desk. Running his hands through his salt and pepper hair, he said, "I thought my committee meeting would never end."

Sitting opposite him, Ben's steel-blue eyes ignited. "Congratulations on the win in the Senate."

"You're welcome."

"My men in the House tell me the bill will pass there on Monday." Ben adjusted the steel-blue handkerchief popping out of the breast pocket of his steel-blue pin-striped designer suit.

"That's the word in the men's room," Max said.

Ben sat back in his chair. "Is it true that you are going to that actress' fundraiser against the bill?"

"I think it will look good for me to be there."

"Why is that?"

"How can I dismiss something as liberal propaganda if I'm not there to witness it?"

"I don't like it, Max."

"I made a reservation for you and your wife as well."

"That was presumptuous."

Max shrugged his broad shoulders. "I'm a

politician."

That's the first thing you've said that I agree with.

Max said, "Why give Jana Lane all the press? Let's go tomorrow night and make our case to the public."

"You think it will work?"

"I do."

Ben thought a moment. "All right. I'll tell my wife."

"Good."

Ben leaned forward in his chair. "The bill should pass the House on Monday, and the president will sign it at the end of the day. On Monday evening, I want you to have the police pick up those two boys I met in your office and bring them to Topower House."

"Ben, I told you, I can't put Topher and Tyler in your orphanage."

"Of course you can. That's what the Protect the Children Act mandates." Ben tented his fingers. "We'll build more orphanages of course, but I want those two boys in Topower House before it reaches capacity. And I want to be notified when they arrive."

You monster!

Max rubbed his forehead. "Why can't we wait until the dust clears from the vote?"

"I'm holding up my end of the bargain. Now you hold up yours."

Max wiped the perspiration off his forehead with the sleeve of his gray designer suit. "Can't you start with *other* children?"

"No. I want Tyler and Topher."

Over my dead body.

"Ben, be reasonable."

"How's this for reasonable, Max? If you want the

backing of the major business and religious leaders for your presidential campaign, bring those boys to Topower House Monday evening." Ben rose from his seat. "We'll be doing them a favor by removing them from their *so-called* fathers."

"Once the press finds out about the H.A. Organization, you'll go to jail."

"Max, I own most of the press. You know that."

"You didn't own Tamaya Stormcloud."

"And now she's gone."

"I don't approve of this."

"Max, the H.A. Organization is continuing the Greco-Roman tradition of wealthy, powerful men assisting boys through maturity. We teach boys how to become men."

Max rose and banged his hand on the desk. "I can't stop your group's perversion of manhood, but I *can* stop you from taking Topher and Tyler."

"Why are Topher and Tyler so important to you?"

Max looked out the window at the cobalt-blue sky filled with gray clouds. "I have my reasons."

"I hope they are good enough to forfeit the nomination for president."

The two men stared at one another like gunslingers with loaded pistols.

"All right." Max finally said, "Topher and Tyler are my grandchildren."

What?

Ben practically fell into his seat. "Care to explain that one?"

Max sat and rested his head in his hands. "That's why I gave Brian Otley and Adam Stokes the contract for the new wing of offices. They're my twin sons."

Brian and Adam!

"Isn't that nepotism?"

"They don't know anything about it."

Ben did a double-take. "You haven't told them?"

Max shook his head no and leaned back into his chair. "I just found out recently."

"How?"

"I looked up the adoption records."

"Why now?"

"I'm running for president, Ben. I wanted to make sure my past couldn't catch up to me."

"Can it?"

"Not anymore. I paid a great deal of money to have the records destroyed." Max sighed.

"Does Cassie Castle know about this?"

"Nobody knows, except you. I was practically a kid when it happened. Seventeen…eighteen years old. It was a girl I knew in high school. Her father was religious and wouldn't let us consider abortion. He sent her to New York to stay with relatives." Max's voice shook. "She died in childbirth and her father put the babies up for adoption."

Brian was adopted!

Max continued, "I brought Brian and Adam here to meet them…to get to know them…and to see their children." He unleashed a melancholy smile. "Wouldn't you know, I liked them."

He's Devon and Ed's grandfather!

Ben sneered. "I don't want the whole soap opera. I only need to know the story won't leak to the liberal press—the little that's left of them. I'm not throwing my money away on a loser."

"I swear to you, Ben. Nobody will know about

this."

Guess again.

Max had to leave for the Senate Chamber, and Ben followed him out. Since Danny and Max's secretary had not yet returned from lunch, Jana made photocopies of Ben's letter of sponsorship for Max's campaign, and copies of the charter of the H.A. Organization. Then she returned the originals to the folder.

Cassie was tied up in the Senate Chamber for most of the afternoon. So Jana watched from the upstairs observation gallery then met Jackson in the south wing for a ride home. It was torturous sharing small talk with Jackson, and not telling him what she had uncovered in Max's office.

Back at home everyone ate dinner and the children were washed, dressed for bed, and read their nighttime intergalactic story. Once the four boys fell asleep, Jana asked Brian, Jackson, and Adam to sit on the sectional in the living room. Standing in front of them like a school teacher meeting her new class, Jana watched Brian and Adam sit next to one another wearing nearly identical jeans and sweatshirts.

How could I not have seen the close resemblance? Jack obviously did, since he's had a crush on Brian for years. Brian and Adam must have sensed something between the two of them. That's why they ruffled each other's feathers at first then became inseparable. And that's how come they act like children around one another—subconsciously recreating a past they were denied.

"What's up, babe?" Brian asked.

"Have you decided to divorce this guy?" Adam asked Jana with a giggle.

Brian pushed Adam's shoulder. "You and Jack show us how, smart guy."

"No way. Then Jackson will come after *you*, Brian." Adam tickled Brian's side, and Brian laughed.

With a concerned look on his face, Jackson asked Jana, "What's going on, hon?"

Jana took in a deep breath. "Adam, you mentioned you were adopted."

Adam nodded.

"And you don't know the identity of your birth parents," Jana added.

"That's right," Adam answered.

Jana continued, "Brian, you always said there was a disconnect between you and your parents."

Adam snickered. "I can't blame them. Imagine having *this* guy as a son."

"Do you want to live to hear what she has to say?" Brian turned toward Jana. "You know about my problems with my parents. But they died long ago. What's this about, babe?"

Jana swallowed hard. "I found out something today." Her hands fluttered like butterflies. "Actually, I overheard something…at the Capitol…about you."

"About *me*?" Brian asked.

Adam said, "Is there something wrong with Brian's plans for the new wing? I thought I corrected all of his errors."

Brian pushed Adam and Adam pushed him back.

Jackson's voice warbled. "Just tell us, honey. What *is* it?"

Jana sat at Brian's other side and took his hand. "Honey, I overheard Max tell Ben Topower that your parents…"

"That my parents *what*?"

"…adopted you."

"What!" Brian looked as if he'd seen a ghost.

Jana nodded. "Max said the records were sealed, and now they're destroyed."

"How does Max know this?" Jackson asked.

Jana bit her lip. "Well…"

"Just say it, honey," Jackson replied.

Jana blurted out, "Brian, Max is your father."

Brian looked out at the black sky and still lake.

"He was only in high school at the time." Jana explained, "Your mother died in childbirth while visiting with relatives in New York, and her father put you up for adoption." She looked over at Adam. "And that's not all."

Jackson rose like a rocket. "Adam and Brian are twin brothers."

Jana nodded.

"When I first met Adam, I thought of Brian. They're so much alike," Jackson said almost to himself.

Brian and Adam stared straight ahead not looking at one another. Jackson put his arm around Adam, and Jana wrapped her arms around Brian.

"I know this is quite a surprise, Brian." Jana squeezed him close to her. "And it will no doubt take some time for you to fully process."

Jackson kissed Adam's cheek and hugged him. "But now you know the truth, and it's always better to get the facts." He smiled. "And isn't it great to have a twin brother?" He looked at Jana. "A brother who is my best friend's husband?"

Brian shook off Jana and rose slowly. "I don't believe any of this. Max probably knew you were listening." He sounded like a child making up an excuse for missing dinner. "Max must have said those things to pay you back for eavesdropping."

"Max didn't know I was there. Why would he fabricate something like that?"

"Because he's a liar and a dirty politician," Brian said. "He must have something up his sleeve."

"Max hired you to do the expansion so he could get to know you and Adam…and meet the boys. They're his grandchildren."

Brian paced the room. "Max must be planning another crazy bill like the Protect the Children Act. It's probably about sending the children of unwed mothers to orphanages." His eyes were wild and probing. "This is all a story…part of a scheme to win political points for Max's run for president." Brian slammed his fist into his hand. "I won't let him get away with it!"

"When's your birthday, Brian?" Adam released himself from Jackson.

"The same days as yours," Jackson replied to Adam. "I thought it was just a coincidence."

Adam walked slowly toward Brian. "Haven't you felt it? Didn't you sense it all along?" Adam was face to face with Brian. "Didn't it freak you out how we each knew what the other was thinking and feeling? How similar we are?"

Listen to him, Brian.

Brian walked backwards away from the others. "This isn't real. You're all falling for a political maneuver by a self-promotional mastermind." His voice broke. "I don't want any part of it!"

Brian ran up the stairs into the guest room and slammed the door. Jana rose to follow him. Adam put a hand on her shoulder and she took her seat. Adam walked up the stairs, opened the guest bedroom door, and closed it behind him.

Jana collapsed into Jackson's arms. She slept on his shoulder on the chaise lounge in the master bedroom while Brian and Adam talked in the guest room all night.

****

Jana and Jackson got the children their breakfast the next morning, then Sancho arrived with Grace in hand. Jana was relieved to find some of the color had returned to Grace's cheeks. While the young woman still had a long way to go, she was not quite as thin as when she left for the hospital. Sancho, looking as casual as Jana in jeans and a T-shirt, stood in the downstairs hallway and kissed Grace's forehead. "Promise me you'll stick to the food regimen and positive thinking exercises the doctor gave you?"

Grace took Sancho's hand. "I promise."

"And promise to call me when you need a ride to see the doctor?"

She smiled. "I will."

Sancho looked at her adoringly. "Now that I finally have you back in my life, I don't want to lose you."

"You won't." Grace kissed his hand.

"I'll pick you up at seven tonight," Sancho said.

"I'll be ready," Grace replied.

Joining them, Jana cleared her throat. "As much as I'd love you to be at the fundraiser tonight, Grace, don't you think it might be too…soon?"

Grace replied, "My doctor said it's all right. Didn't he, Sancho?"

Sancho nodded. "I'll take care of her, Jana." He

winked at Grace. "Now and forever."

They shared a kiss.

Sancho left, and Jana walked Grace upstairs and into her bedroom.

"Where's B.J.?" Grace asked, looking around the empty room.

"Jackson took him out for a walk," Jana replied.

"Where are the four boys?"

"Brian and Adam took them out back to…talk with them." *You'll find out about this in due time.*

"I hope the boys aren't in any trouble."

"Grace, I appreciate how much you care about the boys…and about all of us, but the most important thing right now is for *you* to get better."

Still wearing the new dress from her attempted date with Sancho, Grace sat on the bed. "I know, Jana. Dr. Neville helped me see my problem. I'm nowhere near over the hurdle, but I think I'm on the right path."

"I'm glad."

Grace looked down at her shoes. "And I'll understand if you don't want me to work for you any longer."

Jana sat next to her and took her hand. "Grace, you can work for us as long as you like. The boys adore you, and you're a very good nanny. We are all rooting for you to lick this thing and move on with your life."

She hugged Jana. "I don't have any family left—except my cousin Jolanda. We were like sisters when we were kids."

"She was the one you stayed with after your husband died?"

"Uh-huh. But knowing you and Brian are behind me means so much to me."

Jana returned her hug. "Grace, the other night Sancho mentioned that you and he grew up in the same neighborhood upstate New York."

Grace smiled. "Sancho was ten years older than me, but we hit it off."

Jana returned the smile. "And it seems you still do."

Grace blushed.

Resting her hands behind her on the bed, Jana said, "Sancho also told me you had some trouble back then. With someone in the neighborhood."

Grace rose from the bed. "I better get washed and change my clothes."

Jana held her arm. "You don't have to talk about this with me, but you should discuss it with someone."

Grace didn't look at her. "I am. My psychiatrist."

"Good."

They all spent the rest of the day in bathing suits at the lake for a picnic. Jana was thrilled to see both Grace and B.J. had finished their lunches.

After lunch, a swim, and a boat ride, the four boys sprawled out on the dock as if waiting for Tom Sawyer and Huck Finn, while their parents sat on a long beach towel in the nearby grassy knoll.

Topher threw a rock into the lake. "Now that we're cousins, you two guys can come visit us whenever you like."

Tyler added, "And sleep in our room."

Holding his head up with the palm of his hand, Devon said, "Can our grandfather Max come visit, too?"

Topher replied, "Sure. He lives in DC."

Ed said, "And he can take us to see things in his

big car."

"And out to eat," Tyler added.

While Grace followed B.J. through the woods, Jana closed the picnic basket, and looked out at a tall oak tree waving its emerald green branches in the soft summer wind under the crystal blue sky. She said to the other adults on the blanket, "I'm so happy for the boys. I never had cousins growing up."

Jackson rested his back against Adam's and sipped his lemonade. "Hon buns, you might not have had cousins, but you had a whole studio of people who adored you."

"But most of them weren't family," Jana said.

Lying on his back, Brian said, "I'm happy for the boys, too."

Adam said, "I'm happy for everyone—except me."

Brian threw a carrot cube at Adam and they both shared a laugh.

Jana said, "I'm glad you two talked things out last night."

"After I calmed down and thought it through, it made sense." A new line appeared on Brian's forehead. "I never fit into my family."

Adam smirked. "And you think you fit into *this* one?"

Brian kicked Adam playfully.

"Will you visit us more often?" Jackson asked.

"Well, Brian?" Jana unleashed a smile.

"Sure, so the kids can see each other."

Adam reached over and kissed Brian on the cheek. "And so you can see your *brother*."

They all laughed like children.

Breaking the festive mood, Jackson said, "Max will

be at the benefit tonight."

"Good," Brian and Adam replied in unison.

"Are you two going to do that from now on?" Jackson asked.

"Do what?" Brian and Adam replied in unison.

Jackson said, "Say the same thing? Dress alike? Act the same way?"

"No!" Brian and Adam each threw a celery stalk at Jackson.

"What we *are* going to do is tell Max what we think of him," Brian said.

"I'm right behind you, brother," Adam said.

"People make mistakes," Jana said.

"Not like this they don't," Brian replied.

"He tried to make amends by finding you," Jana said.

"Too little too late," Adam said.

Brian sat up. "*And* Max sponsored a bill to take his own grandchildren away from his own son. I can never forgive that."

Adam added, "And the only reason Max came looking for us now is because he's running for president, and he wants to hide his dirty laundry—us."

"But he *did* find you, and he brought you to *meet* him," Jana said.

Adam clenched his fists. "For forty-one years he wasn't interested in us. That's a lot of time to try to make up for."

"He can rot in hell for all I care," Brian said.

"And take his contract with him," Adam added.

"So you aren't going to build the extension?" Jackson asked Adam.

Adam replied, "The only thing I'd build for that

creep is a coffin."

Jana put an arm around each brother. "I know how much this hurts. As you know my father disappointed me deeply. But you can't wallow in rage. You have to accept what *is* and move on."

"I'm ready to move on," Brian answered. "On and away from that pathetic excuse for a human being named Josiah Maxmillion."

Adam and Brian slapped hands.

"Don't do anything rash tonight," Jana said. "Remember, this is a benefit performance for AIDS and for funding to fight the Protect the Children Act."

"Which wouldn't be necessary if that cretin didn't propose it to the Senate," Brian said. "How can you *defend* him?"

"I'm not *defending* Max," Jana said while wiping sandwich crumbs off the blanket. "What Max did was unconscionable, but it was Ben who put him up to it. And Ben and his wife will be there as well."

Brian grimaced. "As we've often told the kids, nobody can make you *do* anything. We all have free will and make our own decisions."

"Then make the decision to forgive Max," Jana said.

"Not gonna happen," Brian and Adam said in unison. Then they stood and walked into the house.

"Men!" Jackson said.

Jana smiled. "Actually, I have a surprise for Max tonight."

Jackson licked his full lips. "Do tell, girl."

"All in due time."

Back in the house Jackson called to arrange a sitter for the children, then they ate a quick dinner, and dressed for the benefit. Jana, Brian, Jackson, and Adam kissed the children goodnight, left copious instructions with the elderly woman babysitter, and told Grace they would see her and Sancho at the theatre.

****

Jana took in the sight of the historic Ford Theatre with the triangle on its roof. Adam and Brian argued over which space was better, then Adam finally parked in yet another space, and the four of them exited the car. The men looked dashing in their dark suits, and Jackson told Jana she was ravishing in her rose chiffon gown with a lace bodice and matching purse and shoes. She had teased her hair into cascading wings that ended at her bare shoulders. Glancing at her reflection in the car window as she got out, Jana thought the rose eye shadow, rouge, lip-gloss, and pendant necklace added the right touch.

Jana checked in with the theatre manager in the lobby who, after asking for her autograph, reported proudly that everything was under control. She couldn't help but stare at the bar, where Lincoln's bodyguard went for a drink on that fatal night in 1865.

Entering the theatre, Jana marveled at the decorative columns, molding, and carved faces throughout the house. She scanned the empty stage, orchestra seating section, balconies, and the box seats, where actor John Wilkes Booth shot the beloved president.

"Baby doll!" Simon Huckby appeared at Jana's side like a blue jay in spring, wearing a powder-blue jumpsuit, celeste-blue ascot, and teal waist pouch. He adjusted the diaper underneath his pants, a familiar gesture. "The performers are ready backstage."

Jana replied, "I'm so grateful. Entertainers always step up during a crisis." *They almost make up for John Wilkes Booth.*

Cornelius, dressed in an indigo suit with matching suspenders and bowtie, stood next to Simon. "The orchestra members have arrived and will be set up on stage shortly."

Jana kissed their cheeks. "You two are angels."

"Not according to Josiah Maxmillion." Simon sneered.

Jana put her arm around her agent's narrow shoulders. "Believe it or not, Senator Maxmillion is attending the benefit."

"Too bad John Wilkes Booth *isn't*," Cornelius said.

"Right on," Brian and Adam said in unison.

Jana remembered her family. "Simon, Cornelius, you know Brian and Congressman Jackson Mitchell. This is Adam Stokes, Jackson's partner and Brian's brother. Adam, my agent Simon Huckby and his partner Cornelius Chamberlain."

Adam said, "Nice to meet you."

"A pleasure," Cornelius said shaking Adam's hand.

"Hello, Adam." Simon squeezed Jana's elbow and whispered in her ear, "Keeping it all in the family, baby doll? I didn't know Brian had a brother."

"It's a long story," Jana replied.

"One I'm looking forward to hearing—in detail," Simon said.

"And you will, but right now I'd like to get backstage and thank our performers." Jana turned to the others. "Will you gentlemen be all right on your own for a while?"

"We'll be fine, honey," Jackson said with a wink.

"Go do what you need to."

Adam said, "I'll keep Brian occupied by listening to him drone on about the archaic architecture of the building."

Brian put his arm around his brother. "And I'll keep Adam out of trouble by hearing his tirade about how the building needs renovation."

"I'll go see if the bar is open yet." Jackson sighed. "I have the feeling this is going to be a long night."

Jana went backstage and thanked the performers for generously donated their time and talents. Next, she did the same for the orchestra members and the lighting and sound technicians setting up on stage. As the local news reporters positioned their cameras and microphones on the sides of the theatre house, Jana made her way through the patrons being seated by ushers, and thanked them for coming. Her heart fluttered at the sight of Detective Bove standing under the famous house right box, looking incredibly handsome in a black tuxedo with his hair slicked back. She made her way over to him. "Thank you for coming, Detective Bove."

"Thank you for inviting me, Ms. Lane."

Your smile should be labeled a lethal weapon.

His eyes sparkled. "You look amazing."

She held herself back from throwing her arms around him. "So do you. Do detectives always wear tuxedos at the theatre?"

"Only when Jana Lane is the star of the show."

They gazed at one another.

Come to, girl. Your husband is around here someplace, and tonight's a big night. Jana dug into her purse and handed Bove sheets of paper. "On top are copies of a letter from Benjamin Topower to Maxmillion. Following are copies of the charter for the Historical Apprentice Organization headed by Topower. I have one of each hidden safely at home. Please keep a copy of each then give one to every reporter here tonight."

"How did you get these?" Bove asked.

Jana grinned. "They fell into my lap. You'll understand after I make my speech."

"I can hardly wait."

Jana squeezed his muscular arm. She continued welcoming guests, including Sancho in a mint-green suit and Grace wearing a floral charmeuse dress. Standing next to the couple at their seats in the orchestra section of the house, Jana said, "Thank you so much for coming."

"Our pleasure," Sancho said, squeezing Grace's hand and looking at her lovingly.

Grace said, "Thank you for letting me come, Jana."

"Are you feeling all right?" Jana asked.

Grace replied, "Yes, but even if I weren't, I wouldn't want to miss this. Tyler and Topher are such terrific boys. The Protect the Children Act must be stopped."

A crease appeared between Sancho's dark eyebrows. "What Max did in the Senate was unforgiveable."

As if on cue, Jana spotted Max, Cassie, and Lenore heading toward their seats in the same section. Max looked dapper in a navy-blue suit. He nodded at Jana.

"Thank you for coming," Jana said, standing in the aisle near them.

Lenore looked like a different person in a gold silk

dress with her hair done and face made up. "Jana, congratulations. If my father were alive, he would be standing right alongside you."

Cassie, as usual, stole the show in a fuchsia satin gown draped with silver earrings and matching necklace. She pulled down the sleeve of her gown to cover the purple mark on her wrist. "You are a good woman, Jana Lane."

"I doubt Max looks at it that way," Jana replied.

Almost to himself, Max said, "Good people often do misguided things."

Cassie clasped Jana's hand. "I've enjoyed having you visit this week. I'm not looking forward to you leaving us on Monday."

Was that a plea for help?

The lights flickered. Cassie switched places with Lenore to sit between her date and her sister.

Jana excused herself, then noticed Benjamin Topower and his wife enter the house and walk toward their seats next to Max's. Dressed in a black suit and black netted gown dripping with gold jewelry, the billionaire couple did not look happy to be there. Following them were Allan Green and his wife in a worm-gray suit and hip-hugging brown gown.

The house lights went out, the stage lights came on, and Cornelius introduced Jana Lane, who entered the stage to welcoming applause. As she looked out at the faces in the dark—and the lights of the local news cameras—Jana took center stage and spoke into the microphone.

"Thank you. It is my great pleasure to be hosting this benefit tonight. And what better place to do it than at the historic Ford Theatre in Washington, DC, near the Capitol of the country that stands for liberty and justice for all." She looked out at the applauding sold-out crowd. "As you know, tonight we are raising money for two purposes. First, funding to research the disease called Acquired Autoimmune Deficiency. Funding that is so terribly needed, since our representatives in Congress and in the White House have not seen fit to join the war against this deadly illness that has affected so many Americans. And second, to raise money to fight a devastating bill that has passed the Senate and is coming to a vote in the House on Monday—the Protect the Children Act."

She noticed Max squirming uncomfortably in his seat, and Sancho gleaming with pride.

Jana continued. "If this bill should become law, the children of gay parents will be taken from their homes and put into orphanages like Benjamin Topower's Topower House."

Anger filled Ben's face. His wife took his hand.

Jana said, "I would like to thank all of the talented and caring people who donated their time to entertain us tonight, and I would like to thank each of *you* from the bottom of my heart for generously contributing to these two worthy causes. But unfortunately donating your dollars isn't enough. I also ask you to donate your time by phoning the members of the House and asking them…no *demanding* them to vote against this hateful, anti-family, un-American bill."

The applause filled the theatre as Max looked down at the floor, and Ben stared straight ahead like a statue.

When the crowd settled down, Jana said, "Thank you all again for coming, and now on with the entertainment!"

Jana took her seat in the front of the orchestra seating section next to Brian, Adam, Jackson, and Simon. She marveled at the vast talents of the musicians, singers, dancers, comedians, magicians, and ventriloquists that Simon had booked for the evening.

Then Cornelius gave her the signal, and Jana came back on stage and once again addressed the audience. "Weren't they amazing?" When the applause died down, Jana said, "Before we enjoy some liquid refreshments in the lobby during intermission, I would like to share something with all of you about the Protect the Children Act. This bill was proposed by Senator Maxmillion, the majority leader of the Senate with backing from Benjamin Topower of the Multitopower Conglomerate and Topower House. I understand the press members here tonight have become aware of a letter from Mr. Topower to Senator Maxmillion specifying the terms of their agreement regarding this bill. I also understand the press representatives have received the charter to the Historical Apprentice Organization, an organization to which Mr. Topower is a founding member. Senator Maxmillion and Mr. Topower, thank you for being gracious enough to attend this evening. I am sure the members of the press in attendance will have a number of questions for you during intermission. So we will lengthen the intermission time from fifteen minutes to thirty-minutes."

The audience members headed out of the theatre. When Jana arrived in the lobby, she noticed Max and Ben standing at the bar holding their scotches.

"You *had* to drag me to this train wreck." Ben

glared at Max. "Are you satisfied now?"

Max replied, "Calm down, Ben. We can spin this." Max clinked glasses with Ben. "Cheers."

Standing with Lenore at Max's side, Cassie said, "None of this would have happened, Max, if you had pulled the Protect the Children Act."

Max groaned. "Don't push me, Cassie. The reporters are coming."

Cassie put her drink down on the bar, and Max and Cassie posed with frozen smiles. Ben's wife displayed herself next to her husband and took his arm.

Allan Green and his wife made their way over to Ben. Allan said, "Keep calm, Ben. You don't want to come off as a privileged, angry man."

"Don't you think I know that, you idiot!" Ben answered behind a frozen smile.

Bove appeared at Jana's side and whispered in her ear. "Nice job. This should be fun."

"I almost feel sorry for all of them," Jana replied.

Like sharks surrounding their prey, the reporters not under the payroll of the Multitopower Conglomerate encircled the bar and aimed their cameras, microphones, and attention at Max and Ben. As questions flew around them like darts, Max held up his hands with authority. "Mr. Topower and I will be happy to answer your questions, but please ladies and gentlemen, let's have them one at a time."

A Caucasian woman with a huge nose and short-cropped gray hair spoke first. "Senator, your letter from Mr. Topower specifies certain…actions you will take in exchange for Mr. Topower's support for your presidential campaign. One of them is to propose the Protect the Children Act. Do you really support the bill, or was your backing in the Senate merely an example of a politician being bought by a wealthy and powerful lobbyist group?"

The seasoned politician took the floor. "The Multitopower Conglomerate is made up of numerous businesses that each provide jobs, pay taxes, and offer a good many services we all enjoy," Max said.

An African American male reporter said, "But you seem to enjoy these *services* also, senator."

Max put down his drink. "It isn't unusual for a member of Congress to seek contributions from our constituents in the business community. We might request funding for a pet project like the construction of a new nursing home, a super railway, or a children's hospital. Other times it might be a request to support our reelection campaign so we can continue representing the people."

A Latino female reporter said, "It doesn't seem like you are representing *the people*, senator, when Mr. Topower's letter specifies your support of tax breaks and environmental deregulation for his *conglomerate*."

Max replied, "Corporations like those in Mr. Topower's conglomerate bring great wealth and many jobs to the private sector. If we can work with them on lowering their taxes to stay in business, we will." He chortled. "And as for environmental deregulations, my party has always tried to cut the red tape that stifles the growth of businesses, so we can leave a strong business structure to the next generation."

"But will there *be* a next generation if we don't stop corporations' destructive air, water, and soil pollution?" an Asian male reporter asked.

Benjamin Topower took a sip of his scotch then

faced the cameras. "I can absolutely assure you that every corporation in the Topower Conglomerate values the environment and strives for a safe and healthy atmosphere for all families—with *reasonable* environmental regulations that support the growth of business."

The reporter countered with, "Do you mean corporations like those in the conglomerate that pour so much coal dust into the air and chemicals into the water and soil that our children's rate of cancer, asthma, and heart disease have risen two hundred percent over the last five years?"

Ben bristled and glared at Green. The lobbyist took a step forward. "I am Allan Green, representing the Multitopower Conglomerate, and I can assure you the CEOs of our corporations are all family men with strong traditional family values."

"Most of whom are members of the Historical Apprentice Organization," the first reporter stated. "Mr. Topower, your charter specifies that boys will become apprentices to the gentlemen who are members. Can you explain how this program works?"

Ben cleared his throat. "A married man with a thriving business takes a boy under his wing and teaches him the tools of his trade."

The reporter followed up. "Will more than just *business* knowledge be handed off from man to boy?"

Ben held on to his wife. "The H.A. Organization harkens back to the Greco-Roman times when it was a wealthy man's responsibility to take in a poor boy to share his wealth and experience."

Allan Green added, "I would think you, the liberal media, would like the idea of rich men sharing their wealth with poor boys."

Interesting how any reporter not under their employ is labeled, the liberal media.

The reporter said, "Mr. Green, as a lobbyist for the conglomerate, what do you require from members of Congress and the Senate in exchange for funding their campaigns?"

Green stood like a statue in the rain. "Our conglomerate has a wonderful working relationship with many of our…of the conservative representatives in Congress. We fund their campaigns, that is true, but we also work with the legislators to create a healthier, stronger, and more solvent America."

"In exchange for laws being bent to make your corporations wealthier? And for proposing laws like the Protect the Children Act?" the reporter asked.

Before Green could reply, the reporter said, "Senator Castle, you were not in support of the Protect the Children Act. Did that cause difficulty in your…relationship with Senator Maxmillion?"

Cassie faced the camera with a winning smile. "Maggie, you've been around Washington, DC long enough to know that we in Congress disagree on *many* issues, but we still play nice at the end of the day."

You are quite the politician, Cassie Castle.

Lenore broke in. "My father was a respected and admired senator, and he often socialized with legislators from both sides of the aisle."

Et tu, Lenore?

The reporter turned to Sancho—standing with Grace. "Senator Ramirez, you also were not in favor of this bill. And like, Senator Castle, you have been mentioned as a probable vice presidential candidate for the Democratic Party."

Sancho looked earnestly into the camera. "This bill is an assault on everything America stands for—family, individual rights, liberty, and justice. It is an atrocity that it was proposed by Senator Maxmillion, the majority leader of the Senate, and an even worse travesty that it passed in the Senate."

The Latina reporter said, "But Senator Ramirez, some people support the bill because they say homosexuals having children discriminates against their religious beliefs."

Sancho's dark eyes lit up the room. "I respect everyone's religion, but civil law should never boost one religious view over another, or sanction discrimination. That's what this country was founded on." His dimples appeared. "And by the way, that's what many *religions* were founded on—lessons where everyone is loved, served, protected, and treated equally. And *all* families are honored." He moved closer to the camera. "Yesterday, African Americans were told they could not raise families apart from their white slave owners. Jewish parents were separated from their children in concentration camps. Today Senator Maxmillion wants children of gay parents to be sent to orphanages. Who will it be tomorrow?"

And Sancho Ramirez just took the vice presidency for the Democratic ticket.

Simon and Cornelius, standing near Sancho, started the applause and others followed. When the clapping died down, Simon glared at Max. "You are a disgrace to your office, Senator Maxmillion. Gay people are your constituents, too."

Cornelius put his arm around Simon. "And we pay

taxes—and we vote! As do our families and friends."

The African American reporter asked, "Congressman Mitchell, you are one of only three openly gay members in the House. How do you think the vote on this bill will go on Monday?"

Coming to Adam's side, Jackson replied, "I hope and pray it is defeated. If not, we have truly regressed back to the Dark Ages."

"Congressman, do you feel this bill is a personal assault on people like you?" the reporter asked.

Max said, "The Protect the Children Act is not an assault on homosexuals. It is a calling to help and protect children in unhappy homes."

"Where they don't have the benefit of both a mother *and* a father," Ben added.

Adam's nostrils flared like a whipped horse. "And how are you *protecting* children by taking them out of loving homes, *senator*?"

Tears filled Grace's eyes. "Senator, you will never get Tyler and Topher!"

Max turned toward Adam. "Every home is not a loving home."

"That's true," Adam replied. "For example, while my home with my partner and my two children is definitely a loving home, the home I would have had with my birth parents would have been nothing of the kind. Thankfully, I was adopted by a couple who loved me and took care of me."

Max took a step backward and leaned on the bar. Brian grabbed Adam's arm, but Adam pulled away from him. "You see, senator, just recently my brother Brian and I found out the news that *you* are our father, and you gave us up for adoption when you were seventeen years old."

The cameras spun to face Adam and Brian. Max held his head in his hands.

Despite Brian's pleading to stop, Adam shouted, "And based on your so-called Protect the Children Act, I'm pretty damn sure you would not have been the father of the year—even though you are heterosexual."

Max said to Adam and Brian, "I was a kid. I did what her father told me to do. I wanted to make it up to you now." Max's hands shook. He took a sip of his scotch.

Adam came face to face with Max. "Make it up to us? How? By destroying the records of our adoption? By taking our children to Topower House to be with pedophiles like your buddy Ben?"

"Now just a minute!" Ben shouted.

Adam seemed unstoppable. "No, senator, I think you should change the name of your Protect the Children Act to the Protect My Children from Their Grandfather Act."

Sweat dripped down Max's face. "I wanted to get to know you both. I hoped to be a part of your children's lives." He took another sip of his drink.

Adam glared at him. "Senator Maxmillion, you and your bigoted, perverted friend here will never get near my children again!"

Ben's face turned scarlet.

Max downed the rest of his drink. Suddenly, he reached out calling, "Brian, Adam—" Max's eyes bulged, his mouth dropped open, he clutched his chest then fell still into Adam's arms, dying in the Ford Theatre like another famous politician before him.

Chapter 9

Detective Bove ordered everyone in the theatre lobby to step away from the body on the floor then asked the theatre manager to call for an ambulance. Next, Bove asked Lenore to look after Cassie, and Jackson to tend to Adam and Brian.

Jana sniffed Max's glass, careful not to touch it, then made her way over to Bove.

"I checked. He's not breathing," Bove said.

"Max has been poisoned," Jana replied.

"How do you know?" Bove asked while moving her to a corner of the lobby.

Jana explained, "His glass smells of almonds. There are no nuts in scotch." She lowered her voice. "The killer used potassium cyanide, a colorless poison easy to obtain."

"When did you become an expert on poisons?"

"That was the poison the killer used in *The Cutest Scientist*."

Bove smiled. "Lucky me, I have Jana Lane on the case." He bagged Max's glass, then phoned for back up officers. When they arrived, Bove asked one officer to tape off the bar area, another to confiscate the videotapes from the television reporters and bring them and Max's glass to headquarters, and the third to move everyone into the theatre.

Once everyone was seated, Bove stood center stage

and addressed the frightened audience. "Can I have everyone's attention?" When everyone quieted down, Bove said, "I regret to inform you that Senator Maxmillion passed away."

Ben asked from his seat in the center of the theatre, "Was it a heart attack?"

"We don't know." Bove motioned for everyone to be silent. "Senator Castle, I am sorry for your loss."

Sitting near Ben, Cassie and Lenore consoled one another.

"I am sorry for your loss as well," Bove said to Brian and Adam sitting up front. Jana placed her arm around Brian, and Jackson held Adam in his arms.

"The body has been taken away by ambulance," Bove explained. "And the bar area in the lobby has been taped off."

"Did someone kill the senator?" a reporter asked.

Bove replied, "We won't be sure for some time. In the meanwhile, I would like to release the performers and musicians, as well as everyone who was not near the bar during intermission. I will come down now and identify the people who may leave."

"What about the rest of us?" a patron asked.

"Do we have to sit here all night?" another patron chimed in.

Bove took off his tie. "Officer Eads will escort you one at a time to a dressing room backstage, where I will speak with you briefly."

"Then can we go home?" yet another patron asked.

"Yes," Bove replied.

"This is outrageous," Ben said with his cheeks puffed up like a feeding fish.

Bove executed a small bow. "We will start with

you, Mr. Topower." Bove motioned for the young police officer to escort Ben backstage. Then he waved for Jana to join him.

Jana reached Bove on stage as a female police officer was leaving him.

Bove explained to Jana, "She found a small vial in one of the garbage cans in the lobby."

"Did it smell like almonds inside?" Jana asked.

He nodded. "I told her to bag it and bring it to police headquarters."

Jana replied, "I doubt you'll find any prints on the vial, or the glass—except Max's."

"I think you're right. That's why I want *The Cutest Scientist* to sit next to me during the interviews."

Bove released various patrons as Jana thanked the performers again for donating their talents—spending some extra time talking to the magician. Then Jana walked back to her family. "Detective Bove asked me to sit in on the interviews backstage."

Jackson's eyebrows rose toward the chandelier. Adam looked lost and withdrawn.

Brian asked Jana, "Why does Bove want *you*?"

Swallowing his grin, Jackson said, "Our Jana Lane has had a great deal of experience with murder. He must admire your...*talents*, honey."

"I don't like the way that guy looks at you," Brian said to his wife.

"He's a detective interviewing suspects for a murder," Jana said. "I'll be safer in there with him than out here with a possible murderer." *Oops!*

"Thanks," Brian said with a grunt.

Adam said under his breath, "We just found our father and now he's gone. What did I do?"

Brian held his brother in his arms. "You didn't say anything to Max that wasn't true."

Jana patted her husband's shoulder. "If you don't want me to go—"

"Go ahead," Brian muttered. "I'll take care of Adam."

"And *I'll* take care of Brian." Jackson added with a smile, "Go play detective with the football hunk, honey."

Looks like I'm not needed here. "I'll see everyone later."

Jana entered the dressing room backstage.

Bove said, "Thanks for agreeing to sit in on the interviews."

"Thanks for asking me," she replied.

Bove moved a small table to the center of the room, and placed two chairs on one side of the table and one chair on the other. Then he motioned for Jana to sit next to him, took off his jacket, and rested it on the back of his chair. Jana couldn't help staring at Bove's V-shaped back barely contained in his white shirt.

Concentrate on the investigation, girl. Two people have been murdered. You don't want Brian to make it three.

Young Officer Eads entered the room, whispered something to Bove, then announced, "Benjamin Topower doesn't seem too happy waiting out there."

Bove nodded. "Bring him in."

Moments later Benjamin Topower stormed into the dressing room like a lion let out of a cage. "My dear friend has just died. How long do you expect me to be trapped in this theatre?"

"Not much longer," Bove said. "Please have a seat." He opened his notepad and readied his pen. "Mr. Topower, were you angry that Senator Maxmillion asked you to attend the benefit tonight?"

Ben begrudgingly sat down. "Coming here to be ridiculed by Miss Lane and the liberal media was not my idea of a fun evening out, detective." He glared at Jana.

"But you came anyway. Why?" Bove asked.

Running a shaking hand through his designer haircut, Ben replied, "Max felt it was important for us to stand up to our critics. How could I have known it was going to be a hanging?"

Bove jotted down a note. "Were you upset with Senator Maxmillion when your letter to him and your organization's charter were leaked to the press tonight?"

Ben pounded his hand on the desk. "You're not going to pin this on me. Max was my friend and associate. I supported his campaign for president. The last thing I wanted was to see him dead."

"Who ordered your drink tonight, Mr. Topower?" Bove asked.

"I did."

"Did you also order a drink for Senator Maxmillion?"

"Yes. Why?"

"Did you serve the senator his drink, or touch his drink at any time this evening."

"Of course not. I'm not a bartender, man."

Jana asked Ben, "When you were last in Max's office, why did you ask Max to bring Topher and Tyler Stokes to you Monday evening?"

Joe Cosentino

"Eavesdropping are we?" Ben asked Jana with a sneer.

Bove said, "Please answer the question, Mr. Topower."

Ben rose from his seat. "Topower House is a well-respected facility for unwanted youth."

"But these children are not unwanted," Jana replied.

Bove added, "And I'm not so sure your orphanage is all that well respected after tonight."

"What do you mean?" Ben asked with a haughty sniff.

Bove stared at Ben. "One of my officers told me that after Jana's speech hit the airwaves this evening, the police station received a call from an ex-employee of yours who offered some *interesting* news about your orphanage."

Ben's lips tightened. "A disgruntled past employee seeking revenge."

"*And* information from a child who escaped," Bove added.

"Children fabricate tales all the time," Ben said.

Jana said, "The truth about your orphanage will come out sooner or later, Ben. Why not come clean about it now?"

Ben waved his hand at Jana. "This is all *your* fault. You and the rest of the Hollywood elite."

Jana met Ben's glare. "Why do you want Topher and Tyler, Ben? What Greco-Roman man-boy ritual do you want to engage in with them?"

"You bitch!" Ben lunged at Jana, but Bove intercepted.

As Bove pushed Ben out of the dressing room, Ben

216

shouted, "I have the finest lawyers in the country. You will both regret mixing with me!"

A few minutes later Bove returned. "Are you all right?"

"Thanks to my friend the ex-football star," Jana replied with a warm smile.

He squeezed her hand. "I sent Ben and his wife home."

"Why?"

Once we get more on that sleaze-ball, I'll bring him in." Bove asked the police officer to bring in Cassie Castle.

"Again, I am sorry for your loss, Senator Castle," Bove said, as Cassie took the seat.

Cassie replied with mascara-stained eyes, "It's a loss for all of us. Max was a member of the opposing party, but he was a smart and dedicated politician."

Yet no mention of being in love with him.

"I'm concerned about my sister. I'd like to get her home," Cassie said.

"I won't keep you long." Bove said, "You were standing next to Senator Maxmillion before he collapsed. Did you see anything out of the ordinary?"

Cassie replied, "Max was talking to the press, which is pretty ordinary for people like us."

Bove asked, "Besides the bartender and Senator Maxmillion, did you see anyone touch the senator's drink?"

A crease appeared across her smooth forehead. "I don't believe so."

Bove said, "Did you and Senator Maxmillion have words about your different viewpoints on the Protect the Children Act?"

Cassie looked over Bove's head as if Max was standing there. "Max and I argued over politics like cats and dogs—or should I say like elephants and donkeys. Our personal life together was a different matter."

Jana noticed a bruise under Cassie's necklace. "Did Max ever hit you?"

"What!" Cassie did a double-take.

"Did he ever strike you?" Jana asked.

"Of course not."

"Then why do you have so many bruise marks on your body, Cassie?"

"I told you, I'm clumsy."

"But your sister told me she has never seen you bump into anything at home—or in the office," Jana replied.

"My sister isn't at my side every moment of every day and night." Cassie shuddered. "Are you through with me, detective?"

"One more question," Bove said. "Who do you think killed Senator Maxmillion?"

"I have no idea," Cassie replied. "Can you speak with my sister next? I would really like to get her home."

Moments later Lenore sat across from Bove and Jana.

"Are you all right, Ms. Castle?" Bove asked with concern showing on his handsome face.

Lenore wiped her eyes with a wad of tissues. "I can't believe Max was here one minute and gone the next." She blew her tiny nose. "Just like when we lost my father." Her weeping turned into sobbing.

Jana handed Lenore another tissue. "How did you feel about your sister's relationship with Max?"

Between sobs, Lenore said, "I know…they were…different, but Max was a…strong leader…and a devoted civil servant…like my father."

Bove asked, "Were you jealous of Senator Maxmillion's relationship with your sister?"

Lenore's eyes seemed to double in size. "Of course not! Though she's older than I am, my sister and I have always been extremely close. Cassie's relationship with Max didn't change that."

He jotted down a note. "Did you see anyone tamper with Senator Maxmillion's drink tonight?"

"No." Lenore wiped her eyes with the wet tissue. "We all had drinks at intermission. It was hard to keep track of them."

"Obviously."

Jana sensed the tension between Bove and Lenore.

"How can you be so cruel?" Lenore asked Bove.

"Excuse me?" he said.

Lenore replied, "A man has been murdered, and you interrogate and belittle the people closest to him when we should be home grieving in bed."

"Are you one of the people closest to Senator Maxmillion?" Bove asked.

I feel like I'm watching a boxing match.

Lenore replied, "I know what you are insinuating, detective. And regardless of what you think of me, and of my sister, we would never hurt Max."

Bove leaned in closer to Lenore. "What I'm thinking right now may surprise you, Ms. Castle."

"I doubt it, detective."

Bove dismissed Lenore and she left in a huff. Next, Senator Sancho Ramirez sat opposite Bove and Jana. Sancho ran a hand through his slicked back hair.

"Detective, do you have any clues? Who do you think killed Max?"

Bove replied, "Senator, this will go faster if you let me ask the questions."

"Of course." Sancho sat back in his chair.

"You made quite a speech tonight about the Protect the Children Act, senator," Bove said. "You appeared pretty angry at Senator Maxmillion. How do you feel about what happened here this evening?"

"I disagreed with Senator Maxmillion on nearly every issue discussed in the Senate, but I certainly did not want to see him dead."

A few minutes later, Grace Effington answered the same question quite differently.

"I've met men like Maxmillion. He was a parasite. I'm sorry to say this, but thinking about Tyler and Topher, I'm glad he's dead."

Simon, Cornelius, and Jackson had similar answers to Bove's question.

"Bullies like Maxmillion pick on gay people because no other minority group will take it any longer," Simon said.

Cornelius proclaimed, "How long did Maxmillion think he could go on treating gay people like criminals?"

"He was a dinosaur who should be extinct," Jackson said.

Jana had forgotten about Allan Green, Ben's lobbyist, until the small, portly man sat in front of them, wiping his forehead with his handkerchief. "My wife is upset. Can we get this over with as fast as possible?"

"Sure." Bove said, "Right after you tell me if you saw anybody tamper with Senator Maxmillion's drink."

"I did not," Green said.

As Green rose from his seat, Jana said, "Your boss seemed pretty angry this evening when the reporters asked their questions at the bar. Why do you think their questions about Ben's Conglomerate and his H.A. Organization bothered him so much? What does Ben have to hide?"

Green's eyes turned into slits. "Benjamin Topower has absolutely *nothing* to hide. He was ganged up on by the liberal media."

Jana asked, "Do you approve of your boss' business dealings, Mr. Green?"

Green replied, "It is not up to me to approve or disapprove, only to facilitate Benjamin Topower's requests."

"Are you comfortable with the Historical Apprentice Organization's mission and purpose?" Jana asked.

Green glared at her. "I don't judge the actions of my boss. I leave that to you and Cassie Castle."

The last two people to be interviewed were Brian then Adam. After again offering his condolences, Bove asked Brian, "When did you find out Max was your father?"

"Two days ago," Brian replied, shifting his eyes from Jana to Bove.

"How did you find out?" Bove asked.

"Didn't your assistant detective tell you about it?" Brian asked with a cocky stare at Jana.

"I'd like to hear it from *you*," Bove replied.

Brian exhaled. "Jana overheard Max tell Ben that Max had given Adam and me up for adoption. Evidently Max got in touch with us now that he is running for president—to make sure the press didn't find out about his *messy* past." Brian laughed morosely. "I guess the joke was on him."

"How did you find this out?" Bove asked Jana.

Jana replied, "I hid in Max's closet."

"Like you did in *Daddy's Girl*," Bove said with a huge grin. "And that's when you found the papers you gave me tonight?"

Jana nodded.

Bove winked at her. "Good work, *Girl Detective*."

Brian offered Bove dagger eyes.

Back to the case.

Bove said, "I imagine you were quite angry about being kept in the dark all these years, Mr. Otley."

"Wouldn't *you* be?" Brian asked.

Contain the sarcasm, Brian. He's just trying to get the facts.

Bove said, "And your brother appeared angry about the Protect the Children Act."

"Funny how that works when someone threatens to take away your kids," Brian answered.

Bove said, "Senator Maxmillion died saying your and your brother's names then he fell into your brother's arms. Why do you think he did that?"

Brian offered a plastic smile. "I guess he liked my brother best."

Jana breathed a sigh of relief once Bove released Brian. Moments later, Bove asked Adam the same question.

Adam seemed despondent and preoccupied. "Max wasted forty years not knowing Brian and me—and not letting us know each other. I wonder if he realized that at the end?"

"Did you pay Max back for that tonight?" Bove asked.

Adam seemed to focus. "What?" He looked at Bove as if for the first time. "No."

Bove asked, "Then who *did*?"

"Isn't that *your* job to find out, detective?" Adam added to Jana, "Sancho took Grace home as soon as Bove released them. Brian, Jackson, and I will wait for you in the theatre house."

Bove walked Adam out. A few minutes later, he returned to the dressing room. "I'll admit I'm stumped. Lots of people seem to have had it in for Tamaya Stormcloud *and* Josiah Maxmillion. Do we have one murderer or two?" Bove paced the small room. "Everyone had a drink. Was Max the target, or could the murderer have been trying to poison someone else? Lots of people were milling around Max and the bar. Officer Eads just told me nobody was caught on tape putting anything into Max's glass, except the bartender who didn't know Max from Adam—no pun intended." He sighed. "I asked them to continue examining the videotapes at police headquarters."

"The videotapes won't show who poisoned Max," Jana said.

"Why not?"

Jana stood. "Before he left, I spoke with the magician in our show. I asked him how the murderer could have put the poison from the vial into Max's drink."

Bove moved next to her. "What did he say?"

"Nothing, but he showed me how easy it is for someone to hide a small object in the palm of one's hand then discard it. Magicians call it, *palming*."

Bove's dimples appeared. "Are you sure you didn't do a movie called *The Cute Magic Girl*?"

"Very funny."

Bove said, "Have I told you how smart and adorable you are?"

Right back at you, detective. "Have I told you I'm happily married?"

Bove leaned in. With their lips inches apart, he said, "Pity."

I'll say. Jana put a hand on his strong shoulder. "Bove, you're a terrific guy who would make *any* woman happy. You'll meet the right person one day. In the meantime, you have two murders to solve."

They walked to the theatre house.

"Will you and your troupe be all right getting home?" Bove asked.

Jana replied, "I'll make sure the menfolk go straight to bed."

He grinned. "Then do you want to go out dancing with me?"

She laughed. "Call me if you uncover anything."

"*Uncover* anything?"

"About the murders."

"Yes, ma'am."

Jackson, Brian, and Adam looked like three abandoned children in the theatre. Jana said goodnight to Bove and left with her family.

As Jackson drove home, he said, "Based on what happened tonight, my guess is the Protect the Children Act is D.O.A. in the House on Monday."

"I hope you're right," Jana replied from the back seat with Brian.

Jackson winked at Jana in his mirror. "Thanks to

you, honey."

Brian leaned forward and tapped Adam's shoulder. "You all right?"

Adam stared out the front window. "Wouldn't you know, I finally find my real father, and he turns out to be a monster."

"But you also found *me*." Brian rested his hand on Adam's shoulder.

When they arrived home, Brian and Adam shared a beer at the kitchen table. Jackson noticed the elderly sitter asleep on the sectional. So he woke her and offered the woman a ride home.

Jana went upstairs to check on B.J. and Grace, who were both sleeping soundly. Then she peeked into the boys' room, where she found Devon and Ed asleep in their beds, but Topher and Tyler's beds empty. With her heart pounding in her throat, Jana shook Devon and Ed. "Where are Topher and Tyler?"

Devon propped himself up on one elbow. "How come they got to go the benefit and we didn't?"

"What do you mean?" Jana shrieked.

Ed rubbed his eyes. "Ben came over. He said you asked him to bring Topher and Tyler to the benefit, so they left with Ben."

Jana felt as if she'd been punched in the stomach. She hurried to the phone in the upstairs hallway and called Bove. "Topher and Tyler are missing. Ben took them while the sitter and nanny were sleeping."

"Don't leave the house. I'll call you."

"No, pick me up on your way."

Jana flew open Grace's door. "Watch Devon, Ed, and B.J."

"Okay," Grace replied with a yawn.

Jana raced down the stairs. "Ben has Topher and Tyler!"

"What!" Adam jumped to his feet as if his chair was on fire.

Brian stood behind his brother. "Where are they?"

"I don't know," Jana replied trying to stay calm. "Bove is picking me up."

Brian was at her side. "What's going on between you and that guy?"

Really, Brian? You're asking me this now? "I want to help him get the boys back."

"I'm coming, too," Adam said.

"Me, too," Brian added.

Jana replied, "Grace is watching the boys, and Jackson will be home any minute."

Tears filled Adam's eyes. "My boys."

Jana said, "Adam, please try to stay calm. Bove is a good detective. We'll get the boys back." She wrote a note for Jackson and left it on the kitchen counter.

"How do you know so much about Bove?" Brian asked Jana.

Before Jana could respond, Bove arrived and they all hurried into his car.

Bove drove like a racecar driver, and they arrived at Topower's estate in minutes. Bove shouted his name into the intercom, and the ornate front gates parted. When they arrived at the mansion, a Latino butler opened the huge double-doors and informed them, "Mr. Topower has gone out for the evening."

Bove waved his badge, pushed past the butler, then left them in the hallway. A few minutes later he returned reporting his search of the fifteen-room mansion had uncovered nothing except Mrs. Topower out cold in her canopied bed with a bottle of scotch under her arm. Then Bove threatened the butler with deportation and found out Ben had taken the boys to the airport.

Back in Bove's car, speeding to the airport, Bove asked for Devon and Ed's descriptions then radioed them ahead along with Ben's.

Adam's hands were red from clenching them to his seat. "When I see him, I'll kill him."

"Don't make me cuff you," Bove said. "When we get to the airport, all three of you stay back and let me do my job."

"Please do what Bove says," Jana said.

Brian glared at her. "We heard him."

When they got to the airport, Bove jumped out of the car with Jana, Brian, and Adam at his heels. He spoke with a few airport employees, then cased the airport with the others following him. At the information booth, Bove said to Jana, "Nobody's seen them."

"You think the butler was lying?" Brian asked.

"I don't think so," Bove replied.

Adam said through gritted teeth, "We have to get him."

"We will," Bove said.

They split up to search the airport then met up again at a food stand having come up empty.

"Shouldn't we be doing *something*?" Adam asked with a quivering voice.

Bove said, "I put an APB out on Ben, and three officers are surrounding the airport."

In her peripheral vision, Jana saw a mother and her two young daughters on line to board a flight. With her film background, she realized there was something not right about their appearance. "Look over there!"

Bove glanced over. "Stay here." He radioed for back-up, then approached the suspect with Brian, Adam, and Jana inching closer. Bove displayed his badge. "Step to the side, please."

Ben, dressed in women's clothing, followed Bove's orders. Suddenly, Ben thrust a hand up his sleeve and withdrew something metallic and shiny. He lunged at Bove, stabbing him in the side. Adam leapt on top of Ben and the knife flew into the air, landing on the floor. Lying on top of Ben, Adam punched him in the face again and again while passengers screamed and fled the area. Jana reached for the children and brought them to a nearby seating area. Brian pulled Adam off Ben as one police officer cuffed Ben, and another called an ambulance for Bove who lay on the floor with a blood-stained shirt. The police officer pressed his rolled up jacket against Bove's wound, and Bove moaned in pain.

As Ben was brought to the airport doorway, he shouted to the police officer, "Don't you know who I am? I am Benjamin Topower! My lawyers will have your job! I was saving these innocent children from their father's deviant lifestyle!"

Jana asked the children, "Did Ben hurt you or touch you?"

"No." Topher took off his dress and wig. "Ben told us to play this dress up game. We didn't like it."

"He said he was taking us to Cape Canaveral, and you would all meet us there," Tyler explained, shedding his costume.

Adam and Brian appeared next to the children.

Rubbing his sore hand, Adam said, "Haven't I always told you never *ever* to go anywhere with *anyone* without my or Papa's permission!"

Tyler and Topher looked down at the ground.

Tears streamed down Adam's face as he scooped the boys up in his arms.

"Why are you crying, Daddy?" Topher asked.

Adam replied, "Because I'm so happy to see you boys."

"We're happy to see you, too, Daddy!" Tyler said.

Jana rushed over and kneeled at Bove's side. The detective had a large bandage wrapped around his side as the paramedics readied him for transport. "I'll come with you to the hospital," Jana said.

"Stay with your family," Bove replied in a soft voice.

She took his hand. "You did good work, Bove."

"Just like Jana Lane." He smiled weakly. "We solved the case."

Jana squeezed his hand then released it as Bove was carried away on the stretcher.

When they arrived back home, Adam gave another lecture to the boys about not going places with others, and Jana and Brian huddled in the kitchen with Jackson. Once they had filled him in on the events of the evening, Jana said, "Ben will go to prison where he belongs."

Jackson looked fit to be tied. "His plan all along was to take away our children…and other kids to satisfy his own pedophilia."

"And to feed the sick tastes of the other members of his so-called Historical Apprentice Organization," Brian added.

Adam finished his lecture then Jackson, Adam, Topher, and Tyler embraced. Since everyone was emotionally exhausted, after checking in with Grace and the boys, they all went to bed.

Stripped to his underwear, Brian got into their king-sized wood-carved bed. "I hope they put that sicko away for many years."

"Bove will see to that," Jana replied lying next to him.

"What's going on between you and Bove?" Brian asked with a tight jaw.

Jana sighed into her cranberry silk nightie. "We worked on the case together."

"It didn't look like that's all you *worked on together*."

Jana faced her husband and took in a deep breath. "Brian, I'm a human being. Occasionally, I find another man attractive...and sometimes I enjoy speaking with him." She felt her cheeks flush. "Or even flirting a little bit. But *you're* my husband, the love of my life. I don't want to be with anyone but *you*."

He put his strong arm around her shoulders. "It looked like Bove wanted more than that."

"Maybe he did."

Brian's spine stiffened. "Did he come on to you?"

Here goes. "When we went dancing. He kissed me."

"He *what*?" Brian rubbed his fist into the palm of his hand. "Detective Bove will be in the hospital longer than he planned."

"Brian, it didn't mean anything. He was depressed about a recent break-up. Bove knows I'm married, and he understands nothing can happen between us. I'm a one-man woman."

"But who's the man?"

She kissed his cheek. "You are. Whether you like it or not."

He pulled away. "You sure?"

"Double sure."

She scooted closer to him and they shared a kiss.

Brian said, "I don't know if I'm convinced."

"How's this?"

They shared a deeper kiss.

"Convinced now?" Jana asked.

"I'm getting there."

Jana wrapped her arms around her husband's muscular back. He ran his hands down her body.

"Now?" she asked.

"I'll tell you later."

Jana and Brian made love until they fell asleep in one another's arms.

****

Jana Lane ran down the Capitol hallway out of breath. She turned the corridor as fear gripped her like a vice. Who was behind her? Why was she being followed? Arms reached out for her waist just as—

Waking alone, Jana heard Brian in the bathroom. She wiped the perspiration off her face with a tissue and tried to shake off the recurring dream. She heard a knock at the door.

"Yes?"

"Jana, it's me. Are you all right?"

Jana opened the door to Grace. "I had a bad dream," Jana replied, fastening her silk robe.

"No wonder, after what you all went through last night."

"Where's B.J.?"

"Sleeping late this morning after being woken up last night when you all came upstairs." Grace sat on a wood-carved easy chair.

Those jeans and that blouse don't hang off you. Thank goodness you're getting well.

Grace put her head in her hands. "I'm so sorry, Jana."

"For what?" Jana sat on the bed.

"I should have woken up when Ben took Tyler and Topher. I was just so wiped out after the benefit and the interrogation."

"I assume Ben was as quiet as a snake," Jana replied.

Rage filled Grace's young face. "That's the perfect word for him. He should be shot in the desert." She rose and paced the room. "I knew someone like that in my hometown when I was a kid. Poor Tyler and Topher."

Jana stood and placed her hand on the girl's shoulder. "Grace, it was a terrifying experience. But Tyler and Topher came out of it unharmed, and Ben is in jail where he belongs."

A tear stained Grace's cheek. "If anything had happened to those two little boys while I was sleeping, I would *never* have forgiven myself."

Jana put her arm around Grace, happy to feel more than skin and bone. "Grace, we appreciate your loyalty, but you need to take care of yourself, too."

"I am."

"And you should spend more time with Sancho."

"Sancho is picking me up later to go out to dinner."

"Good."

"I really like him, Jana."

"I'm glad."

They shared a smile.

Grace asked, "Do you think it's too soon for Sancho and me to become…serious?"

"I think it's *just* the right time. And after so many years, I'm happy for you both."

They shared a hug.

"Mommy!"

Hearing B.J.'s morning call, Jana went into the next room to get B.J. washed and dressed. While Grace dressed, Jana went downstairs with B.J. to fix his breakfast, and ran into Brian and Adam in the kitchen.

"Adam made us breakfast to go. We're having a men's meeting at the lake," Brian said.

"To process everything that happened last night with the four boys," Adam explained.

As she prepared B.J.'s oatmeal with B.J. running around her, Jana replied, "And mothers aren't good at processing?"

Brian said like a kid asking for an allowance, "Do you mind if we handle this one without you, babe?"

"Go for it," Jana said. "After B.J. and I eat breakfast, I'll leave him with Grace, get dressed, and go to church."

"Mommy dressed!" said B.J.

Adam said, "There's a liberal Christian church a few blocks away."

"Sounds perfect." Jana added, "Afterward I'll do a couple of errands."

Brian's face fell. "Will you visit Bove in the hospital?"

"That's the plan," Jana replied.

"Tell him I hope he gets better soon," Adam said.

"I won't stay long." She kissed Brian's cheek. "Let Jackson know I'm borrowing his car."

Jana changed into a lavender sweater and matching skirt, then drove to the quaint church with a steeple, stained-glass windows, and a pipe organ. As was the case at her church in New York led by Reverend Heather, Jana was moved by the congregation's welcoming of everyone, including gay and lesbian couples, and by the outpouring of love and acceptance that filled the small church in the true spirit of Christianity.

When the service was over, Jana shook hands with the minister as she exited the church then drove to Simon and Cornelius' hotel. She met them in the lobby, surrounded by enough pieces of luggage for a trip around the world. As usual Simon wore a loud jumpsuit, and Cornelius sported a matching bowtie and suspenders over his shirt and slacks. Upon exchanging air kisses with them, Jana asked, "Do you need a ride to the train station?"

"We called a taxi," Simon replied. "I wasn't sure if we'd be seeing you before we left," he added like a martyr.

She rested an arm around each of them. "Thank you both so much for producing the benefit show. You did a wonderful job. The theatre manager told me we made close to a hundred thousand dollars. I hope the performers understood about cancelling Act II."

Simon answered, "They were disappointed." He grinned from wrinkled ear to ear. "But the murder of Josiah Maxmillion made up for it." Simon adjusted the yellow and pink polka dot scarf around his neck. "Did your hunky football player find out who did it?"

"He thinks he did," Jana replied.

"But you're not so sure," Simon said.

Cornelius pinched her waist. "It sounds like it's up to *you* to solve the case again, Jana Lane."

The taxi arrived, and the driver grumbled as he loaded the luggage into the trunk and back seat.

"We will see you back in Hyde Park, baby doll," Simon said. "Take care of yourself. You have a movie to shoot soon." He winked. "Remember, ten percent of you belongs to me, but I love the other ninety percent, too."

Jana waved goodbye to the departing taxi, drove to the florist, then to the hospital, where she found Bove in a private room on the second floor. The detective sat up with a white bandage around his torso. Jana tried unsuccessfully not to stare at his incredibly muscular shoulders as she placed a vase of flowers on the windowsill. "How's the hero today?" Jana asked.

Bove put down his pudding container. "In need of some food from my parents' restaurant."

"Would you like me to cater it?"

"They're coming later. But since you were the *Little Candy Striper*, can you fluff my pillow?"

Jana giggled and went to work. *He still smells like the outdoors.* "When can you go home?"

"My doctor's a football fan. In exchange for an autograph, he said I could leave tomorrow. Thanks." He motioned for her to take the seat next to the bed. "How are Topher and Tyler?"

"A bit shaken, but they'll be fine." She sighed. "Thank goodness Ben didn't get his hands on them."

Bove leaned back on his pillow. "The lab results are back on Max's glass. Just as you said. Potassium

Joe Cosentino

cyanide. Ben's legal team got him out on bail, but we have an officer guarding his house. We'll get him convicted in trial."

Jana looked out the window.

Bove said, "Care to tell the sick guy what you're thinking?"

"I don't want to disagree with you—"

"But?"

"I don't think Ben is our murderer."

Bove did a double-take. "You were the one who spotted him in the airport."

"I know he took Topher and Tyler, but kidnapping and murder are two different things."

"Ben knew Tamaya Stormcloud was researching his shady conglomerate and man/boy organization. And you saw how angry he was at Max for making him come to the benefit. Not to mention Ben was standing next to Max at the bar last night. It must have been easy for him, as your magician friend said, to palm the vial and pour the poison into Max's drink without anyone noticing."

She nodded. "Ben was also unhappy with Max for not bringing him Tyler and Topher."

"See?" Bove said with a proud smile.

"But it doesn't make sense that Ben would want Max dead."

"Why not?"

She tented her fingers. "Ben was set to fund Max's campaign for president in exchange for Max proposing and supporting the Protect the Children Act to fill Ben's orphanage."

"Which Max *did*."

"But the *other* part of the deal was for Max to

236

support tax breaks and the deconstructing of environmental laws to profit Ben's companies."

"Which Max hadn't done *yet*." Bove rubbed his forehead. "And that leaves us with no fingerprints, a useless video, and no eye witnesses."

"What did you make of the interviews at the theatre?" Jana asked.

"Topower's number two, Allan Green, sure seemed nervous," Bove replied.

"Do you think Green killed Tamaya to stop her investigation of the Multitopower Conglomerate then killed Max because Max wouldn't play along with all of Ben's demands?"

"Could be." Bove scratched the area around his bandage.

If I watch your abdominal muscles, I'll never be able to concentrate.

Bove said, "But a lot of people didn't like Maxmillion, thanks to the Protect the Children Act, including your agent and his partner."

"Simon and Cornelius wouldn't murder anyone. And they had nothing against Tamaya. They didn't even know her."

"As far as you *know*." Bove ate more of his pudding. "Your friend Adam Stokes seems like *Oedipus* material."

Jana laughed. "A theatre reference from an ex-football player and current police detective?"

"Hey, just because I played sports and I'm a cop doesn't mean I'm not cultured." He licked his spoon loudly. "Adam sure wasn't pleased with his father, and I'll bet Tamaya's article about Adam's ex-wife didn't make Tamaya his favorite reporter."

Joe Cosentino

"Adam would never hurt anyone. Neither would Jackson."

"Maybe you don't know them as well as you think." Bove pushed his tray away. "Ramirez made an impassioned speech against Max for the cameras. And his skinny girlfriend seemed hot under her size two dress. My guess is they also weren't happy about Tamaya's threat to write an article about Sancho's stripper days. Just like Cassie was unhappy with Tamaya for breaking the story about Cassie and Max's relationship."

Jana remembered the marks on Cassie's body.

Bove continued, "And did you notice how Lenore seemed so upset over Max's death?"

"So did Cassie."

"But Cassie was dating Max. Lenore wasn't." He shrugged his broad shoulders. "Ouch."

"Are you all right?" She sat next to him on the bed.

"I am now." He smiled. "Do you think there was something going on between Lenore and Max?"

"Tomorrow's my last day shadowing Cassie. Hopefully, Lenore will be there, and I can talk to her about Max."

Bove exhaled. "Josiah Maxmillion. Another crooked politician goes down in history."

"If only all politicians could be like Senator Castle."

"You mean Cassie Castle?"

Jana shook her head no. "Cassie and Lenore's father. Samuel Castle was a champion of anyone or any group without power, money, and hope. *He* was a true hero. Just like you." She took his hand. "You're quite a guy, detective."

"But not the guy for you."

She smiled. "Things might have been different in another place and time."

"But not *this* one." He looked like a boy who lost a puppy. "I guess we won't be going out dancing again."

"I guess not."

"And here I was practicing my moon walk."

Jana kissed his forehead then rose from the bed. "Feel better soon. I'll call you before we go back to Hyde Park."

Jana left the room, realizing she had only one more day to expose the murderer.

Chapter 10

Jana woke the next morning and dressed in a blueberry pants suit with a white ruffled blouse. Blueberry eye shadow and a silver necklace with a sapphire stone completed her ensemble. She got B.J. washed and dressed, then headed for the kitchen to put away the dinner dishes and the board games from the night before. Since Brian, Adam, and the four boys were outside boating, she ate a bowl of cereal and fruit with B.J. then left him with Grace.

On the drive to the Capitol, Jackson looked every bit the congressman in his sea breeze suit. Stopping at a red light, he turned to Jana and smiled. "I love it that we're in-laws."

Jana giggled. "I can't think of anyone I'd rather have as my brother-in-law."

Jackson squeezed her hand then continued driving. "It seems like Adam is working through his issues with Max...and with Max's death. We stayed up and talked about it last night."

"Same for Brian." Jana sighed. "I guess it was honorable of Max to try to meet his family."

"Too little, too late."

"How are Topher and Tyler doing?"

"Kids are so resilient. It was all a game to them."

"It could have been a deadly game."

Jackson turned a corner. "Will Brian and the kids

come with you to DC when you shoot your movie?"

"It's only a week's shoot—for exteriors."

"Topher and Tyler would love to see their cousins again."

"I'll ask Brian."

As he made another turn, Jackson said, "Adam is driving over to meet me for lunch today. He's giving Grace a lift so she can do the same with Sancho."

"Sounds like Brian's the designated sitter for the kids."

"*And* the designated packer since you'll be leaving us tomorrow." Jackson feigned hysterics, weeping into his forearm.

"Good thing *I'm* the actor," Jana said with a laugh.

"Let's make a pact to see one another more often."

"Done."

They shared a smile.

"How's Bove the body doing?" Jackson asked with a sexy wink.

"I went to see him in the hospital yesterday."

"*Did* you now?"

"You can wipe the smirk off your face, Jackson. I told Brian all about Bove kissing me."

"A kiss-and-tell gal. I like that."

"There wasn't all that much to tell."

"And Brian is okay with it?" He glared at her. "Don't lie to your brother-in-law, honey."

Let me choose my words carefully. "Brian...understands the situation."

"I'm glad *somebody* does."

"And Brian knows I'm a one-man woman."

"Yeah, but which man?"

Jana hit Jackson's shoulder.

"Owww," he shouted. "Are you sure you weren't *The Little Boxer*?"

"Lucky for you, I wasn't."

When Jana and Jackson arrived at the Capitol, they noticed a group of protestors waving signs.

Jackson parked his car, then led Jana to the entrance of the building. "The gay groups you funded from the benefit are demonstrating against the Protect the Children Act."

"As they should," Jana replied as she and Jackson walked up the many steps. "If the government threatened to take children away from their heterosexual parents, straight people would wave more than signs."

Jana arrived at the Senate wing of offices, and found Lenore sitting at her desk in Cassie's outer office with Cassie and the secretary nowhere in sight.

"Jana, hi," Lenore said with a shaky voice.

"Hi, Lenore. Today's my last day to shadow Cassie. Did she come in?"

Lenore wiped a tear from her cheek with a tissue. "Cassie's in the Senate Chamber. You can watch from upstairs if you like."

Jana sat on the loveseat. "I'm surprised."

"You've watched from upstairs before."

"No, I mean that Cassie came in today."

"Cassie's like my father. Her duty to her constituents comes before her own feelings." Lenore walked to a side table and poured herself a cup of coffee. Jana noticed the young woman's hands were shaking. "Would you like a cup, Jana?"

"No, thank you." Jana patted the place next to her on the loveseat. "Lenore, please sit with me a moment."

Once Lenore was seated, Jana said, "I can see how upset you are over Max's death."

Tears filled the young woman's eyes. "Last night was horrible. Why would anyone want to kill Max?"

You have an hour? Jana shifted on the loveseat to face Lenore. "I know this isn't any of my business, and I know Max was a great deal older than you, but I can't help wondering if you and Max…"

Sancho Ramirez entered the outer office wearing an avocado-colored suit and cherry-colored tie. "Jana, we'll miss you around here."

Jana smiled. "You'll miss my son's nanny more."

"You're right," he replied. "Cassie's in the Senate Chamber. I'm headed back that way now. Come on, I'll walk with you."

"I'll speak with you later, Lenore," Jana said.

Lenore nodded, wiped her face, and sat at her desk.

Jana and Sancho walked down the hallway together.

Lobbyist Allan Green passed by them. "Senator Ramirez, Ms. Lane."

"What are you doing at the Capitol today, Mr. Green?" Jana asked.

Green replied, "Max's secretary has some papers for me."

Pouring salt into the wound, Jana said, "You must be devastated about what happened to Max and Ben."

Green snarled into his jowls. "They were fine men brought down by the liberal agenda." Green hurried down the hallway.

"Poor guy doesn't look too well," Sancho said looking after Green.

"He is anything but *poor*," Jana replied.

Jana and Sancho continued walking down the hallway.

"I'm so glad Grace is getting well," Jana said. "I hope you aren't too upset about us leaving tomorrow."

Sancho's dimples appeared. "I'll get to see Grace when I'm in New York, and now that Brian and Adam have made their connection and you'll be shooting a film here, I hope you will all come visit DC again soon."

"I hope so, too," Jana said.

"I'm so lucky to have Grace back in my life. She is an amazing woman," Sancho said. "I knew that the first time she came to my door when she was eighteen." He took in a deep breath. "She's a real survivor."

They turned a corner and Jana asked, "Sancho, what happened to Grace when she was eighteen?"

"She doesn't talk about it much."

"I know. And I don't mean to pry. But given Grace's fragile health, as her employer…and as her friend, I'd like to know what happened, so I can help her." She touched his forearm. "Please, Sancho."

Sancho stood still. "Back in the old neighborhood in upstate New York, Grace's neighbor, a friend of her parents…took advantage of Grace." Pain filled Sancho's handsome face. "Grace didn't tell anyone, including her parents."

"Why not?"

"To protect her younger cousin, Jolanda."

"I don't understand."

Sancho exhaled. "The guy told Grace that if she said anything to anyone, he would go after Jolanda."

Jana shuddered. "How horrible."

Sancho rubbed his forehead. "I wish she had told

me. I'd have taken care of the guy myself. Instead she…"

"What did Grace do?"

"One afternoon when her parents were out, the guy had Grace cornered in her bedroom. He pushed her onto her bed. She screamed but nobody came. As he mounted her, Grace picked up a letter opener from her desk next to the bed…and she stabbed him in the chest." Sancho wiped the perspiration off his neck with his handkerchief. "The guy fell on top of her…dead."

"How horrible!"

They continued walking. "It was self-defense. Grace was found not guilty."

"And your lives took different directions after that?"

Sancho nodded. "But I never stopped thinking about Grace…and caring about her."

Jana and Sancho arrived at the door to the Senate Chamber and Sancho opened it.

Grace. Oh my God! The pieces all fit together. "Sancho, I think I know who killed Tamaya and Max."

"Who?"

"I have to call Bove!"

"You can use the phone in my office."

Jana hurried down the hall searching for Sancho's office. After making two turns, she realized she was lost. Jana felt as if she was caught in her dream. She walked faster. The distinct sound of breathing filled the hallway. Jana looked around her. All the doors were shut and no one was in the hallway. She ran just ahead of the sound of footsteps behind her. Jana looked back and gasped—at the sight of the murderer. She ran faster, and so did the murderer. As the murderer's arms reached out for Jana's neck, Jana remembered a move from *School Spy*. She turned a corner and stuck out her foot. The murderer came around the same corner and fell to the floor. Then using a hold from *Jungle Girl*, Jana leaned over and pinned the murderer's arms to the floor.

"Enough!" Cassie Castle's voice echoed in the empty hallway. "Enough fighting, enough running away, and enough killing."

A few minutes later, Jana and the junior senator from Ohio sat on an empty stairwell in the vacant hallway. Still catching her breath, Jana said, "I'll ask Bove to help you if you tell me the truth."

Cassie rubbed her sore arm. "I overheard you tell Sancho you knew it all."

"I think I've figured out most of it," Jana said.

Cassie rested her head in her hands. "What do you think you know?"

Jana's mind was racing. "You idolized your father, and you wanted to be just like him. You were the apple of his eye."

"Everyone knows that."

Think fast, girl. "And once you became a teenager, when your mother wasn't around, you seduced your father."

"That's absurd."

Keep fabricating. Make her angry. "And when Lenore tried to follow in your footsteps with your father, you got jealous and killed him. Then history repeated itself when Tamaya went after Max. You got jealous and killed them both."

Cassie looked wild and angry. "You don't know what you're talking about."

But the more lies I spout, the angrier you'll get—and the more likely you'll tell me the truth. "Like Max, Samuel Castle was a highly revered senator who was good looking, charming, charismatic, and famous. Even as a teenager, you wanted a man like that."

"This is insane."

Jana's face was inches away from Cassie's. "How old were you when you first seduced your father, Cassie? What did you do to make such an honorable man do such a dishonorable thing? Did you sit on his lap and giggle into his ear?"

"No!"

Jana was like a bloodhound at a carcass. "How did it first start, Cassie? Did your father come home late one night when your mother was in bed? Did you compliment his new suit? Help him off with his jacket? Run your fingers through his hair?"

"I won't listen to your lies." Cassie rose from the step.

Jana grabbed her arm. "Did you fix your father a drink? Try to get him drunk? Take a sip then raise the glass to his lips?"

"Stop!"

"Did you put your mouth on his and place his hands around your waist?"

Cassie screamed, "Never!"

Jana stood and shook Cassie by her shoulders. "If you don't want me to tell Lenore what I know, you'll be honest with me about what you did with your father."

Cassie blurted out, "I didn't do anything. He did! I begged him to stop, but he wouldn't!"

She finally said it.

"Night after night I lay in my bed crying with him

on top of me. Is this what you want to hear, Jana?"

Jana clutched her stomach, trying to keep from vomiting.

"Would you also like to hear about how he forced himself on me? How the pain in my heart matched the agony between my legs? Would you like to hear about how he grunted like an animal in my ear? And how his breath stank of liquor when he dribbled onto my cheek?"

Jana took Cassie's hand. "I'm so sorry, Cassie."

"Me, too."

"How did it all start? Please tell me."

Cassie sat back down on the step. "The great Senator Samuel Castle had a drinking problem. And when he drank, he became a different man."

"Tell me, Cassie. So I can help you." Jana sat next to her.

Running shaky hands through her hair, Cassie replied, "He shouted, swore, and pushed my mother around. When my mother shunned him, he came after me." Tears flowed freely down Cassie's cheeks. "As I told you the day we met, my mother died when I was nineteen years old, and my father passed away when I was thirty. My father molested me from the time I was fifteen until he died."

"And Lenore was thirteen."

Cassie's eyes and cheeks turned red. "I couldn't leave Lenore alone with him. She loved him—and still does. She saw him drunk and angry, but he never—"

Jana leaned forward on the step. "Until the night you killed him."

Cassie nodded. "I went out on a date—with a pharmacist. When I got home, Dad was in the living room, drunk out of his mind. I couldn't calm him down. He threw things. Ranted and raved about how I wasn't attentive enough to him. How I was dating too much."

"And when you could no longer dissuade him from doing so, he went after Lenore."

"But he never got to her room."

"Because you gave him another drink—loaded with potassium cyanide."

Cassie said through a tight jaw, "Since Dad had a heart condition, and because I scrubbed his glass clean, our doctor assumed it was a heart attack."

Jana rested her elbows on her knees. "And eleven years later, when talking to your closest girlfriend, you let down your guard and slipped—telling Tamaya Stormcloud the entire story."

"Enough of the story for Tamaya to threaten me in my office with printing it," Cassie said.

"So you stabbed Tamaya with your letter opener."

"I couldn't let Lenore know the truth. She idolized my father. And for some reason she looks up to *me*."

Moving on to the next murder victim. "You dated Max. Though you two were total opposites, somehow you complimented one another. Lenore liked him, too. Everything went well—for a while. You liked rough sex, and he was able to do that for you. You even trusted him enough to tell him a bit about your troubled past—but not the whole story. Max got curious, and one night during sex he wouldn't stop hitting you until you told him everything about your secret past—which you did."

"Though Max and my father were leaders of opposite political parties, they were alike in many ways. Maybe that's what attracted me to Max."

"And when you became frightened and wanted out of the relationship, Max blackmailed you. He said he'd go public with the story about your father. So you stayed with him. But when Max turned his attentions to Lenore, you'd had enough."

Cassie wiped her eyes with her pink satin sleeve. "Lenore was taken with Max, not romantically, but she saw him as a father figure. I knew Max was growing tired of me, and despite the difference in their ages, he wanted Lenore. I couldn't let that happen."

"So you poisoned Max in the same manner you poisoned your father, and for the same reason—to protect Lenore." *Just as Grace killed her neighbor to protect Jolanda.*

Cassie nodded.

"But that isn't the only reason you killed Max." Jana took Cassie's hand. "Watching you and Lenore together, knowing the difference in your age, seeing how you took care of her and how she looked up to you, Max figured out you aren't Lenore's sister. You are her mother."

Cassie looked away, her face wet with tears.

"If you don't tell me, I'll ask Bove to investigate this."

Cassie rested back on the step. "I was only sixteen years old. I was so frightened. At first I thought I had the flu. But when the nausea and vomiting continued, and my bust and waist size increased, I panicked."

"Did you tell your mother?"

Cassie nodded. "She didn't believe it was my father. She told me I was trying to blame him for my 'slutty ways' with some boy at school."

"And what did your father say?"

Cassie laughed bitterly. "Always the powerful senator, he told me to leave everything in his hands." Cassie shuddered. "His disgusting, cold, clammy, groping hands."

"What did your father do?"

"Everything." Cassie faced straight ahead as if watching a horror movie. "He told my mother I admitted the boy was a private in the Army passing through town on leave. Playing the role of the kind-hearted father, he talked my mother into *forgiving* me for my *indiscretion*. Next, he visited the principal at my school, and told her I had come down with tuberculosis and needed to be home-schooled. After my father hired a tutor, and slipped him some extra money to keep his mouth shut, I did my studies at home—until the well-paid midwife came to deliver my baby. Since my father was such a powerful man in Washington, he was able to call in a few favors, and grease a few more palms, and bingo, Lenore's birth certificate listed him and my mother as Lenore's parents. And he convinced my mother to play along in order to protect *me* from scandal." Cassie turned to Jana with a look of fear in her eyes. "You can't tell anyone, Jana, especially Lenore." Cassie clutched onto Jana's arms. "I'll…I'll…do *anything* to keep her from knowing."

"But I have to tell Bove enough of—"

Cassie grasped her fingers around Jana's neck and squeezed. Struggling to breathe, Jana remembered a move from her *Girl Detective* movie. Jana rammed her knee into Cassie's stomach and thrust her arms from below into Cassie's arms, forcing them away from her neck. Cassie collapsed, weeping on Jana's shoulder. Jana rocked Cassie back and forth like a child, then

Joe Cosentino

helped Cassie to her feet. Finally she led Cassie to her office, where Jana phoned Detective Bove.

Minutes later Bove entered the outer office in a white shirt with navy pants and blazer. Jana noticed he moved stiffly. *He's still wearing the bandage.* She stood next to him. "Cassie is resting in her office. Please go easy on her. She's had a rough day."

Before Bove could respond, Lenore entered from the hallway. "I was in the ladies' room. Jana, what did my sister say to you? Is Cassie in some kind of trouble?"

Jana replied in a soothing voice, "Cassie needs to speak with Detective Bove."

Lenore blocked the door to Cassie's office. "My sister didn't do anything wrong. Don't go in there, detective, and put words in her mouth!"

He came face to face with Lenore. "Ms. Castle, I'm going to ask you to trust me. Can you do that?"

"Why should I trust *you*?" Lenore asked.

Bove looked into the young woman's eyes. "Because I want to do what is best for your sister—and for *you*."

Lenore looked away as tears filled her eyes.

"Do you believe that?" Bove asked.

Lenore looked at him. As she nodded, tears ran down her cheeks like raindrops.

Bove squeezed Lenore's arm, entered Cassie's office, and shut the door behind him.

Jana put her arm around Lenore and sat her on the loveseat.

"My sister killed Tamaya Stormcloud and Max, didn't she?" Lenore said.

Jana sat next to her. "I'm afraid so."

"Why would she do that?" Lenore asked as she wiped her eyes with a tissue.

Jana rested a hand on the young woman's quivering back. "Sometimes good people do bad things to protect the people they love."

"Whatever she did, I know Cassie will always love me, and I will always love her."

"Good. She'll need your love now more than ever."

Lenore nodded. "I know a lot more about our past than Cassie thinks. I pretend not to, because I know it's what Cassie wants." She stared into Jana's eyes. "Mothers are always overprotective of their daughters."

Jana embraced the young woman as Lenore wept.

Bove opened the door to Cassie's office and joined them. "Ms. Castle, your sister would like to speak to you."

Lenore looked at Bove with tear-stained eyes. "Thank you, detective."

When they were alone in the outer office behind Cassie's closed door, Jana asked Bove, "Did you get Cassie's confession?"

He nodded then winced from the pain in his side. "She confessed to the killings, but I don't believe her motive was jealousy over Tamaya Stormcloud's affair with Maxmillion."

"Does her reason for doing what she did matter all that much? Cassie confessed to the murders. Isn't that enough?"

"I guess it will have to be." Bove grinned. "For everyone, except Jana Lane."

Jana smiled. "I don't know any more than you do, detective."

"Not true." He winked at her. "Jana Lane solved

the case."

Cassie came out of her office with her arm around Lenore. "I'm ready to go to police headquarters, detective."

"I'm going with her," Lenore said at Cassie's elbow.

"Of course," Bove replied.

Cassie said to Bove, "Take care of my sister, will you, Bove?"

"I will," he answered.

The three of them left the office.

In the car with Jackson driving home, Jana sank into the passenger seat and moaned.

"You look as if you've fought in a war."

"Pretty close."

Jackson's bright smile emerged. "You should be happy, hon buns. The Protect the Children Act was defeated today."

"Good news." Jana leaned her head back and closed her eyes.

"What's wrong, honey?"

Jana said, "Cassie Castle confessed to killing Tamaya Stormcloud and Josiah Maxmillion."

Jackson nearly swerved off the road. Upon regaining control of the wheel, he said, "When was this?"

"Today in her office with Bove."

"Why did Cassie kill them?"

"Max had his eye on Tamaya. In a jealous rage, Cassie killed them both."

Jackson's eyes narrowed. "I know you are lying to me, but that's okay. I'm sure you have a good reason."

"Thanks, Jack."

He smiled. "And I know one day you'll tell me the truth."

Guess again, chum. "I hope they go easy on Cassie."

"And hard on Benjamin Topower." Jackson chuckled. "You did good, girlfriend. You're becoming a regular sleuth."

Jana rubbed her sore neck. "I'm just glad this is over."

Jackson replied, "Until the next time."

Epilogue

The following February, Jana Lane Otley, wearing a rose-colored satin gown, sat in the third row center aisle seat at the Dorothy Chandler Pavilion in Hollywood, California for the fifty-fifth annual Academy Awards. Sitting by her side, Brian Otley, looked handsome in a black tuxedo. A number of rows behind them, Brian's brother, Adam, and his partner Congressman Jackson Mitchell sat looking equally dapper in their matching gray tuxedos. Next to them sat Simon Huckby in a lemon and cranberry swirled jumpsuit, and his partner Cornelius Chamberlain in matching swirled suspenders and bowtie over a white tuxedo. In the row behind them sat Senator Sancho Ramirez in a sea-green tuxedo, and his wife Grace who was just beginning to show in a maroon maternity gown. A number of rows behind them sat Detective Christopher Bove and his fiancée, the junior Senator from Ohio, Lenore Castle.

The butterflies in Jana's stomach had butterflies. She reached for her husband's hand and held it tightly.

The previous year's winner for Best Leading Actor read the five nominees for Best Actress in a film released in 1983: Sally Field, Jane Fonda, Jana Lane, Susan Sarandon, and Meryl Streep.

When the actor read the name of the winner, the audience erupted into thunderous applause. Jana couldn't believe her ears. As Jana sat in shock, Brian threw his arms around her, kissed her, and motioned for her to go on stage to accept her award.

Simon Huckby jumped to his feet and led the audience in a standing ovation.

The room was a haze in front of her as Jana made her way down the aisle, up the stairs, and to the microphone, where she was handed the award.

As if getting her wish from a fairy godmother, Jana looked down at the statue and could not believe her eyes. When the applause finally died down and the distinguished-looking audience members returned to their seats, Jana Lane said into the microphone, "I made my first movie at six years old. I guess it took me thirty-five years to get it right."

When the audience's laughter faded, Jana said, "I would like to thank my producer, director, and co-stars in *Madam Senator*, as well as my agent Simon Huckby."

Simon and Cornelius applauded wildly.

"On a personal note, I would like to thank my best friend Congressman Jackson Mitchell." Jackson winked at her. Jana added, "And of course I want to thank my husband and our three sons who should all be in bed by now. I mean my three boys should be in bed, not my husband." Jana blew a kiss at Brian. When the laughter ceased, Jana looked out at Bove. "And there is one other person I would like to thank. He knows who he is."

Bove smiled from ear to ear.

Jana continued, "Finally, I would like to dedicate this award to families everywhere. Families in all shapes and sizes." Thinking of Cassie and Lenore, Jana said, "To sisters." She looked out at Brian and Adam. "To brothers." Locking eyes with Jackson she said, "And to all children—whether they have a mother and a father, one mother, one father, two fathers, two mothers, grandparents, or guardians. They say love makes a family. And I am so fortunate to be surrounded by so much love."

Jana returned to her seat, and to her family, as the applause swelled.

A word about the author…

Joe Cosentino is the author of three Jana Lane mysteries and numerous other novels and novellas. His next Jana Lane mystery is *China Doll.*

As an actor he has appeared in principal roles in film, television, and theatre, opposite stars such as Bruce Willis, Rosie O'Donnell, Nathan Lane, Holland Taylor, Charles Keating, and Jason Robards.

His one-act plays, *Infatuation* and *Neighbor*, were performed in New York City. He wrote *The Perils of Pauline* educational film.

Joe is currently Head of the Department/Professor at a college in upstate New York, and is happily married.

http://www.JoeCosentino.weebly.com

Other The Wild Rose Press titles by Joe Cosentino:
Porcelain Doll

Thank you for purchasing
this publication of The Wild Rose Press, Inc.

If you enjoyed the story, we would appreciate your
letting others know by leaving a review.

For other wonderful stories,
please visit our on-line bookstore at
www.thewildrosepress.com.

For questions or more information
contact us at
info@thewildrosepress.com.

The Wild Rose Press, Inc.
www.thewildrosepress.com

Stay current with The Wild Rose Press, Inc.

Like us on Facebook

https://www.facebook.com/TheWildRosePress

And Follow us on Twitter
https://twitter.com/WildRosePress

www.ingramcontent.com/pod-product-compliance
Lightning Source LLC
Chambersburg PA
CBHW070334260626
47160CB00003B/1042